EYEV

The picture before ... moonlight. On the ground, its hands and feet twitching, lay the body of a man wearing a knit golfing shirt. Above him stood the assailant: a tall, muscular man of almost aristocratic demeanor, his silver-gray hair combed straight back. And piercing through the whiteness of his face were steel blue, panic-stricken eyes, wild and frenzied; eyes that had lost all rationality.

The assailant ran past him and quickly disappeared into the hillside shrubbery.

Colon wanted to run too. Fast. But he had done nothing wrong. His obligation was to stay. To call for help. Why could he not bring himself to just yell?

His predicament was resolved by the glint of metal on the ground. He retrieved the spray can Slic had dropped. In scrawled letters, he wrote directly above where the body lay:

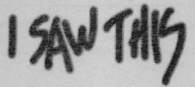

Then he shoved the can in his pants pocket and fled to safety.

Other Avon Books by
Patricia D. Benke

GUILTY BY CHOICE

FALSE WITNESS

PATRICIA D. BENKE

AVON BOOKS ◆ NEW YORK

FALSE WITNESS is an original publication of Avon Books. This work has never before appeared in book form. This work is a novel. Any similarity to actual persons or events is purely coincidental.

AVON BOOKS
A division of
The Hearst Corporation
1350 Avenue of the Americas
New York, New York 10019

Copyright © 1996 by Patricia D. Benke
Back cover author photo by Kira Corser
Published by arrangement with the author
Library of Congress Catalog Card Number: 95-94721
ISBN: 0-380-78184-0

First Avon Books Printing: February 1996

AVON TRADEMARK REG. U.S. PAT. OFF. AND IN OTHER COUNTRIES, MARCA REGISTRADA, HECHO EN U.S.A.

Printed in the U.S.A.

RA   10 9 8 7 6 5 4 3 2 1

For my husband, Don,
and Mike and Peter

I would like to extend my gratitude to my agent, Pat Teal, for her unfailing encouragement and impeccable advice; and to Lorna Luthy, without whose patience and dedication nothing would get done.

No true secrets are lurking in the landscape, but only undisclosed evidence, waiting for us.

No true chaos is in the urban scene, but only patterns and clues waiting to be organized.

—GRADY CLAY

Prologue

───◆───

FROM THE BACK of the courtroom, Judith Thornton watches as Alan Larson rises from his place at the defense table that has been his post for the last two months. His client, a young woman on trial for murdering her parents by bombing their car, sits stone-faced. Larson exudes a confidence that overpowers his baggy brown tweed sports coat.

Judith notices Larson's jacket pockets are bulging. The hapless investigator for the district attorney's office, the office she works for, is about to be blindsided. Larson crosses his arms against his chest and rests his hand under his chin. He approaches his witness.

"Let's see now, Mr. [he does not use the title detective . . .] Tague. If I recall correctly, you testified this morning that these two screws here . . ." He picks up the plastic envelope containing two pieces of metal. ". . . these two tiny little screws here in Exhibit 4 are pretty hard to come by."

The unsuspecting Tague shifts his weight, tilting confidently backward on the brown leather witness chair. Judith is watching the prosecutor. He's young. Two years out of law school, and he hasn't the foggiest what is about to happen.

"Yes sir, those screws are rare. Very rare."

Larson places the plastic envelope in front of the witness, on the witness stand.

"And these are the two screws you found in my client's garage?"

"Yes sir, the same ones. See the bag here is sealed with tape that has my initials on it and the date I personally collected them."

"These are the same rare, excuse me, I think you said very rare screws used to assemble the bomb that blew up the victims' car?"

"Yes, sir, the same."

Larson steps back and reaches into his pockets, producing two tiny metal objects. He hands them to Tague.

"Take a look at those will you Mr. Tague. If I'm not mistaken, they're the same kind of screws you found in my client's garage . . . the same type that are in Exhibit 4."

Tague holds the two screws together not six inches from his face and squints at them.

"Take your time, Mr. Tague."

Larson, his hands behind his back, turns toward the jury and smiles. He turns back as Tague begins to speak.

"They appear to be the same."

Larson reaches into his pockets again, producing two more of the tiny metal objects.

"How about these?"

Tague's face flushes red. Larson leaves no silent interval. Timing is now all important.

"And how about these?" *Larson asks, again dipping his hands into his pockets, this time producing two handfuls of the tiny screws, all Judith assumes identical to the two rare, no very rare, screws Tague collected from the defendant's garage.*

Larson deposits the metal on the witness stand from

*a height sufficient to hear them fall against the wood
and roll about. As the startled witness gropes for words,
Larson again reaches into his pockets.*

"And how about these?"

Another spray of metal hits the stand.

"And these?"

*Yet another handful spills onto the floor and the in-
vestigator's lap. And yet another, until Tague is sitting
in a shower of screws.*

"I have no further questions Your Honor."

*Larson sits down, his pockets still bulging. In the
background the prosecutor is yelling, "Objection." The
judge sustains the objection and tells the jury to disre-
gard what it has just seen.*

But the damage has been done.

*The day after the not guilty verdict, Judith runs into
Larson in the courthouse. She is gracious, congratulat-
ing him on the impressive win. On his proving his client
is not guilty.*

*Larson, a slight smile appearing, leans toward her,
whispering, "She's as guilty as hell." Then he walks
away, leaving Judith standing in a near-silent hallway.*

*That he would admit to his own client's guilt does not
leave Judith numb. Or even surprised. Because this is
the way the system works. No . . . her sudden discomfort
. . . her growing disdain . . . is with him. Larson. With
his arrogance. His "take that" tone. There was not even
a hint of ethical remorse. This was a time for remorse.
Or if not remorse, then at least silence. Finding the
guilty innocent was something you at least kept to yourself. You don't flaunt those kinds of wins.*

*He should be careful, she thought. Someday that ar-
rogance was going to be his ruin.*

PART ONE

SASSING
THE NIGHT

1

THE YOUTH FORCED his way through the shrubbery lining Montgomery Road until he located the dirt
footpath that would lead him up through the narrow canyon toward the homes along the rim of Silverado Estates. He tried to stay low, stopping short now and then
to evade the occasional glare of headlights from the cars
speeding southward past him toward the freeway.

He avoided the flat rubbery disks of prickly pear cactus mixed randomly with the shrubs—mostly witch's
broom and raphiolepis—at the edges of the path. As he
had occasion to personally discover, the cactus was covered with minute, deceptively benign needles that caused
sufficient pain to immobilize whatever limb was unfor-
tunate enough to have made contact with the plant.

It had been an unusually wet winter for San Diego.
A record rainfall had bathed the canyons in greens and
forced out the April purples and golds in the southern
California wildflowers and shrubs. Tonight, the hillside
was in full bloom and the smell of jasmine was strong.

But the colors and smells of the season were of no
interest to him. The excitement, the adrenaline-charged
assault on the hillside, was for a singular purpose, and

every step, every one of his animal instincts, was calculated to accomplish that purpose.

His objective was to tag, to write his initials over the huge new retaining wall above him, and to inscribe his moniker on as many parts of that wall as he could as fast as he could.

Killing all points!

Sassing the night!

A decidedly unattractive, gangly five-foot, six-incher with protruding cheekbones and ears slightly too big for his thin face, he shed his earthly identity at the base of the canyon. He was Antonio Enrique Perez no more. He was "Slic," the name he tagged by.

This afternoon, he'd been in a classroom listening to some gringo whose name he'd forgotten try to teach him to speak Spanish—the language he'd spoken all his life.

Now, under a full moon casting an eerie argentine glow on the hillsides he was a whiz-bang cactus dodger enclothed in the hip-hop I-don't-give-a-fuck uniform of the day—blue plaid flannel shirt, gray pants baggy enough to hide a friend in, and a designer label baseball cap worn cockeyed backward. The sum total message of this time and place, this dress and mission was unambiguous: I do it my way when I want where I want how I want.

He didn't much give a damn if the owner of the wall painted over his tag as soon as he put it there. He would climb the hillside again and rewrite it. And if they covered it yet again, he would write it yet again. He could match their attempts to stop him at whatever pace they chose. And unless they found some way to stop him he would, in the end, prevail. They would give up and his tag would remain until other taggers found ways to replace his initials with theirs.

Writing—he did not like the word "tagging"—was not a casual pastime.

It was a passion.

It was his life.

His past as far as he cared to remember was writing; his future as far as he could predict was writing.

His idols were other taggers; guys like Cool Earl who had tagged the tallest water tower in Philadelphia, and Chaco, who tagged twelve train cars in one night up in Los Angeles.

His writing offered escape from a house full of his parents' drunken arguments. And it had, in its own perverse way, given him hope, replacing failure with self-esteem, boredom with the excitement of courage. Anonymity with fame.

Fame.

Fame was the name of this game. He would tag the best, the most. The highest. No more significant was his message than to declare to the world, "I was here. *I* was here!"

No one could stop him. Or even keep up with him. Not the city maintenance crews. Not the department of transportation, which angrily lamented that a few minutes of tagging could take a whole day and three thousand dollars to remove. And not the other writers he competed with for space.

He'd go bombing—tagging walls—for two, even three days without really going home except to eat and change clothes. Whatever it took to keep control.

He owned the city.

He never thought about the damage he caused. It never occurred to him that writing was bad for the neighborhood.

After all, he could be getting his thrills doing far worse things.

Far worse things.

They all should be thankful he'd found such a creative way to express himself.

Now midway up the footpath he saw his destination—
the wall anchored to the side of the slope. It was flaw-
less! It would be a clean hit.

Slic whistled under his breath. What a landmark! The
wall overlooked all of Mission Valley and even if his
tag was there for only a day, thousands of drivers would
see it from the freeway below.

Pretty good for seventeen years old. Damn good! Shit
he was it! He was all city now!

Slic had tagged from central San Diego to Chula Vista
since he was thirteen—writing mostly on vacant buildings and retaining walls along the freeways—battling for
space with other taggers—dissing them by crossing out
their tags and writing his over them—watching over his
tags to keep them from the humiliation of being dissed.

And he'd mapped the heavens!

Oh how he had mapped the heavens!

Climbed the twenty-five feet up freeway posts! Shim-
mied out along the tops of the large green traffic signs
hanging over the middle lanes of Freeway 8 down in
Mission Valley where he would write his name above
the traffic directions. Hanging out! It had scared the hell
out of him the first time he'd done it. And my God, Cal
Trans was going crazy trying to catch him and keep up
with erasing his tags.

And he'd done it all alone! A oner! No crew of
squealing fatuous kids backed him up.

He never thought . . .

Slic's concentration was momentarily broken by a
rustling sound to his right. He froze in the darkness then
forged onward. He could run faster than whatever or
whoever it was and he knew it couldn't be the police.
He'd done his homework. He'd watched the area police
patrols for days and he knew their schedules. He could
get up before they came around again.

At the base of the wall, the mass of smooth gray-white

concrete stood illuminated by the moon—so much bigger than it looked from the street below. Maybe six hundred feet across. Fifty feet high. Earth and concrete molded together, each holding back the other.

Slic reached into the pocket of his pants, feeling for the can of ultra-flat spray paint he'd stolen—racked—that afternoon. You only tagged with paint you stole. Stealing the paint was part of the tagging.

The cold feel of the metal spray can started his heart beating faster.

This was no fifteen-second scribble, no throwup. Five minutes. Maybe ten. That's what he needed for a fifty-by-six-foot-tall piece; one as high as he could reach.

The paint he'd brought wouldn't be near enough to do any kind of major piece, but that was cool. He'd hit it again.

Slic's hand poised mid-air, his whole body feeling the day's warmth radiating from the wall, inviting him closer. He tested the can first, scrawling "Slic" in foot-tall red letters. There were no paint drips. It was perfect.

Then suddenly, from nowhere it seemed, an unnatural breeze brushed his face.

There was no time to react. An arm from nowhere reached around his neck and another pulled his own arm sharply, painfully, behind him and up. The paint can fell, rolling a short distance down the hill into the darkness.

As his body lifted off the ground, the smell of alcohol and cigarettes enveloped him; a deep, strong voice whispered in his ear.

"Toy! This canvas isn't yours. Not one of you toys has any idea good enough for this wall. Not if you thought about it for a whole year!"

Toy.

It was an insulting word. It was a term he and his homies—his friends—used to describe a writer with no style.

This was no police officer.

"What's your name, Toy?"

The boy choked out, "Slic."

"What the fuck you think you're doing with that can, Slic?"

The hold around Slic's neck tightened. He gasped. The man was a bull; his grip a vise. The hold tightened again. Then, when he thought he was about to lose consciousness he was released, shoved roughly away and to the ground. He turned his body and looked up to meet his assailant—a man he would later describe as a short old man with mean and angry black eyes.

"I don't want to see your skinny body up here again. Eh, Slic Toy?" the man growled. He spoke with an accent. Not Chicano like him. More like Italian—but not Italian.

Slic didn't answer. He crawled several feet, rose, and as the man stretched out his leg to kick him, Slic half-crawled, half-rolled as fast as he could down the hill to the busy street and safety below.

I'll be back, Slic thought. But not tonight. The lack of oxygen had left him with a headache. And his neck hurt bad. He'd wait to see if this guy dissed his tag and laid claim to the whole wall. If he wanted a piecing battle he'd get one. But Jesus! The dude was too old to be writing! Who the hell was he? Maybe the property owner! If he was the owner, Slic would have to be careful. He'd seen the results of some of the beatings his homies had received from property owners and police. It would never happen to him. The next time he came back it would be even later, past the old man's bedtime—but that old man sure had a hell of a grasp.

This was just a temporary setback. He'd catch the trolley back home to southeast San Diego and scribe his tag on a seat or two along the way. Definitely. He'd chisel tonight. It wouldn't be a complete loss.

At the wall, Gui Colon stood watching until Slic dis-

appeared from sight. He was breathing heavily. No punk
toy was going to destroy what he had planned for the
wall by covering it with layers of multicolored scribble-
scrabble that no one wanted to see.

Gui Colon painted murals—pieces. His own plans for
the wall lay askew at his feet. He could see the sketches
clearly in the moonlight—four pencil versions of the
same thing—the frontal view of a golden eagle in flight;
its wings outstretched, talons extended. When fully ex-
ecuted, the painting would be two hundred feet across,
soaring high above Mission Valley.

Colon had come here tonight to begin chalking the
bird's dimensions on the wall. But after his skirmish
with the toy, Colon was going to find it hard to concen-
trate or do any physical work. He looked at his shaking
hands. His fingers, whose joints bulged with arthritis,
had stiffened from the tension caused by the scuffle with
that kid. He was sixty-six. Too old for such games.

Maybe he'd been too harsh. What did he say his tag
was? Slic? He squinted in sudden recognition. He knew
who that was! The toy who'd been trashing the freeways! What garbage that kid wrote. He hadn't choked
him hard enough! Colon grunted in disgust as he envi-
sioned the wall covered with big red S's.

Yet despite the disdain, there lay understanding. He
was that hungry for recognition, and, hell, hadn't he
even quit high school and tagged up and down the trolley lines over on Adams Avenue for a year before finally
burning out on tagging? That's what happened to all
taggers. That's what would happen to this Slic toy. He'd
survive. And maybe go back to school or join the army.
If he didn't get himself mixed up with some gang or
killed trying to do something stupid like hanging over
traffic going by at sixty miles an hour. These new toys
were prone to doing stupid things though. They gave
everyone a bad name.

Still, this Slic—or some other toy—would be back. The wall was vulnerable.

A year—even six months—ago, Colon would have simply gone elsewhere to paint. Turf fights were the sport of gangs and taggers, not him—not the muralist's. Tranquility. Reflection. That was what his painting required.

But he would not give up this wall.

This was his last canvas. This was where he would paint his last mural; a masterpiece worthy of the sheer size and visibility of the wall. And if he could paint fast enough—before the arthritis crippled him—and well enough, maybe this work would appeal to something in the public's heart and it would be left untouched, respected. He had seen that happen before, but it had never happened to him.

Colon retrieved his sketches, followed the base of the wall, and climbed to the street above. Tierra Verde Drive was the only way into Silverado Estates and the only way out. Lined by lush green hedges of cape honeysuckle and covered by a loose canopy of pine and jacaranda branches, the two-lane street ascended gently from busy Montgomery Road past two scrupulously maintained wood signs at the entrance to the area; the smaller announcing SILVERADO ESTATES followed a respectable distance by a warning to the uninvited: PRIVATE SECURITY PATROL 24 HOURS. Two miles from the signs, at the top of the hill, Tierra Verde disappeared into side streets of one-acre estates, their sprawling earth-tone homes camouflaged artfully into the hillside by an army of gardeners. Residents of neighboring Kensington could live four minutes away all their lives and never know Silverado Estates existed. And the Estates homeowners liked it that way.

Colon appreciated the anonymity of the area. The homeowners who caught glimpses of him walking up

Tierra Verde early in the morning or late in the evening
never bothered him, believing him a gardener or handy-
man. He seemed at home in the area; seemed to fit in.
More than they could know, their instincts were right.

Colon was no stranger to Silverado Estates. As a child
he had climbed the hill every day, his mother leading
him by the hand up Tierra Verde Drive where he played
in the empty fields while she cleaned the homes of area
residents. The area was more built up now. There were
only two empty acre lots along the canyon rims and they
were being held by the homeowners' association to pre-
serve the canyon greenbelt surrounding the hilltop. Silverado Estates was and always would be country in the
middle of the city.

Confident he had seen the last of Slic, Colon crossed
an unlighted section of Tierra Verde Drive and slid
down the canyon on the other side. When he reached a
small plateau approximately fifty feet below the street
level, he removed a large, dried piece of shrubbery from
the front of a two-foot wide opening in the canyon wall
and pushed his body through. Inside, he groped for then
lit the small camping lantern he kept on the ground to
the immediate right. A sleeping bag, pencils, and sketching pad were just where he had left them. On its side,
half-empty, lay a bottle of vodka.

Colon unrolled the sleeping bag and reached for the
vodka bottle.

The cave was not as comfortable as his one-bedroom
house on India Street. But his instincts and feelings sur-
faced here. He could stand at the rim of the canyon,
watch the brown falcons circle above during the day,
and savor the smells of the night.

The caves were Colon's secret. A forgotten part of
San Diego's colorful folklore, the underground chambers Colon had played in as a child, and now used as
an artist's retreat, had once earned Silverado Estates

considerable notoriety. As Colon remembered it, in the early 1900s William Young, a druggist who lived across the canyon in Kensington, developed consumption and was told he could live longer if he engaged in some form of physical activity. Like digging. And dig he did. Young surveyed the Silverado hilltop and day after day, stripped naked to soak in the hot sun, dug with pick and shovel; first into one side of the hill, then the other, eventually completing a tunnel that stretched 240 feet between the canyons on either side. When he finished, he embarked on an even more ambitious project, expanding the tunnel into an extensive network of rooms and hallways, eventually reaching the size of an eight-room house. Some of the rooms were ten to twenty feet across. The doctor's advice worked. Young, who was sixty-eight at the beginning of the project, died at the age of ninety-three when he was struck by a car near his house.

Over the years, Young's caves had been relegated to the status of public nuisance attracting teenage runaways and mischievous kids. Even a group of youths calling itself The Sons of Satan had used the tunnels briefly as a meeting place. In the 1950s the owner of the land on the hill offered the tunnels to the city for use as a bomb shelter in the event of nuclear war. The city declined and ordered the entrances dynamited closed. With the advent of luxury homes on the hill, the tunnels had long since been forgotten.

Except by Colon. On his first trip to the hill to survey the mural wall, he had poked around the canyon rim until he relocated one of the cave entrances.

Now, as Colon sat on the sleeping bag, debating whether his hands ached too much to work on yet another of his eagle sketches, he heard muffled voices. He put down the drawing pad and stepped cautiously from the cave. It was a clear night. Voices were carrying easily. They were coming from above his location, across the street, in the direction of the wall.

Colon climbed up onto Tierra Verde Drive. They were men's voices; one deep and measured in tone, the other higher, and growing more excited. He needed to be careful. If someone caught him watching, they might call the police. So he stood, listening as the argument grew more heated and the man with the higher voice began yelling obscenities. Colon moved still closer. He could catch a few words here and there—"lines" and "thorns." The men seemed to know each other, that much he could tell. They were standing in almost the exact place where half an hour earlier he had confronted Slic.

Colon inched closer, curious to see if one of the combatants might be the young tagger, caught in a confrontation with an irate neighbor. One look, however, satisfied him that Slic had not returned.

Colon crouched behind a thick growth of prickly pear and cape myrtle only to witness an escalation of the fight. There was a shove. Then another.

The two men fell awkwardly, slipping heavily part way down the hill. As Cólon struggled with whether to interfere or let this skirmish run its course, the taller of the two men lifted something over the head of his now prone adversary, and, before Colon could think to react, the man brought the thing crashing down on the head of the other.

There was a hideous sound. The contents of Colon's stomach rose to the base of his throat. He slipped backward as the man suddenly turned his attention toward Colon who, too late, realized he was now standing in full view—no longer hidden by the shrubs.

The picture before him was frozen in the moonlight. On the ground, hands and feet twitching, lay the body of a man wearing a knit golf shirt. Above him stood the assailant, a tall, muscular man of almost aristrocratic demeanor, his silver-gray hair combed straight back from his thin, triangular-shaped face. And piercing through the whiteness of the assailant's face were his steel-blue eyes; panic-stricken eyes that had lost all rationality and were wild; wild and frenzied.

Colon's mind raced. Should he subdue this murderer? Too late again. The assailant ran past Colon and although Colon reached for him the man quickly disappeared into the hillside shrubbery.

Colon's reaction was to run too. Fast. Before someone happened on the scene and pointed the finger of guilt at him. Yet he had done nothing wrong. His obligation was to stay. To call for help. Why could he not bring himself to just yell? To run for the security patrol he evaded nightly? His predicament was resolved by the glint of metal. The spray can Slic had dropped!

In spontaneous compromise, Colon retrieved the can and to the left of Slic's tag, in scrawled letters of his own, wrote directly above where the body lay, "I saw this." Then, he shoved the can into his pants pocket and fled to the safety of the cave, where he gathered his papers, turned off the lantern, and left, carefully replacing the shrubbery in front of the cave opening.

Colon could not risk being seen running down Tierra Verde Drive. He slid as fast as he could down the height of the canyon to Montgomery Road, where he caught the first bus and rode without caring where it took him.

Colon finally reached his house well after midnight and waited nervously in front of the television for the late-night news. Maybe there would be a story about the man's murder. When there wasn't, Colon poured a glass of vodka, drinking long swigs. He needed something to stop the dull throbbing in his head.

Colon sat for what seemed hours, lamenting his predicament.

All he had wanted to do was paint something good to go out on.

Just paint.

And now look.

When he'd drunk enough vodka he passed out.

2

JUDITH THORNTON'S PHONE rang at 7:10
A.M. The ringing sounded far away, a fragment of some
departing dream. It triggered a burst of adrenaline as
there was a sudden awareness of place but not time. Her
heart raced as a sudden fear seized her and the thoughts
came rapid-fire. *She'd overslept! Court had started. She,
the chief prosecutor for the San Diego district attorney's
office, hadn't appeared for trial! The judge had ordered
the clerk to call her office and the office was in an utter
panic now the way it was when some Ivy League rookie
failed to properly calendar a case and the office was left
unrepresented in front of an unhappy judge and impa-
tient defense attorney . . . and now they knew she, the
most celebrated member of the office, hadn't come in at
all and she would have to publicly embarrass herself by
apologizing in open court. . . .* And in the middle of this
terror, the temporal aspect of life returned. No . . . no . . .
it was . . . Saturday. Yes . . . she was positive it was Saturday . . . so this call was . . . too early.

Without unfurling herself from the pink flannel bed
sheets, Judith reached for the phone at the top of the
headboard and pulled the receiver to her face. She rec-

ognized the voice immediately. It was Lawrence Farrell. District Attorney Lawrence Farrell. After the Bobby Engle murder trial, Farrell had been appointed district attorney and with his appointment, Judith had been promoted from head of the major offender unit to chief assistant district attorney . . . the first woman to ever hold the office.

"Judith? It's Larry. I didn't get you up did I?"

He didn't wait for her to answer because his question was one of courtesy only. He knew damned well he'd gotten her up. But there was always a reason for his early calls. When the big cases broke the police notified him first regardless of the hour and when he got up she got up.

"It's nice hearing a man's voice so early Larry but I'll bet this isn't a social call. What's happening?"

"A major homicide went down last night Judith. Right there in Silverado Estates . . . in fact it happened almost in your backyard. . . . "

Judith was suddenly alert. She shifted and sat up, pulling the bed pillows to her back.

"Who was it Larry? Someone who lives up here?"

There were only a hundred homeowners in the Estates. She knew most of them and could identify all of their names.

"Threadgill. A William Franklin Threadgill. You know him?"

"Oh, no. . . . I don't know him real well, I've met him a couple of times, Steven and I . . . before our divorce . . . were invited to a housewarming Threadgill gave when he moved into his new home. Nice man. Rich man."

"How rich?"

"Rich enough to own lots of racehorses. Rich enough to hire a fifteen-man mandolin orchestra for his housewarming. An impressive man too. Very articulate, and kind. He owns . . . owned . . . a chain of pharmaceutical companies. They were socially active but not with the folks up here . . . mostly with the La Jolla scene I think. Where was his body found?''

''At the base of a retaining wall near the west canyon.''

''I know the one. It overlooks Mission Valley. Who found him?''

''Some man out walking his dog this morning. Threadgill's wife didn't know he was missing until the police officer knocked on the front door with the bad news.''

''That's awful Larry. They're good people. Any idea who did it?''

''No. We have a sketchy preliminary report here. His wife couldn't think of anyone who'd want to kill him. But then she's in a pretty bad emotional state right now. Relatives are staying with her. We'll try questioning her again in a few days after the funeral when things settle down. Her memory might improve. We want to take a look at the company books right away but from what little we know he was doing very well and the firm was on the up and up with plenty of cash. He was a one-man operation with no partners so we have no one to call in right away for fast information.''

''What do we know about the cause of death?''

''His skull was smashed in. It wasn't a pretty scene.''

''Was the murder weapon recovered?''

''No. Couldn't find it. Or them.''

''Or them?''

''Uh-huh. There are slashing and cutting marks on Threadgill's scalp along with the heavy crushing blows so either two murder implements were used or the weapon's got a real interesting shape. We think we might have a witness but that's not a sure thing.''

''Someone could have heard something. Things at that

end of the Estates are a little closer together.''

"No . . . nothing that simple. There's a very strange message spray-painted on the retaining wall just above Threadgill's body. It's fresh and looks like it was painted last night.''

"Graffiti?''

"That's what it is, apparently.''

"We don't have graffiti in Silverado Estates. I've never seen any up here. Ever. We have a twenty-four-hour patrol.''

"Go take a look if you can Judith. The case is all yours if you want it. You can pass it on to a line deputy but it'll be a good supplement to your PDQ.''

PDQ referred to the thirty-page personal data questionnaire Judith filled out when she applied for the one remaining vacancy on the San Diego Superior Court. She had sent the questionnaire to the governor's office where it had gone the way of most judicial applications and languished for months. Then, after her successful prosecution of Bobby Engle for the murder of Kelly Solomon and her thorough annihilation of Engle's highly touted defense attorney, Alan Larson, Judith was promoted to chief assistant district attorney and in so doing assumed the role of San Diego's leading trial prosecutor.

A week earlier, she had received a phone call from Peter Thomason, senior partner in the law firm of Thomason, Edmonds, and Dymer, known affectionately to the legal establishment as TED. Thomason was also a personal friend of the governor and was widely rumored to be chairman of the governor's informal judicial screening committee for San Diego, a group of hand-picked confidants of the state's chief executive—a chief executive elected on a strong anticrime platform. The committee, like those said to have been established by the governor in other counties throughout the state, was composed of people the governor trusted to both give him truthful information about judicial applicants and recruit judicial candidates who fit his own anticrime profile.

Despite occasional attempts to learn the identity of the San Diego group's members, its composition was still rumor only—its anonymity itself an indicia of its power. The only thing certain was that the governor would not send a judicial application on to the state bar's commission on judicial nominees for formal evaluation by the governor unless the candidate first got past his own group of local advisors.

Thomason had called Judith and, in ambiguous language, had asked her for six personal references "in order to process her judicial application." One of those references had been Farrell, and he had called her immediately after Thomason called him, breaching Thomason's confidence by confirming she was being evaluated by the local committee.

Farrell's reference now to her PDQ was a reminder that her personal resolution of the Threadgill murder would be just high profile enough to earn smooth sailing through the local committee.

"Do you want a report from me today Larry?" Judith asked, avoiding prolonged discussion of her application.

"No . . . no . . . I've promised Janet I'd take her out to Julian for the day to do some shopping. Just go eyeball the scene will ya before all the evidence gets carted away or someone up there decides to clean up the writing on the retaining wall. . . . We'll talk on Monday."

Then he hung up. Just like that. He briefed her, asked her to assess the case, and that was it.

Threadgill was an important man, important enough to merit a high-level investigation, but he wasn't so important that the district attorney himself needed to sit by the phone and assume a personal, hands-on approach to the case. He could take his wife out to the east county to shop, and turn the case over to Judith. She was on her own to pick the approach she wanted. That's how she liked to work. That's the only way Farrell worked.

Judith looked at the radio alarm next to the phone. Seven forty-five. She laid back down and pulled the bedspread up over her shoulders, almost over her head. Her six-year-old daughter Elizabeth was spending the weekend with her father, and this was supposed to have been Judith's morning to sleep in.

She wasn't the kind of person who had ever spent much time feeling sorry for herself. Not when her husband announced he needed some time to separate, or when they divorced. That had been coming for two years. She'd seen it and dealt with it as well as any then-thirty-five-year-old with a child. Nor had she felt the martyr when her mother came to live with her then lapsed into a progressive dementia. That was divine fate. She and Steven had bought this big beautiful house with the unconscionably large one-acre lot with its unconscionably large mortgage just in time to provide her widowed mom with a proper home and care.

And who was she to be complaining, anyway? A gorgeous home, healthy child, successful career in high gear . . . everything else, all the pressures, came with the territory. And there was no doubt she could handle the big things coming at her. They required organization, strong intestinal fortitude, and endless patience. She had all that.

But her private moments, her time for herself, *her mornings to sleep in*, they were all disappearing with all of her successful management of life, leaving her to wonder whether she was running her life or it was running her.

She looked up at the radio clock. 7:50.

First thing coffee. She needed a cup in her hand before she did anything else. She'd put the coffee in the coffeemaker and filled it with water the night before. All she needed to do was push the start button.

Judith quickly dressed in a blue velour sweatsuit and tennis shoes. She quietly walked the fifty-foot hallway to the kitchen. Her mother's apartment area and guest quarters were at the far end of the hallway, just past the kitchen.

The sun had begun to creep into the breakfast nook and the polished ash stain on the wood cupboards took on a warm reddish hue. The blues and pinks of the dry straw flowers and brown earthenware jars on the white-white counter tile exuded the serene look of French country.

Judith pushed the button on her coffeemaker and walked to the end of the hallway, to her mother's quarters. She peeked into the bedroom and heard her breathing. She was still asleep.

Her mother's nurse had slept over. There was relief knowing she would be there to take care of her mother as soon as she awoke.

Over the last two years, multiple strokes and a suspected but unconfirmable case of Alzheimer's disease had gradually destroyed her mother. Bit by bit, minor stroke by unpredictable minor stroke, her brain was shrinking. Two expensive MRIs over the span of six months confirmed what the first neurosurgeon diagnosed in minutes two years ago when she had suddenly but temporarily lost her ability to speak.

Now, her mother was bedridden and quadriplegic; unable to do even the simplest of things for herself. Unable to swallow all but pureed foods, the daily struggle was to blend enough solid foods with enough calories to keep her alive. Just alive. To get enough sips of water into her to keep her hydrated and stable.

Judith had talked to her mother's doctor a year ago. He told Judith then that her mother would hold on as long as her body was strong enough. But they all knew what was coming. What was coming was a losing battle. Her mother was slowly starving into an ever-weaker physical state. Eventually she would die of pneumonia.

And so Judith watched and waited; a facilitator of her mother's death. Helping her mother get from here to there, wherever *there* was.

Death seemed to be approaching like that. There were times she thought she could see it coming and got set for it. Then it would take a quick side-step and was gone, around her. At first Judith was prepared to grab hold of it, fight, and wrestle it to the ground. Now she was resigned to meeting it halfway; she just wanted to be there when it finally came. But it was strange, this waiting. Everything, even the mundane things in life, took on a new perspective. Not of appreciation, but of timing. She would look at her cat and know in all probability it would outlive her mother. News of the sudden death of some famous person struck her as incongruous. Useful life snuffed out; her mother staring in silent victory over death.

At one point, before she decided her mother would die at home, and not in a hospital, Judith had even packed an emergency overnight bag. All plans were in place for whatever emergency might arise. It was not unlike giving birth, she thought at times. Like when she was waiting to go to the hospital to have Elizabeth. Except mother was going, not coming. And the end result was certain pain, not joy.

Of all the pressures in her life, it was her mother's condition that periodically threatened to push her over the emotional edge. There were mornings when Judith didn't think she could possibly go on a day longer balancing the going and coming of life, home, job, and child. And then one of those moments would happen— when Judith hugged her mother tightly to say goodnight and her mother's face went from deadpan to elfish smile . . . or when her mother, her body torturously stiff, turned her eyes to the bedroom door at the sound of Judith's voice . . . when Judith knew, she really knew, that if she had to she could go on like this forever.

At times Judith found herself envious of people whose loved ones died quickly. Then she would wonder if the pain of not having been able to say goodbye was the same as grieving the loss in segments, grieving a loss every day for an indefinite period of time.

So on mornings like this, in the calm quiet of the first rays of light, Judith loved her mother desperately and at the same time loathed the never-ending pain she caused to surround them. Life and death were all one inside her house. A moment away from each other. Sometimes she wondered, would there be a difference, ever again, between the two?

In the midst of the specters and dilemmas, Judith poured herself a cup of coffee and tucked a pencil and small pad of paper into her pants pocket.

Outside, the circular driveway was damp from the sprinklers. The smell of newly cut grass and canyon flowers filled the air. It was hard to believe death lay so close.

Judith decided to walk rather than drive the distance even though walking on a morning as nice as this one seemed too casual, too enjoyable for the job that awaited her up the street.

As Judith rounded the curve just past her immediate neighbor's house, the blue stucco of the Thuli home stood out in the distance. The house was new, just six months old. The retaining wall where Threadgill was murdered belonged to the Thulis; it circled the base of their hillside.

Overlooking Fairmount Avenue and the freeways below, the Thuli house had already achieved notoriety. It was blue, contrary to the Silverado Estates Covenants and Restrictions, the C&Rs, as they were called. The C&Rs of Silverado Estates required house and roof colors to be muted earth tones. The Thulis' stucco color had been approved by the development committee of Silverado Estates based on a color chip submitted with the house plans. But no one, not even the Thulis, expected it would dry such a bright blue. The board of directors for the Estates held two emergency meetings to debate whether the Thulis should be required to strip the stucco and start over. Several neighbors gathered signatures on petitions demanding the Thulis plant more shrubbery to completely hide the exterior of their house. In the end, a resolution was passed ordering the Thulis to restucco within ten years in a color agreeable to the board of directors, and plant five full-sized trees in front of their home to mask the blue. The board of directors, for the time being, was not concerned with the eight thousand square feet of blue facing out over the canyon toward Kensington.

As Judith approached, she could see a circle of bright yellow plastic police tape linking all five of the mandatory trees, warning away the curious with its admonition, "Police Line—Do Not Cross."

Three uniformed police officers were guarding the scene. Judith recognized one of them, homicide field sergeant Tim Engersoll.

"Sergeant Engersoll . . . good morning."

He recognized her, even in her casual attire.

"Mrs. Thornton! What are you doing here?"

"Same as you. Investigating the homicide. But I also live down the street. I knew that guy down there. Not well but I knew him."

"He's not down there anymore. Coroner took him away about half an hour ago actually. We got the photos. There really isn't a whole lot left here. We're securing the scene til we get the word the photos are good.''

''My office tells me there's graffiti, or some kind of writing on the wall above the area where the body was. Can I take a look?''

''Sure, come on down.''

Judith ducked under the yellow tape and followed Engersoll down the pathway on the side of the house to the wall. She stopped just short of the obvious location of the death. A large oily blackish pool of liquid lay on the ground. That's what a head wound left. Not the bright red stuff you saw in the movies. Oily stuff. Thick.

''Did anyone see or hear anything last night?'' Judith asked.

''Not around here. The Thulis have been in Italy for the last two weeks. The maid was in the house last night but she didn't hear anything.''

Judith turned her attention to the writing on the wall. It was not clear to her that the writing was that of two different people. What she read was a message signed by Slic. She read the words aloud.

'' 'I saw this . . . Slic.' Did you get a good photo of this writing, Sergeant?''

''Plenty of them. From every conceivable angle and five distances. Homicide's taken chips of the paint to track down the type and manufacturer.''

Judith stepped closer to the wall, trying to make some sense of the scribbling.

''What do you make of it, Sergeant?'' she asked. ''Do you think this really has something to do with the homicide?''

''Given the way it was placed just over the body it may be this Slic saw the murder or committed it. We talked to the guy who found the body. He walks his dog around here every morning and he says this wasn't here yesterday. He's positive of that.''

''Sergeant, this Slic, what could he have been up to

here? Burglary? He's a gang member, maybe?" The gang crimes were handled by a special unit within the office.

"Slic's the guy . . . or gal . . . probably a guy . . . we don't know for sure, who's been tagging up and down the freeways. It isn't the work of any gang we know of from around here. The closest gang turf is down on El Cajon Boulevard. The 1922s rule down there."

"1922s?"

"Sorry, Mrs. Thornton. This is all a separate language when you're talking about graffiti and tagging. You have to translate 1922. That's the nineteenth letter of the alphabet . . . S . . . and the twenty-second letter . . . V . . . SV stands for Shell Village gang. They sign 1922. All those 1922s you can see plastered on the walls along El Cajon Boulevard east of Fifty-fourth? They've been put there by the 1922s to keep people informed of what's going on in the neighborhood . . . graffiti's the newspaper of the streets. For example, our gangs around here have been known to use their graffiti to brag about their crimes . . . and we've found graffiti at the scene of at least one murder. But we'd expect to find something explaining why the murder happened . . . you know . . . like 'Fuck With the Best Die Like the Rest.' Pardon the language. We found that one written on a wall near the homicide of an ex–gang member turned businessman. Naw . . . this Slic's a tagger. A tagger's only goal is to paint his initials to tell the world he was there, at that spot. Taggers and gangs aren't the same thing. Taggers don't claim territories. Gangs do. Taggers are a major irritant to gangs. They get in the way of communications."

Judith's attention turned from the wall to the footpath that led down to Montgomery Road.

"Did you check out the path there? Were there any paint cans or markers anywhere?"

"We checked our standard three hundred yards every direction from the body and a hundred yards either side of the path. We raked the area too. Nothing. It's clean. Whoever used the paint brought it with him and took with him."

Judith took a sip from her coffee cup.

"Like I said, the way I figure it Mrs. Thornton, this was probably left by someone who came up here to tag the wall . . . not a gang member or anything."

"Sergeant, has anyone suggested we watch the wall and question him if he comes back up?"

"Sure. But if he sees us maybe we get nothing from him. Who's going to be the investigator on the case, Mrs. Thornton?"

"I'm not sure yet but it's probably going to be Pike Martin."

Pike had been Judith's investigator in the Kelly Solomon murder case. She trusted his skill but he needed to be watched carefully. He was prone to stretch the limits of propriety. And his stretching the limits had almost cost them their chief witness in the Bobby Engle case.

Judith had not taken out her writing pad. There was nothing she could do until the police evidence reports came in and the coroner completed an autopsy report on Threadgill.

"You need any coffee or anything, Sergeant? My house is just down the street. . . . I can bring you something."

The officer looked at his wristwatch.

"No. Thanks anyway. I'm about to wrap it up here. We just need to get this place cleaned up a bit, you know, in case kids or someone comes down here." He cast a quick look toward the oily substance on the ground.

Judith walked the area, careful to avoid the immediate

vicinity where the body was found, until she was satisfied she had seen as much as there was to see. Then she
set back for her house. She needed to get up to speed
quickly on graffiti. Who was this Slic? What was he
doing up here last night? She knew enough about graffiti
to know the kids who tagged lived in their own world,
a world whose language she didn't speak.

They needed to find this Slic. But if she was going to
find him she was going to have to learn his language.

Guillermo Colon could identify the events that defined
and destroyed his life. They had always moved in and
out of his dreams, haunting him with undefined grief,
silently rendering impotent the part of the human spirit
that maintains life's stability.

It was New York City, 1932. Past the bedroom door
somewhere that seemed far away, women were crying
the way they did when someone died. There was a
knock. Then another. In silence he watched his mother
lift the frail little body close to hers and hold it tight.
The five-year-old watched as their neighbor gently
pulled his mother from the younger child and led her
out the door because the men had come to take his
brother to the undertaker. The influenza had killed him,
just as it had killed other children in their close-knit
Portuguese neighborhood.

Outside the bedroom, in the hallway with the floral
wallpaper, his mother had paused, suddenly remembering something important. She stared at the wall where
her husband had punched a hole with his bare hand
when he was told of his youngest child's death. In a
voice devoid of emotion, she had asked where her husband was. Colon remembered the neighbor's eyes nar-
rowing to slits as she mercilessly announced Guillermo's
father had disappeared that morning. "He ran like the
drunken coward he is. He cursed everyone," she had

said. "Me. The cats. Everyone." His mother was un-shaken. She pulled him close as she explained with su-perb intuition and understanding of human nature, "His heart is broken and he is mad at God. He will come back."

But his father never did come back. In the weeks that followed, Guillermo heard the hushed whispers. His fa-ther had broken under the strain of poverty and death. He had fled to California.

Life though went on and past events found their proper place in their lives. His mother took a job in the textile mill and the neighbors helped care for him when she worked. The baby portrait of Guillermo's brother— a black and white filmy depiction of a naked child on a white and gray cloudlike background—was hung at the base of the living room stairway next to the portrait of a young uniformed soldier, Guillermo's uncle, who had been killed in the First World War.

Guillermo never spoke of his brother's death or of his father's flight. He never dealt with it, withdrawing in-stead to the large mulberry tree in his backyard where he would sit for hours drawing pictures, listening to the neighbors' concerns over his withdrawal and their plac-ing of the blame for it on his father. Their wrath stood unresolved by time's passage. "Guillermo sits and mopes up there. . . . He holds his arms out like he's try-ing to fly. He's so skinny . . . so white. Is he sick? Have you taken him to a doctor? I think he wants to be a bird now like his brother and fly away. Do something before he kills himself. Find out where he's flying to or from if you know what's good for you . . . and him."

Then one cold October afternoon just before Hallow-een, Guillermo did what they were waiting for. He tilted his thin body forward and sailed over the heads of his mother and one of the neighbors, escaping unharmed except for a broken ankle. With that act of flight, his

mother packed their few belongings, tearfully left her
neighborhood friends, and moved to San Diego to stay
with her second cousin. She never said it, but Guillermo
knew she secretly thought that if she was closer to where
his father was, he might find his way home.

Colon and his mother settled quickly into the growing
community along the waterfront of southern California.
The neighborhood stretched high up into the nearby hills
overlooking the bay. Back then, the area was predomi-
nantly Italian with a strong representation of Portuguese
and Japanese. Many of the residents were fishermen who
supported tackle shops, boat repair, and canneries, and
who swore that if you squinted, the streets resembled
Naples.

Times were good. The air was filled with the rich
smell of provolone and bread, and with an electric energy, a purpose. In the midst of such life and purpose,
Guillermo was content to walk on the ground, padding
through the mudflat that lay between the thriving community and the heady sights and sounds of the fishing
boats at the water's edge.

Colon's mother took jobs where she could . . . baking
bread, cooking and cleaning in high-priced homes as
Guillermo grew up in the streets, drawing the activity
around him on scraps of the thick white paper used to
wrap fish.

Eventually testing his drawing talent in art classes, he
ultimately rejected the discipline school forced on him,
preferring instead the freedom to draw and paint what
he wanted as his moods struck him. He could live without complaint slightly above the poverty line painting
signs, window advertisements, murals, anything anyone
would pay him for. Three Italian restaurants still displayed the murals he had painted well over a decade ago.
He was known to some local artists familiar with his

street art, artists who at one time had sworn he was on the verge of greatness.

Greatness that never came. Greatness that could never reach above restaurant walls. Greatness whose one last chance had been a golden eagle on a retaining wall, a golden eagle that had taken flight with the sudden, untimely death of a man he had never met.

The morning after the Threadgill murder, as Judith Thornton stood examining the cryptic note he had left on the retaining wall, Gui Colon woke with a hangover to the irritating whine of his neighbor's electric weed whacker.

His first thought was of what he had seen. Hot and sweaty, still in the same clothes he'd worn the night before, his first act was to collect the newspaper from the front porch. Spreading the paper on the small round wood table in the kitchen, he quickly checked the front page and the local section. Nothing. The killing happened too late to be reported. Maybe, he thought, the body hadn't even been discovered yet. He needed to think about what his next act would be. He'd seen the murderer and he was the only person who could help identify him. That would mean going to the police.

Colon staggered into the pink tile bathroom and slapped cold water on his face. He needed a shower badly. But he needed something to eat more. His stomach rumbling, he made himself a cup of instant coffee. The little house on India Street, all that his mother left him when she died, was flooded with bright sunlight . . . a stark contrast to the black caves of Silverado Estates.

The icebox was near empty; the eggs he wanted he'd already used for dinner the night before last. Colon could walk two blocks to Leno's Pub and buy a good breakfast for two dollars. The eight quarters he needed were laying on the television set.

Colon stood outside for several minutes on the small

porch, its white paint peeling in large petals from the aging gray wood. The house was a small box with a wood banister. The pink and red geraniums in the clay pots lining the porch and stairs were tinged in brown; they needed water. The distant sounds of Freeway 5, the freeway that had sliced his community in half, hummed in the distance. Not six blocks south lay the outskirts of downtown San Diego and the business lunch trade that kept the remaining restaurants and delicatessens alive.

Colon had been eating at Leno's Pub for ten years, since the place first opened. He was one of Philip Leno's first customers. And vice versa. At the time, Colon was doing odd jobs for anyone who would hire him for anything they were willing to pay. Colon offered to paint signs on Leno's restaurant windows in return for a few dollars. In return, Philip Leno offered him a job painting the daily specials on the windows, and, impressed with the work, had allowed him to paint the name of the restaurant on the doors of one of the vehicles he owned . . . a small station wagon. It was Phil Leno who began referring Colon to other restaurants where he eventually landed work painting wall murals.

Philip had been dead for three years, but the new management kept the restaurant's name and its steady customers. It still catered to a neighborhood that over the last few years had changed very little.

In the corner of the restaurant, in the red leather booth he always sat at, Colon quickly ate the eggs, toast, and potatoes he liberally sprinkled with Tabasco sauce. Finished, he pushed his plate away and began motioning the waitress for refill after refill of coffee as he sketched on the pad of paper he had carried in with him. The man's face was imprinted in his mind. He could close his eyes and see him. Thirty minutes later he dropped his pencil and held his pad up to the light. It was the same man, the same eyes staring at him. All the police needed was a name to go with the face. He could send his portrait in with a note describing what he'd seen. Let the police track down its owner. They could have the killer before the next day had passed. That would end this thing he was in the middle of.

Colon left the restaurant momentarily to buy the mid-morning newspaper from the rack outside the door. He returned and spread it over the table. He did not need to look further than the front page: WILLIAM THREADGILL, NOTED BUSINESSMAN, MURDERED.

It was all there. Photos of the dead man with his wife and grown children. A history of Threadgill's numerous civic accomplishments. And the sketchy details of the man's death. No clues, it said. No clues except a strange note written by someone who might be known as Slic.

Colon's body jerked back, struck by the impact of the shock.

Slic was wanted for questioning!

"My God," Colon whispered under his breath. "They think that kid saw it."

Colon stared at the sketch before him on the table. His loss, his personal tragedy, had taken an incredible twist.

He had information. Valuable information.

He could use it . . . trade it . . . for what he wanted, a mural to paint. At the same time he would give the police what they wanted.

It was ingenious. He would have to give up the painting of his eagle, but if he could have the wall, he would paint a mural that included the killer's face.

This man he had sketched, whoever he was, could be his ticket. And he, Gui Colon, held the cards. He could demand the space . . . demand that wall. It was a guarantee he could paint this one last time. If they wanted the portrait he was holding in his hands, they would have to pay for it and they would have to pay in concrete and time. And they would have to leave him alone to do his work. It was like immunity. Just like the criminals got for the information they gave to the police.

He wanted immunity from artistic interference.

Colon reflected. He was not, he had convinced himself, acting of ill will, or any desire to see this murderer escape. With the information he would supply, the murderer, he was convinced, would be captured. This was a use of coincidence, of a power handed him unasked for.

God would not have given him talent and put him in a position where he could never use it. He had been placed in a position to use his talent right now.

Gui Colon smiled. This could be his greatest work. And a triumph for art because, by God, for once art would control the critics.

Gui Colon waved away the waitress's offer of a sixth coffee refill. He needed to think about just how he could make his demand.

3

SUNDAY MORNING.

Judith looked through the four-inch pile of papers and documents before throwing them away, just to be sure the pile contained nothing of importance.

It was mostly old school work of Elizabeth's and a week's worth of junk mail. Nothing in the house ever got thrown away until it was examined twice, maybe three times. So much paper piled up from the mail and came home from school and work that a fail-safe system had been put into place to assure some important document didn't get tossed by accident. Anyone cleaning or straightening the house had to place any papers collected into a pile next to the bar sink.

Somehow a certificate of achievement, which had been presented to her the month before at a luncheon, had found its way into the pile. Judith carried it into her library office and slipped it into the top drawer of her desk; another piece of paper. On the walls of her office at work she had the obligatory diplomas, and the certificates from the courts she was licensed to practice before, but that was it. The memorial walls built up by those who accumulated and displayed awards was not for her; an anomaly given the number of awards she had garnered over the last three years as the first woman to do a whole list of things, including her becoming the first female chief deputy in the district attorney's Office. Nothing had ever quite moved her to visibly display her success.

Judith's small wood-paneled office at home likewise minimized the outwardly legal appearance of her work and her personal achievements. The deep red-brown tones of ash wood were a strikingly classical balance to the shelves lined with Shakespeare and Charles Dickens, her favorite writers. Dickens's *Mystery of Edwin Drood* sat on a shelf of its own next to a large silk fern. The shelf was balanced by a statue of a bearded sea captain stooping next to a small girl whose long flowing cape was wrapped around her. The man and girl were facing into the wind; his left arm around the child's shoulder, his right arm extended outward, index finger pointing to the horizon. Everything in this one room had been hand-picked by Judith. It was the only room Judith had made a point to tell her housekeeper to touch nothing in and move nothing in.

The design of the library was the only control Judith had demanded when the house was being built. Steven, a successful attorney, had surrendered its design to her, engaging her in heated debate only once when he instructed the electrician to place the light switch on the wood-paneled wall nearest the entry door. Judith had come upon Steven as he was giving the order to the electrician and she had politely but in no uncertain terms insisted it be moved to the wall between the two book-shelves nearest the entry. Granted, it was awkward reaching back between the shelves to turn the light off and on, but she ultimately prevailed; her sense of the room's feeling left undisturbed by utility.

At 10 A.M. sharp, Elizabeth burst through the front

door, followed by Steven. She yelled hello and disappeared down the hallway toward her bedroom.

"Hey! No hug?" Judith called after her. There was no response.

"She was very anxious to get back to her horses today," Steven said, closing the door behind him. "She was telling me all about them. I promised to come in and take a look at them. Hope that was okay."

"Sure, of course," she said waving him in. "There's some coffee left. Help yourself. Elizabeth and those horses. They're the good plastic ones. She's got seven of them now. They're expensive but she takes good care of them."

Judith and Steven were still friends. Despite the pain of the sudden realization they had permanently drifted away from each other, they had parted amicably. They'd worked out the finances themselves and settled on visitation for Steven and Elizabeth without intervention of the courts. Steven had visitation every other weekend and they shared holidays and summer. Child support was never late and with the spousal support Steven gave her, there was just enough to pay the mortgage and cover the costs of running the house. She was living on the edge of financial disaster, but as long as Steven could help and her mother's health and expenses remained steady, Judith was making ends meet.

"How's your mom, Judith?" Steven asked, pouring himself a cup of coffee and settling onto one of the wood chairs at the circular glass dining table nearest the bay window overlooking the pool and yard. Judith sat down across from him.

"The same. Just hanging on. She's still sleeping. I'll tell her you came by . . . but bless her heart . . . I don't think she'll understand."

"Give her a hug for me anyway."

Steven was the first to notice Judith's mother's failing

health. After she singed her bathrobe while cooking it was he who had suggested they get her into their house and out of her home in the northern part of the county before she injured herself. He'd been patient through the worst of times with her mother, living through the loss of their own privacy as soon as they had moved into the house, and adjusted to the pressure of having a terminally ill member of the family surrounded by an incessant flow of aides, nurses, and housekeepers. He'd helped keep it all together at the outset when the going was roughest. He'd done it not from an artificial sense of obligation, but out of genuine concern and caring. For that she felt a profound respect and an abiding love.

"How's your judicial application coming along?" he asked.

"Oh, it's moving along . . . slowly . . . you know how they go. It takes months, even years sometimes. The timing's got to be right, the *right* party in the governor's office, the *right* age, the *right* background."

"I hope it happens for you. I know how much you want it, and you're in the right spot at the right time. A Republican woman prosecutor from Stanford Law School."

Only a few people, among them Steven and Farrell, understood how deeply she wanted this judicial appointment. It wasn't the increase in salary a judgeship would bring—that was only a few thousand more dollars net a year than she was already earning as chief assistant DA. It was something more, reaching far back into her childhood, maybe her genetic code: a need to achieve, attain the highest goal possible. She had loved the law since ninth grade when her social studies teacher set up a mock court system in class, complete with bar exam, prosecutors, and defense attorneys. Prophetically, she'd been selected prosecutor, then judge for her class. A judgeship now would catapult her again into a realm few women had entered. And those watching her knew that once she entered it, she would scale it the same way she'd conquered the district attorney's office. If the timing were right, she might just go the distance, all the way to the court of appeals or even Supreme Court.

"Elizabeth tells me she has a science fair project due in a week," Steven said.

Judith corrected him. "An *invention*. She has to make an invention."

"She's got a great one," Steven said, reaching for another spoonful of sugar for his coffee.

"Oh yeah?"

"Yeah . . . I asked her what you needed around the house and she told me the cat's been scratching the wallpaper in the living room."

"I'll never forgive you for insisting we put up that grass cloth on the wall in there. The cat attacks it whenever we're not watching."

"Well, your daughter's got something that'll help." He was chuckling.

"Okay, what is it? You can tell me. I'm her mother."

"It's great, really."

"I can imagine. You know how terrible I am at building things. I do law, the house, Mom, nurses, dance classes, shopping, schoolwork, and cooking. I don't do mechanics. Is this something I can manage?"

"Relax, I offered to help her put it together and we have it out in the car. It's called 'Cat-Away.' It's a box. We put an electric eye in it and a tape recorder's attached. You plug it all in and if the cat or anyone else walks past the eye, the tape recorder comes on and scares the intruder away!"

"Ingenious. What's on the tape?"

"Barking. Actually, it's me barking. We tested it on Terri's cat and it freaked."

Terri was Steven's new wife. Judith had met her and

even liked her. Terri was blonde, pretty, and she treated Elizabeth very well. According to Elizabeth, she even spoke highly of Judith. Still, she bristled when Terri's name was mentioned; an automatic reaction to Steven's having made a preferential choice in the face of her celibate lifestyle. Hers though was a lifestyle thrust upon her. For now, the possibility of any kind of relationship with a man was out of the question. There were no candidates for the part and besides, she didn't have the time. Not with work, Elizabeth, her mother, and a huge house to worry about.

"Well, we can plug it in and try it. It meant a lot to Elizabeth . . . and to *me*. Anything but inventions!"

Steven looked at his wristwatch. "Gotta go. I have a meeting set with a possible client over in Mission Hills." He disappeared down the hallway. She could hear him and Elizabeth in animated conversation. Then he reappeared. "I'll get the Cat-Away. Try it out for the week and see if it has any kinks in it that need fixing before she has to turn it in. I'll be home early tomorrow night and Tuesday. I'll come over if there's a problem."

"You're a good dad, Steven. Why'd I ever let you get away?" she asked sarcastically.

"I was too mechanical," he flatly explained.

"You're right," she relied in equally flat tones.

Steven retrieved a large cardboard box from the trunk of his silver BMW convertible, carried it into the living room, and set it down on the floor next to the targeted wall.

"The barking dog tape is in there. Elizabeth keeps trying out new tapes to see the kind of reactions the cat has. So far the barking dog tape has had the best results. You want me to plug it in?"

"Plug away!" Judith said. "We'll let you know how it works."

After Steven had gone, Judith walked in front of the

box. Elizabeth and their gray tabby cat, Claws, came running as soon as the loud barking began.

It stopped when Judith stepped out of the path of the electric eye.

"Congratulations," Judith said, patting Elizabeth on the shoulder. "Looks like you have a winner."

They watched as Claws sniffed the box, circled it, and finally hunched down warily next to it.

All afternoon Claws explored the perimeter of Cat-Away, periodically setting off a frenzy of barking. By mid-evening, as Elizabeth was getting ready for bed, Judith went into the living room, drawn by the hint of a familiar odor. Claws was still perched next to the box. The odor was unmistakable. Convinced an intruder inhabited it, Claws had marked her territory around the box.

Judith removed the Cat-Away to the dining room table, scrubbed the carpet as best she could, and sprinkled a powdered floral deodorant on the area. When she was done she stood looking down at the area where the Cat-Away had been.

"Hope this doesn't get to the marketing department," she whispered aloud to herself.

4

JUDITH'S CAR PULLED onto Freeway 15 and
headed north toward Clairemont Mesa. It was 10 A.M.
and the heavy Monday morning traffic into north county
was over. Whenever she could, Judith tried to avoid the
early-morning and late-afternoon bumper-to-bumper au-
tos traveling the north-south corridors of the county.
With any luck now, she would make her ten-fifteen appointment with Melody Harmon, the newly appointed
director of the city graffiti abatement task force.

It had not taken long to connect with the task force.
Judith had dropped Elizabeth off early at school so she
could reach her office in time to talk with someone in
the gang prosecution unit before they headed off to
court. She was most interested in determining how she
might locate the person who had written the strange note
that had appeared on the wall, above Threadgill's body.
While the gang unit attorneys had vague memories of
seeing Slic's moniker around the city, their jobs centered
around prosecuting gang violence, not graffiti writers.
She was, however, supplied with a list of fifty-five city
and county agencies and individuals involved with the
graffiti problem. The description of the task force had

47

intrigued her, promising a clearinghouse of information on monikers and writers. By eight-thirty Judith had an appointment with Melody Harmon.

The directions to Harmon's office were explicit. Harmon's secretary instructed her to exit on Clairemont Drive and look to the left for the frontage road and the row of new office buildings next to the local radio station. Within ten minutes of entering onto the freeway, she'd parked in a visitor space and was climbing the stairs to Harmon's second-floor office.

Even before she reached the midpoint of the staircase, Judith could hear a woman delivering a frenzied oration from the second-floor lobby, her voice sporadically modulating from shrill to bass and back again.

Judith instinctively stopped to evaluate the woman's emotional condition and decide if she should walk into the middle of whatever fracas was going on. One too many office shooting sprees by distraught employees and deranged stalkers cautioned conservative approaches to public exhibitions of anger. But having paused to listen, Judith was now intrigued with what was clearly an irate member of the public venting some obviously righteous steam.

Judith entered the lobby and stood a few moments next to the lady, a tall, heavy-set black woman who looked to be fifty-five or sixty and punctuated her comments by pointing her beautifully manicured index finger at the face of the receptionist, a woman half her size who listened in rapt attention.

"I tell you those kids they got me up at five-thirty. Five-thirty in the morning mind you! Yesterday I finally says to myself, *That's it. I done had it.* I grabbed my husband's shotgun—it wasn't loaded—he don't trust me with it loaded—and I just marched out there to my fence with this gun—and there's this bit of a girl no more than sixteen or seventeen years old with this can of spray

paint. Mind you it was red paint! Right there with that
can at my white fence.''

Unable and unwilling to wedge her way into the
monologue, Judith took a business card from her purse
and slipped it onto the receptionist's desk. The receptionist read it and nodded an acknowledgment as Judith
chose a seat behind the woman, on one of the four gray
tweed office chairs that served as the waiting area, and
continued listening.

''I told her, 'I know you. You're a gang member!'
She never would admit she's a member of the 942's
gang but I told her she is because they're painting their
names on everyone's houses and walls all up and down
the street. And I tell her if she ever comes back—if I
ever see her again I'm goin' to blow up her car—the
big blue one that plays the loud rapping music up and
down the streets at every hour of the day. And I tell her
I don't give a damn if'n she's in it either. She's lucky
she left. And I did see her this morning but she was
walking on the *other* side of the street and that's where
she better stay if she knows what's good for her. She'll
leave me be but I don't know about everyone else. I
talked with my neighbors and they wanted me to come
up here and tell you all that if you don't do somethin'
about these kids, someone's goin' to get hurt. And it
ain't a goin' to be me or my white fence.''

Sensing a convenient stopping place the patient receptionist stuck her own index finger into the air and
announced, ''Just one minute ma'm I have to deliver
this.'' She picked up Judith's card and carried it into the
office area behind the reception desk, returned, and
handed the woman a sheet of paper across the top of
which was written in bold letters GRAFFITI HOTLINE.

''The next time these kids hit a spot in your neighborhood, ma'am, give us a call at this number and we'll
try to get someone out there right away to help you erase

it. You can't give them the satisfaction of seeing their writing. You can also call and schedule a meeting with our representatives. We can come out to your neighborhood and give you some tips on how to handle this problem.''

Satisfied she'd made her point, the woman politely but loudly thanked the receptionist and left.

Peace settled on the office and within a few minutes a short, thin, blonde woman who appeared to be no older than thirty and was dressed casually in denim blue jeans and pink sweater top strode quickly toward Judith, extended her hand, and introduced herself as Melody Harmon.

She led Judith back into her office, a large utilitarian cubicle with a picture window overlooking the freeway Judith had just traversed.

As they settled into chairs, Judith caught the younger woman's furtive glance at the wall clock.

"I appreciate your meeting with me on such short notice. I'm not going to take much of your time. I'll get right to the point. We're investigating a murder that occurred this past weekend. There was graffiti found at the scene. We think the person who wrote it is a tagger who may have seen or even killed the guy. I specialize in homicides and a few of my cases have involved gangs but none involved taggers. My immediate problem is that I need to find our witness and to do that I need to learn as much about graffiti as I can. I'm starting here because more than one person suggested I talk with you.''

"Anything you need. Where shall I start?''

"Maybe you can tell me something about what your office does.'' Judith glanced at the clock long enough to punctuate her sincerity.

"Let's see . . . what's abatement like. Well I've been here since seven this morning. I was here till ten last

night and I'll be here till eight tonight. I'm getting off
early because I need to speak to a whole bunch of neighbors in southeast San Diego who are as mad as that lady
you heard out front. They're having their walls and
fences decorated nightly by tagging crews and need
someone to tell them how to stop it. I can't. And there's
no one I know who can. So I'll talk fast and run if I
have to. Let's see . . . I do have a staff but right now,
that's good news and bad news. The good news is that
I've got a five-member patrol that does nothing but erase
graffiti from eight a.m. to eight p.m. The bad news is
they're the only five I've got.''

She pointed out the window next to her.

''They're all that stands between that garbage you all
see scribbled over the stop signs and freeways out there
and . . . civilization. Today I have one of those five out
with the flu, one on vacation, and one's developed an
allergy reaction to our paint removers. That leaves . . .''
She held up the two fingers. ''That's what stands between us and them. And,'' she added with slight sar-
casm, ''there's a good chance we'll get the budget ax
next fiscal year.'' She dissolved into a friendly laugh.
''Now, how else can I help you?''

''I . . . I'm trying to locate a tagger calling himself
Slic.''

''You need to locate him?''

''I need to talk to him.''

The phone rang, for the moment relieving Judith of
the kind of detailed discussion she needed to avoid. She
wanted to keep any information given out to a minimum
and as general as possible.

''Tom! Heh. Yeah I need to conference with you desperately. We've got those two openings coming up and
we need some diversity. I got three Hispanics, two black
and two white. A great group but we need to schedule
interviews. We need to talk on this for a while but can

I call you back? I've got someone with me now. Good. Three o'clock today my office."

She hung up and dialed the receptionist.

"Hold my calls for a while April, will you?" She returned to Judith. "Sorry. It's like this all day."

"If this isn't a good time . . ." Judith began.

"No, no, if you don't mind interruptions . . . we'll work around them. Now . . . this Slic. I know the kid you mean. He paints the heavens. Regularly."

"Paints the heavens?"

"It's a tagger's term for writing one's initials on anything up high. Like freeway signs and building walls. Nothing seems to slow him down. This kid's got Cal Trans hopping. They put razor wire around the top of one of his favorite freeway signposts to stop him from shimmying out over the traffic sign, and somehow that weasel still got his initials up there. Then they tried to get him by greasing the pole. Some other kid probably trying to match the skills of this Slic tried to climb it. He fell thirty feet into oncoming traffic and just about killed himself. The week after the fall? The parents of the kid who fell filed a lawsuit against the city, and Cal Trans for creating a nuisance that injured their kid. Cal Trans ungreased the pole. They can catch 'em and deter 'em, but just don't hurt 'em. I don't know what, if any, plans they have for catching your Slic."

"Unfortunately, he's our only lead in a crime right now. I have to find him."

"It's not going to be easy for you to do that. As far as we know in this office, the kid's a 'oner.' That means he works alone. And that's getting to be pretty unique because the days of the lone tagger in this city are gone. Long gone. Taggers work with their crews now, that's a group of usually four to ten kids that go along to support the activity. Some members of the crew steal the paint, some do the tagging, some serve as lookouts for the police. We know the names of the most active crews around and with the help of the police, we'll have them all identified and on computer in a couple of months. It's harder to track down the loners like Slic though. The police can always put the word out in the street and see what comes back. But don't count on it. There's a real strong ethic out there. The crews sure don't talk. As far as I know we here at the city have nothing on who this Slic might be. But then our chief job isn't to chase and catch. It's to organize the public to stop graffiti from happening and help clean it up when it does.''

''Anything you can tell me will help.''

''You need to understand this is an incredible onrush of subculture you're up against here. Tagging's the 'in' thing. And it's affecting every ethnic group. Every economic level. Every area of the city. Almost every age group of kids too. In fact, our taggers are getting younger and younger. We get some in the third grade. Imagine, your Slic might be nine years old.''

''Take a look at this,'' she said. Reaching into her desk drawer she retrieved a child's white t-shirt. On the front was a cartoon character, a rabbit glaring angrily. The rest of the shirt, front and back, was covered in multicolored graffiti.

''A bunny with an attitude. Guess where I got this?''

''Some street stall downtown?''

''Nope. I got it at Markel's, that's no third-world store, it's a major clothing store for middle America. They got lots of negative feedback on this one. They pulled it off the shelves. We do other things here though. We're starting a free paint giveaway next month so folks can get rid of the graffiti they find on their property as soon as they find it. The key for the public is to erase it as soon as it's gone up. Taggers need their tags to be seen. If we can get their painted tags erased fast it's what they call 'wasted paint.' They'll leave the wall alone eventually. They put themselves on the line to steal the paint. They don't like it wasted. But that puts the onus on the public. People like that poor lady who was out there when you came in. It's war out there but we don't take the prisoners here.''

Melody reached to the right, to a credenza stacked high with magazines and files. She grabbed three of the magazines off the top and handed them across the desk to Judith.

''You want to curl your hair, read these. I have a memo here that needs delivering. Browse through those for a few minutes. I'll be right back.'' She left, taking with her what Judith surmised was more than one memo.

Judith started with the magazine on the top, a black and white ink job on medium-quality paper. The name was *Lip*. As in don't give me no lip. At the very top was written the subtitle ''The Hoodlum's Zine.'' She struggled with the word zine. What the hell was a zine? It took a moment. It was short for magazine. As in reading material. As in the part of the gun that holds bullets.

She quickly leafed through the black and white compilation of advertisements that ran the gamut from polished to amateur freehand, and two-page interviews with musicians. The faces of the models with hands in their pockets and fists in hands and record groups vying for dollars stared out directly at the reader. Cocky faces. Smug grins. Angry eyes. All men—all with, what did Melody call that look? An attitude. They had an attitude. In this magazine, there were a few white, a few Chicano, but mostly black faces.

The language of the plentiful record album advertisements sporting the young black men with attitudes grabbed her. ''Lyrical bullets to the brain!'' ''Twelve shots in the dome!'' ''Reload your clips!'' Obviously, they referred to songs, cuts on records. Playful double entendre until she got to the advertisement for the album *Kill the Postman.*

The name brands on the clothing ads, like the one for the "Pimping" design line, were as unconventional as those for the music.

Scattered liberally in the art and ads was the graffiti. It was there, unashamed. A cartooned character on the inside cover of the first magazine said it all. He stood with gun in one hand, marking pen in the other. Two pages into the magazine a report on the graffiti art scene implored the reader to be sure to catch the graffiti art exhibition in Los Angeles. A photograph of one of the showpieces struck Judith with its powerful message. "Uprising," by Coax of the A. W. R. Crew, depicted a larger than life, bald, thin, and muscular black man struggling with a helmeted, riot-geared police officer. The officer was swinging his baton at the ribs of the shirtless man, who was simultaneously stretching his arm toward the head of the officer; in his outstretched hand was his weapon, a large spray can. In the background of the painting, a column of smoke rose ominously.

"Interesting reading, huh?" Melody rushed past Judith and sat smiling across from the absorbed prosecutor.

It was all making a little more sense to Judith. "It's not just about making money, is it?" she asked.

"Oh, there's lots of money to be made. You can see from the ads in those magazines and the hundreds like them. It's the selling of a subculture image. There's big, big money in marketing that culture. It's in the music the kids listen to, the clothes they wear. The stores sell it to them, pump 'em full of it, and a lot of them go out and paint the neighborhoods. How's that for commercial responsibility? What entrepreneur could blame them. Any name-brand hip-hop baseball cap sells for twenty-five bucks. But you're right. It's not just about selling products, selling an image. It's selling an attitude. Hip-hop glorifies telling the whole world to go to hell. It's being sold to a whole generation of kids eager to stretch its wings in freedom's behalf. That's not new. But look at the ads in there. Youthful freedom's won with violence. That's new. Freedom of expression protects the right to violence. That's new too. Lots of the ads remind the reader they have a First Amendment right to freedom of expression. So if a cop jacks up your shirt, he's violated your freedom. Not your right to be free of unwarranted seizures. Your right to express yourself through your clothing. And sure, it sells the shirt, but like I said, it sells it with violence.''

Judith continued fingering through the magazine until she reached a page that made her freeze in astonishment.

It was a half-page ad. A young Caucasian boy, about six or seven, stared out at her, his eyes dazed, mouth grimacing. What looked like an ice cream stick lay at his feet. His left hand was clenched, but empty. In his right hand he held a grenade.

Judith blinked. There was a name in small bold black print under the photo. "Felicity amps." Below the name, almost at the bottom of the page, there was a phone number.

Melody saw Judith's eyes widen. She leaned across the desk and focused on the ad. "Record store," she said matter-of-factly.

Judith stacked the magazines. "I would like to read these." Then, as an afterthought, she added, "Can anyone stop this?"

Melody barely paused, "Ask me in about ten years. I don't mean to be flippant. It's just that we're civilized because we agree to be. If enough of us stop wanting it . . ." She laughed, lapsing into humor. "Hell, I say we make all those guys in those magazines rich. Filthy rich. See 'em move into La Jolla and Mount Helix. I'd feel a heck of a lot safer! Come to think of it, maybe there is some hope. I recall reading somewhere this week that the lead singer in Trash—the rap group that sings about killing lawyers—just bought a big mansion on Martha's Vineyard up with the Kennedys and film producers and . . . rich lawyers." She was writing as she spoke, and barely slowed long enough for a response from Judith.

"If you want to find out how to catch Slic, if you *can* catch Slic, talk to this man." She handed Judith the paper she was writing on.

"His name is Nick Margolis. City transit office. That's his telephone number. Those guys over there were chasing down taggers long before we were involved. Nick's an old-timer. And a mean SOB. If you need an advisor, he's the guy you want on board. Tell him I sent you. And good luck. If you've never chased someone down out there in that other world, you're going to need it."

"Mind if I telephone him from here?"

Melody pushed her desk phone toward Judith. "Be my guest."

Within the hour, Judith had checked into her office, answered her calls, and was on the freeway again headed toward the city transit office and a meeting with Nick Margolis.

5

JUDITH WATCHED NICK Margolis empty several inches of the ketchup bottle over the small mound of French fries on a paper hamburger wrapper, alternately picking the potatoes out with his fingers and noisily sucking the ketchup off his fingertips.

"You want to do what?" he asked in mock disbelief.

"Catch a tagger."

Judith said it calmly, watching intently as Margolis dug the last potato out of the red mound. Margolis was a large, rotund man, one whose midsection shirt buttons, she could not help but notice, was straining hopelessly against the pressure of his obesity.

His voice was low, monotone. "Do ya mean a specific tagger?"

"Yes."

"Can't be done," he said quickly, running his hand through his straight black hair as a grin spread across his wide lips. He motioned around the room, at his office walls; all were covered with large maps of the city bus and trolley routes.

"We've got thousands a miles of streets and tracks.

Can't be done. Not if your tagger operates randomly along those routes."

Nick Margolis was the guru of the graffiti transit police. If he said it couldn't be done, it probably couldn't be done. But just as surely as she knew he had far more experience than she, Judith also knew that she needed Slic, needed him badly enough to risk challenging impossibility.

Margolis crushed his hamburger wrapper into a ball and tossed it a good twelve feet across his chest to his left, a bank shot that landed squarely in the middle of the small wastebasket against the wall.

"Wadaya need this tagger for?" he asked, turning back to Judith.

"He wrote 'I saw this' on a wall over a dead body. We'd like to find out what exactly he saw."

Margolis reached for the heavily coffee-stained white mug at the corner of his desk and took a short drink.

"Cold," he said. "Nothing's worse than cold coffee." He put the mug down and slid it back to the precise location he'd taken it from. "For a murder investigation, maybe we could help; give some supplemental support. It's not the kind of thing we've ever done here at transit. We just don't have the manpower to go looking for a specific person. Hell, we don't have enough officers to even watch what's goin' on in the main bus stops downtown." He leaned back and stretched his hands clasped behind his head. Judith's gaze involuntarily shifted to his shirt. The button pushed sideways, half out of the buttonhole.

"We spend almost twenty thousand dollars a month cleaning up graffiti. There's nothing left for tagger manhunts."

"I know—at least I'm beginning to understand—that what I'm asking may be difficult."

Margolis unclasped his hands and folded them on top of his large desk.

"When was the guy killed?'

"A couple of days ago. William . . ."

"Oh yeah, that doctor or something?"

Close enough, she thought. "That's the one."

"You have any leads?" he asked. Judith hoped he was talking himself into giving the investigation some help.

"No really solid leads. Just the writing like I mentioned, on the wall. The initials written were S-L-I-C."

Margolis leaned back and closed his eyes. The mention of Slic's byline had the same effect as if some large caliber bullet had suddenly knocked him slightly off-balance. His reaction was not unexpected given her discussion with Melody Harmon concerning the torment Slic's freeway signing was causing transit. It was clear Margolis was familiar with the kid.

"Mrs. Thornton . . . mind if I call you Judith?"

"No . . . please do."

"Judith, I think there are a number of people around here, me being one, who would like to talk to Slic as much as you would. He's one of our own targets. Drive down Interstate 5. You'll see his tag at the overpasses, and now he's appearing nightly on retaining walls and freeway signs. But now a murder? Hard to believe unless he bungled into it somehow. Frankly it doesn't fit the profile."

"Maybe he got caught in the act by Threadgill and they fought," Judith offered, more interested in his general response to her comment than his agreement with her theory.

"Interesting idea but why'd he tag that he saw it?"

"We have a few theories to work with but none are going to help us if we can't get to him. We have to take a chance trying to catch him and we have to take a chance pretty soon. Homicide cases can get cold quickly. If it's not Slic, someone else out there did it and Slic's our only way to him right now. Pretend for a moment you don't feel the way you do about tracking a specific tagger and tell me how we could do it . . . if we could.''

Margolis's tone softened considerably. ''Like I said before, we haven't had any luck trying to trap specific taggers. We can only hope we get the ringleaders if we set out to do a net. I mean we can create . . . let's call it an opportunity, for taggers to come out to a specific location and we can just hope we get some of the major offenders. We haven't had a whole lot of success. In fact we've created messes sometimes.''

''Like?''

Margolis glanced at his wristwatch. ''How much time you have?'' he asked.

''The afternoon if I need it.''

''I have a couple of things in mind that you'd be interested in trying maybe. If you wanta drive around a little I can show you some things we've tried and maybe we can kick around an idea, or two or three. I'd sure like to see you catch this one.''

''I can drive,'' Judith offered.

''Naw,'' he said, rolling his chair backward and rising from behind his desk, ''I got my car just out the back door. I like a lot of leg room.'' Judith gathered her purse from the floor next to her chair, and followed him out the back of the building into the parking lot.

She could hear Margolis breathing heavily as they walked to the car. ''Hope you don't mind,'' he said, motioning to a white Chrysler New Yorker circa 1964. ''It's an oldie but runs like a tank.''

Judith opened the heavy passenger door and slid onto the blue satin cloth benchseat that rose slightly when

Margolis sat behind the wheel and wrestled with his lap-belt.

By the time he had pulled the car from the lot, he had just regained normal breathing.

"Beautiful, ain't they Judith?" he said, nodding toward the seven-block-long blankets of soft lavender flowers dropped by the jacaranda trees lining Ash Street. "Like I said," he continued, "we ain't had any luck trying to trap specific taggers. Even when we've tried to catch groups of taggers we've sometimes created messes."

He abruptly turned right up India Street toward some of the city's better known Italian restaurants. "I wanna show you one of the messes here." He slowed the car and pointed to three neighboring billboards whose advertisements for beer, tennis shoes, and pizza had been defaced with tag after multicolored tag.

"We allowed this to happen," Margolis said in disgust. He drove on a block and pointed to a low retaining wall. It had been tagged, but with nowhere near the obvious fervor of the writing on the billboards. "That's the culprit there, our last free wall."

"What's a free wall?"

"Something I hope you don't want to use to snag Slic. Free walls were clean walls we used to invite taggers to come to and paint what they wanted. We'd even give the kids legal permits to carry paint cans to the wall. You know," he said parenthetically, "there's a city ordinance prohibiting them from carrying cans of paint. That's why they wear the baggy clothes . . . they can hide the cans on themselves. About a year ago, some kid actually had five cans hidden in his pants and was hit by a car . . . the damn cans exploded. It would be funny except he was dead on impact. Anyway, the free wall idea was to give the kids a chance to paint something legal. But we were fooling ourselves."

"It failed?"

"It failed failed failed. And it fails every time we've used it. The kids had this legal paint and they trashed the area . . . tagged every billboard and fence around the free wall, like those three we just saw. Left the wall itself pretty clean. It's no fun paintin' legal. If we tried to stop 'em in the other areas for carrying illegal paint, they'd flash those permits at us . . . the ones *we* gave them. No, I wouldn't suggest free walling as a way to locate anyone."

"Has anything worked?" Judith asked.

"Shit, look around you. Nothin's worked. We greased the poles. Too messy. Too risky. We tried rat guards, you know, those metal funnels we used years ago to keep rats from climbing onto ships? The taggers brought ladders and climbed over 'em. Some guy wanted us to try puttin' electricity through the poles to shock 'em. We didn't want any part of that business! Imagine the fun the lawyers for electrocuted kids would have with that one! Razor wire's being used up in Los Angeles around the freeway sign posts to keep 'em from climbing the polls, and it was workin' pretty good til they started throwing ropes up around the signs to pull themselves up. We could coat the freeway signs with stuff that lets us wash the paint away, but it costs a fortune."

Margolis accelerated onto Freeway 5 north.

"There's a way that might work. We've only experimented with it a couple of times. We set up a nice clean wall or freeway sign, way up high like taggers like to go after, then we advertise the hell out of it . . . sending out the word on the street that there's a nice new high canvas for them to try, and they'll all be like wild bunnies hopping around it. Trying to get up to the heavens. The problem is, it's damn labor intensive for us. It won't guarantee you're going to end up catching the tagger you want, but for now I don't know of anything else you

can try short of waiting til some officer picks him up by
coincidence or he falls off a freeway sign somewhere.''

"I don't have the time to wait for coincidental
events," Judith said.

"Then I'd suggest there's a promising wall in Old
Town. I have an appointment there with the property
owner in oh"—he glanced at his wristwatch—"ten
minutes. I can drop you back at your car or you can
come on over with me and explore.''

"Let's explore," Judith said. "The sooner we get
moving with some plan the better for me." He was
hooked. He was on board.

"It's going to take some coordinating with local agencies. We'll need police support and city help too.''

"That can be arranged through my office. It might
take a day or two but we can do it.''

"Like I said before, Old Town's one of Slic's favorite
hangouts. We find his tags all over. Hey! Look over
there!" Margolis pointed to the wall of a gelato shop on
the corner. "Lookie lookie." A big red "S-L-I-C" stood
out on the white stucco. "I haven't seen him on restaurant walls before. Might not be him. Might be someone
copying him.''

"We're going to need some kind of plan for what
happens if you catch him," Judith said. "Because we
may not be able to hold him for very long.''

"Sorry, I don't know much about you folks' procedures over there at the DA's office.''

"Penal code Section 594 controls vandalism. Tagging
is considered vandalism and it's still a misdemeanor. Six
months in jail or a thousand-dollar fine. But the jail's so
full you know he won't go there on a property-related
misdemeanor. And in fact, if this is a juvenile, he can't
be sent into the jail at all. He could go to juvenile hall.
But if they can reach his parents they'll send him home
and have him appear later up at traffic court. That's

where we're hearing these cases now. If he's caused five thousand dollars' damage we can charge a felony but most tagging probably doesn't amount to that much.''

"Yah, Judith, it's usually less and we can never tell if an initial was really done by the person the initials claim to be. That makes it hard to come up with the amount needed for a felony.''

"But you know, even though we wouldn't hold him long for misdemeanor tagging, we can hold him for questioning as an accessory to murder. It's a stretch given we have nothing but what he wrote, but playing around with that charge for awhile can buy him forty-eight hours in custody and buy us an interview if he doesn't ask for a lawyer right away.'' Judith, suddenly realizing they had left the downtown area and were almost at the east-west intersection of Freeway 8, asked, "Where are we headed, anyway?''

"That's it, over there,'' Margolis replied. "Looks like a war zone, doesn't it?''

To the right, above the freeway, along the rim of the embankment was one of San Diego's more infamous and recurring examples of graffiti. The long retaining walls separating the row of office buildings from the embankment were covered with initials. Near the middle, in large red letters were the initials SLIC. The wall stood in stark contrast to the view to their left—the San Diego International Airport runways and beyond, the dark blue of the Pacific Ocean. Must be embarrassing and frustrating as hell for the chamber of commerce. Freeway 5 was the major artery for tourists seaward just to the north and Mexico to the south.

"I've been working the Western State Law School up there trying to find a way to keep their wall clean. We've been talking about maybe baiting it. You-know-who's initials keep popping up on it. Maybe we can combine both your needs, ya know, and end up with a clean wall *and* Slic. They seem to be related.''

Western State University College of Law had been a fixture in San Diego's Old Town since the school's establishment there in 1983. The three-story tan stucco building, with its arches and red tile roof, fit well into the early California architecture of the area.

Dean Alice Lee Stottler stood on her tiptoes and peered over the edge of the garage surveying the damage to the law school's retaining wall. For too many consecutive nights to remember, the wall had been plastered with taggers' initials, including the recurrent initials of someone calling himself Slic. The fact it was a law school's wall had not kept the vandals at bay, or put the fear of apprehension in them. Nor had the private security guard hired by the school to patrol the area. If anything the wall seemed to have become the favorite target in the row of retaining walls separating the freeway from the businesses on the rim along San Diego Avenue. All four of those office buildings had been hit repeatedly and no matter how determined or organized the buildings' owners had been in covering the unseemly painting as quickly as possible, it reappeared with nightly vigor.

Finally, fearing the wall had begun to affect the school's reputation, Dean Stottler called the Freeway Transit Department, and they had referred her to Margolis. It was Margolis she was waiting for, watching the planes take off across the freeway and wondering what approach the school should take in curtailing the vandalism now that the first physical assault—of sorts—had taken place. The victim, the uniformed security officer hired by the school, stood next to her shaking his head.

''I tried to chase them this time with my gun *out* and it didn't stop them. They laughed at me. Laughed and ran. Look at my shirt.'' He turned around, his arms outstretched, a model pirouetting for his audience; on the back of his gray shirt, a large red Z.

"You still have the same shirt on?"

"My only other uniform shirt's at the cleaners. The company says they'll send another one over to me today. I'm expecting it any minute now. I can't work without my uniform on. That's why this is still on."

"Very brave of you, but please don't go over the wall after them again and don't unpack that gun unless you have some kind of backup with you, okay? With all the concrete in here we could have a ricochet. I just don't want to see anyone hurt. And look, it's only a wall. I'd rather see it marked up than see anyone hurt over it."

"I didn't think about it. They just made me so mad." He waved his fist. "I'd have loved to cuff one of them. Someone just sneaked up and did this. They've got to be coming up from along the freeway down there. They can't get through the garage with those iron bars we just put up on the open areas. My guess is they're moving in from the sides along the neighboring buildings' retaining walls."

"We could try . . ." The last part of her sentence was drowned out by the sound of an approaching car. She watched it park in one of the visitor spaces and observed Judith Thornton emerge from the passenger's side.

The women had met several times before at one of the seminars conducted annually by the law school for its entering class. Both times, Judith had been a guest speaker on the subject of career opportunities in government and civil service. They were about the same age, and this alone would bring an instant camaraderie. Both had attended law school in the mid-seventies, when less than two percent of their co-students were women. Both savored the success now of being at the top of their professions; success which they found at times so much more easily shared amongst their female counterparts than their male co-workers.

As the security guard retreated to the second floor of the garage, the two women exchanged greetings, each feeling and looking short and thin next to the corpulence of Margolis, who stood mute, watching the guard walk away.

"What happened to him?" he asked, pointing to the red Z.

"A tagger got him last night when he tried to shoo them away from the wall," the dean offered.

"Geez they dissed a person."

"I'm sorry, what did they do?" she asked.

Judith was pleased she could offer the explanation. "They dissed him. Diss with a *d* as in dog. Crossed him out. Taggers do that to be disrespectful to another tagger. They cross out his initials. It's called dissing."

"Ya," Margolis said, his voice higher, his eyes still on the departing figure. "They dissed a *person*. First time I seen that." He looked at Judith. "I hope that's not a new trend."

They watched silently as the marked man disappeared into the elevator. Then Judith took the lead, explaining the nature of her visit in what was otherwise supposed to be the dean's brainstorming session with Margolis.

"We need to use the wall for a sting operation. A tagger who's been signing off down there on your wall is a kid we're looking for."

"You're welcome to it. But I hope it's going to be fast because next week we have a new automated water sprinkler system going in. The wall gets treated with a paint resistant sealant and motion detector lights turn on the water when anyone gets close. Any paint gets easily washed down and the kids go home wet. It's worked pretty good up in Orange County."

"Actually," Margolis added, "we were hoping we

could put this all together for tomorrow night. We'll come over first thing in the morning with a city crew to paint over the tagging and then we sit and wait. Hopefully our friend Slic will turn up as one of the group that comes to paint your wall again. It might work if we're lucky. If it's okay with you, I'd like to look around, see what it looks like down there and figure out where we'll put the police units."

As Margolis flexed his elbows back, stretching, Judith's eyes moved to his shirt. The button, still postured to pop, held, but only by a breath. Her eyes met the dean's. She had seen it too, and for a moment their attention shared a focus, distracting them from Margolis's invitation.

"Ah . . . ladies?"

Judith snapped smoothly back, speaking but eyes still on the errant plastic disk.

"Just tell me where to step."

Judith looked down at the dean's feet. She was wearing tennis shoes with her suit, the modern indicia of the physically fit executive whose heels were reserved for the boardroom but whose lunches were spent on power walks in tennis shoes.

"I'm ready," Stottler declared.

Within the hour, the three had walked the outside perimeter of the school and ventured as far down the freeway embankment as caution and the stinging nettle bushes permitted.

The stage was now carefully set. Judith would request the San Diego Police Department provide four police units and six officers. Three of the four police cars would be unmarked and positioned at the front, north, and south sides of the school building. One standard black and white would be positioned in the neighboring office building parking lot. If a street chase ensued, the easily identifiable black and white would be a necessity.

It was 3 P.M. by the time Margolis and Judith returned to the transit parking lot and Margolis walked Judith back to her car. She unlocked the door and slid in behind the wheel, feeling slightly uncomfortable as he closed the door for her. She hit the electric switch on the door handle, lowering the window.

"Nick, I'll call you later this afternoon to let you know if the police units are confirmed."

"If I'm not in, have 'em beep me."

"I will. And, oh, by the way," she said, pointing to his stomach, "your shirt button's open."

6

COLON SAT SULLENLY at the booth of the Ensenada Bar on San Diego Avenue. He sat nearest the window hoping perhaps he might catch a glimpse of the boy. He would recognize him if he ever saw him again.

Colon was convinced it was in this part of town he'd have the best chance of finding Slic. He'd seen his tags everywhere but especially along Freeway 5 at the Old Town exit and near the law school. He wasn't sure how or when he'd find him, only that he wanted desperately to find him.

Colon had a plan. He had been reading the papers. He knew Slic was being sought for questioning in the Threadgill murder, a murder he hadn't seen, and unless he read the newspapers, didn't even know had happened. It would be easy for him to extricate Slic if he were to come forward and explain it was not Slic, but he who had witnessed the murder and left the note on the wall.

But while Colon's ability to exonerate Slic existed, his desire to do so immediately was less pronounced. Colon knew he would never be allowed to paint the mural unless he had the wall and he couldn't have the wall unless he *made* someone give it to him. Now, he needed to communicate his demand. But not on the phone. That was too easy. And they would come after him fast. Before he could get them to agree to give him the space he wanted, they would find him and he would have to do what the police wanted. No, he needed his demand painted across the heavens, painted someplace high. Someplace the police couldn't miss seeing it. Someplace it couldn't be removed from too easily.

But his body, his fingers, could never get him to such a place now. Not at his age. He needed someone who would help him do that. Slic could help him. Didn't Slic need him, Colon, to tell the police what really happened and that Slic had seen nothing? They needed each other.

Colon looked at his wristwatch. It was 11:30 P.M. He would have one more beer and take a walk along the edge of the town. As he sipped his last drink, he noticed one police car, then another, driving slowly eastward along San Diego Avenue. Something was up. He finished his drink and sat looking out the window, waiting for something to happen.

At the law school, four blocks from the bar where Colon sat, the police waited patiently at the now clean retaining wall. 11:30 P.M. So far no one had approached the wall. The unsightly writing had been covered that morning with Navajo white paint by the graffiti removal volunteers of Graffiti Clear, a nonprofit organization dedicated to removing the blight of graffiti from the city.

That the police and Colon, each for their own reasons, were hunting him down that very night, was unknown to the skinny kid who was carefully making his way along the hillside toward the law school's retaining wall; oblivious to all but the clinking sounds of the two cans of flat red paint tucked into the inside pockets of his knee-length flannel jacket. He'd smuggled them out of the house past his mother as she stood at the stove, imploring him to sit for dinner. He'd brushed aside her demands, hurled at him in Spanish, promising he would be back to sleep at home tonight.

Above him the officers stood in previously assigned positions: two in the garage, two on each end of the school's retaining wall, and two in a black and white patrol car concealed in the darkness of the neighboring business parking lot. On Slic's approach, the officers began coordinating their observations by radio until one of the two in the garage turned on his halogen flashlight and waved it, signaling the time had come to seize the intruder.

The spotlights swept the walkway along the retaining wall. Someone up above, inside the law school's garage, began to whisper into the walkie-talkie.

"Someone's down there. I can see him. He's wearing a long jacket and moving south at the wall."

Another voice responded.

"Yeah, I have him in sight. You! There! Stop and put your hands on your head."

Too late Slic realized a trap had been set. There had been the routine police patrols, seemingly at their usual times. Nothing had been out of the ordinary. Now he would have to run it out. He could. He'd done it before.

Slic reversed his position and ran back along the wall away from the school. They'd have to follow him on foot. That gave him an advantage. He could outrun them.

At the base of the last building before he had to climb to the street above, Slic pulled his jacket off and let it fall to the ground. What a waste, he thought! All that paint lost, and racked just that day. But he couldn't afford to save it. They'd be up on the street looking for a guy in a jacket. That was the description one of them had yelled. As far as he knew, no one had seen what he was wearing under the jacket, and his white silkscreened t-shirt might be enough to throw them off his track.

Two blocks away a siren started to wail. His face wet with perspiration, Slic climbed toward the street above. If he had to, he'd head back down the embankment again to the freeway and cross it. Traffic was light. But crossing a freeway was a last resort.

He emerged from the embankment between a business supply store and a small real estate office. In the three-foot gap between the two, he edged sideways toward the street, his back against the wall of the store.

Standing breathless against the building, he had almost regained a sense of security when he heard voices coming from behind him, down in the embankment. He couldn't hear all they were yelling but he did make out the words "paint" and "jacket." They were sweeping the area around the retaining walls. He was trapped. He couldn't move back down toward the freeway. He couldn't run into the street or he would attract too much attention.

Slic stepped slowly and deliberately from the safety of the darkness into the well-lighted street and forced himself to walk away from the law school toward the restaurants two blocks away. If he could get to the tourist shopping area he could step into one of the bars or stores that were still open and disappear into anonymity. He almost made it.

"Stop right where you are. We want to talk to you."

Slic never looked toward the direction of the command. He knew they'd never shoot him. Deadly force couldn't be used for a property crime, and an attempted one at best. He started to run as fast as he could toward the restaurants now a block away.

He never hesitated, never looked back. Ahead, just past the small parking lot on the right, was a side street. He'd duck down it and maybe make a turn into the back of the bar he knew was there at the end of the cul de sac.

He was faster, much faster than the foot officers. He rounded the corner and saw the square outline of the bar's trash bin. The siren was a block away. The unsavory thought crossed his mind that his only chance of escape might be to dive into the bin. But as he headed straight for it his body came to a violent stop.

An arm seized him around the throat and pulled him hard into someone's chest. The pain had a strange feeling of familiarity.

Slic was half-dragged, half-pulled into the back door of the bar, and held immobile against a wood utility closet as a siren passed. The vise around his neck loosened and as he struggled to face his attacker-savior, he heard a voice as familiar as the stranglehold.

"Don't fight. Just come with me," he whispered. "Move to my booth there, Toy. And smile like we know each other all our lives."

Colon's grip around the boy's neck loosened. It hadn't been tight enough to completely cut off his breathing, just immobilize him. As Slic rubbed his neck Colon, pressed against him, moved him toward the seating area of the bar, a captive of sorts but better a captive of this man than handcuffed in the back of a police car.

At the black Formica table Slic abruptly stopped. The booth was in front of the window facing the sidewalk.

"Here," Colon said, taking off his leather jacket. "Put it on and sit."

Slic quickly followed directions, and slid onto the sagging brown leather seat.

Colon sat opposite him, and slid as close as he could toward the window. He wiggled his index finger at Slic, summoning him nearer to the window.

"Stay still and look friendly-like, Toy. I come in to have a drink and the sirens sounded. I think, go out and see what happens, and look who I find. The toy from the hill.''

"My name's Slic . . . remember? Toys are amateur writers."

"No, *all* you writers are toys. You want something to eat . . . Slic?''

Slic shook his head, but pointed to the glass of water the waitress brought earlier. The ice had melted and the coolness condensed, leaving beads of moisture around the outside of the glass. Colon picked it up and ceremoniously placed it in front of the boy. As he did, two uniformed officers walked past the window in front of them and looked into the seating area in search of the furtive movement, the guilty look. Colon smiled at Slic and gestured widely, as though caught midstream in some complex conversation that had been underway for some time. Slic sat frozen, a strained smile spreading across his face. Two friends, out for a drink.

"Why'd you help me?'' Slic whispered.

"Who says I helped you. It was fate. I was looking for you. And look. Here you are. Delivered right to me.''

"Why are you looking for me? There's nothing you and me have to talk about.''

"Ahhh . . . but yes, there is.'' Colon reached into his pants pocket and retrieved a square of folded paper. He handed it to Slic, who unfurled the half-page newspaper article that appeared two days after Threadgill's death. He watched the boy struggling to read it using his fingers to follow each of the words. Midway down the first column the boy stopped and looked up at him.

"Hey! That's me in this paper! It has my street name here. It says . . . it says I saw this murder? I didn't see no murder! I didn't do no murder!''

"I know you didn't do it.''

"That makes me feel real good like, but it don't help me. Those police they want me for this thing here.'' He threw the paper on the table toward Colon.

"*I* saw it." Colon paused to let the statement sink in, as Slic's eyebrows pressed together.

"I saw it," he repeated. "I saw the killer. After you and me . . . we can say spoke . . . up on the hill at the wall I saw someone kill that man there. They think *you* saw it or did it because you wrote your name on the wall and I wrote a note near your name."

"What kind of note?"

"I just told them I saw it. Now they think you saw it. They think you signed my note."

He leaned back and triumphantly declared, "They think you're me."

Colon sensed the growing panic as Slic's eyes widened and a grimace spread across his face; a bug, a helpless little bug caught in a very big web.

Colon reached over the table and rested his arm on the boy's shoulder. "I can help you. If I tell the police what I saw. If I let them know you aren't the person that did this to that man. But."

"But what?"

"But I need you to help me write to them."

"You can't *write*, old man?"

"Colon. Gui Colon. Colon to you."

"You can talk to them! Tell them."

"No! I'm not talking to them. That's too easy. I want to put a message up where they can see it." Colon jabbed his index finger into the air. "Up in the heavens."

"Why?"

"I want something from them. I want the wall. I want it for a painting. And I won't tell them who did it unless they give me my wall to paint on. I need to tell them this. I want you to write it for me, maybe across the freeways so they know what I want; what I'm doing. I need someone like you . . . I can't do this myself. I can't climb.''

Colon held his gnarled fingers out for the boy to see.

"And when I tell them what I saw, they will know you saw nothing. They'll know you killed no one."

For a moment defiance flashed across the boy's face. He would go to the police himself. And do what? Tell them some other dude did it? No. He needed Colon as much as this old man needed him. The dude wanted the wall. Like, he could dig that. It was something that on a different but strangely similar level, he understood.

"What are you going to tell them?"

"I'm going to paint the picture of the man who did it! Beautiful eh? And my writing to them will tell them I, Gui Colon, saw the murderer, not you, toy."

Slic's voice was a low whisper. "How do I know you're on the level?" Slic was merely being cautious. He knew of cases where writers had been lured into helping people who then turned them in to the police for rewards.

"Why would I sit here smiling at you when the police were right outside the window here?"

"You're crazy, old man. Crazy."

"Will you help me?"

"Do I have a choice?"

"Not really, you don't."

"Then tell me what I have to do."

PART TWO

PAINTING
THE HEAVENS

7

THE SMELL OF Jungle Gardenia perfume accompanied the firm tapping on his right shoulder. Slic vaguely remembered he was in his English class. As he drifted back to consciousness, the unmistakable voice of Mrs. Claris Morton whispered so close to his ear that he could feel the warmth of her breath.

"Late night last night, Mr. Perez?" She had lowered her face to his and now stared directly at him, her blue eyes magnified to a grotesquely large proportion behind her quarter-inch-thick glasses.

He shook himself awake.

"Uh, I was up late. Studying." The excuse rolled off his tongue without a hint of hesitation.

Giggles turned to laughter as Slic smiled in mock helplessness; to his classmates offering a weak, "Really."

"And I suppose *that's* your homework?" the woman asked, pointing to the pencil drawing on the sheet of paper before him on his desk. She had been teaching in the center city schools for thirty years and was no longer exasperated by any response she heard because she'd heard them all.

Slic had fallen asleep over a drawing he'd completed in the bus that morning on his way to school: a woman's figure with flowing hair, exaggerated breasts, and exaggerated small waist and ankles. Under the pencil sketch he had written in large balloon letters, "Linda." Linda was no one in particular, a figment of his postadolescent imagination. He'd hoped to spend his class time filling in the letters, but hadn't been able to stay awake.

"Try to stay with us for the next ten minutes, Mr. Perez," Mrs. Morton said, stepping back from the boy. "I'm going to be giving you some indication of what's going to be covered on the spring final next week. I can't think of anyone here who would benefit more."

She walked on, toward the front of the room, leaving Slic's artwork on his desk. He shifted, leaned back, and folded his arms across his chest. He struggled to stay awake until exhaustion overcame him again and his half-closed eyes shut firmly.

From the front of the classroom Claris Morton looked on, shook her head and let the boy pass back into unconsciousness. In the early years of her teaching, two generations ago, she would shake the sleepers, and, if her efforts failed to revive them, she would send them off to the principal's office. Her practice stopped one afternoon when she icily asked a sleepy young man why he was chronically slumbering. Choking back tears, he whispered to her that his mother had "visitors" at night and when she did, he had to sleep in the car. She never asked the "why" question again, content to make an impact wherever she could on a population of youngsters whose personal problems at times so overwhelmed an immediate need to teach the difference between pronoun and adjective. Every now and then, when something important was about to happen, she would awaken a chronic sleeper to remind him there was work to be done. Sometimes they actually stayed awake, but more often they went back to sleep, as Slic had done. And so she shook her head, but let him slump forward again across his art project as she prepared the class for the spring final.

Claris Morton could not have known how misplaced her compassion was. She did not know that Slic, like the youthful outcast of yesteryear who had slept in the car, spent wakeful nights. But there the similarity of circumstances ended. Slic, like most all writers, needed to sleep at school so he could tag into the early morning hours, so he would have enough energy to seek and destroy, to tag everything in sight. Like most writers he moved from class to class throughout the day, sleeping.

At 2:30 P.M., having missed the class review, Slic rose slowly and stuffed his English book into the backpack he uselessly carried around. Mrs. Morton, he could tell, was curious as to what it was that required he sleep in class. She eyed him warily as he left the room, but refrained from comment. He wondered, had she seen the small holes around the waist of his gray t-shirt, holes caused when the paint cans stored under his waistband rubbed his shirt against the walls he was bombing? Had she seen his Adidas shoes with the paint drips on the tops of them? The shirt and the shoes, both of which he was wearing today, were dead bang giveaways that he was a writer. Another writer would notice immediately. Even some of the teachers at other schools had become wise to writers' clothing and directly questioned some of his acquaintances about their extracurricular activities. But if Mrs. Morton suspected anything, she never shared it with him.

Across the street from the school, on busy El Cajon Boulevard, groups of students, at last free of the day's academic duress, congregated at the takeout windows of a small taco shop to relax, flirt, and discuss the things high schoolers discuss on Wednesday afternoons. Except for his two days' worth of beard, the older man in their midst was unremarkable in his oversized blue denim pants and baggy white t-shirt. Colon, a large taco before him, sat alone at one of the circular concrete umbrella tables, waiting for Slic. He was largely ignored by the wave of students, who, if any noticed, probably fashioned him to be one of the elderly inhabitants of the center city.

Colon had an appointment with Slic. Following their fortuitous meeting at the bar in Old Town the previous night, they had agreed to meet here, across the street from Slic's high school, to plan just how and where Colon's message would be delivered to the police.

At last the boy ran toward him and took the pedestal seat across the table.

"You look sleepy. You go to sleep last night after we talked?" Colon asked.

"Sure, I slept."

Colon eyed him suspiciously. "No, you didn't. Your eyes are pink. Like a rabbit's."

"So, what's it to you?"

"So, I have this special interest in you now, you know. I have to be sure you take real good care of yourself. My success, it depends on you."

Slic's eyes rested on Colon's taco.

"You eat any lunch today?"

"I forgot my money at home."

"Uh, huh, take this, I won't eat it. I already have a burrito before you come." Colon pushed the food toward the boy and watched him consume it in five large mouthfuls. The boy was hungry. He hadn't had lunch and probably hadn't had breakfast either. "You want another one kid?"

"You buying?"

"Sure. I'm buying. You left your money home, remember?"

Colon bought three more tacos and a Coke and watched in silence as Slic took the bright yellow paper from each one.

"I've been thinking," Slic announced as he finished his Coke, "we need a message that we can do two, three times, close to each other, maybe on southbound Freeway 163 you know, and Freeway 5 downtown where the police can't miss it."

Despite the freeways being the obvious choice, Colon was guarded in his acceptance of Slic's suggestion.

"I think," he ruminated, "we need something closer to where the killing took place, so we can be more certain they can make a connection."

"I say 163 and 5. Maybe even Freeway 8. I know the areas. The messages are gonna be read right away. We gotta try it and if there's no action by anyone, we can change our direction and move near the place the dude was killed."

Colon had no immediate response.

"Hey, old man . . ." the boy whispered, leaning forward across the table, "it's my ass hanging out over the traffic. I don't, you know, *have* to do this."

It occurred to Colon that he was indeed asking Slic to do something he probably hadn't done before. Taggers didn't send messages through their writing. Their short, cryptic initialization was only to announce they had been there. What Colon was asking of Slic would take more time and be far more dangerous.

"Okay." Colon conceded. "We try it. Maybe we can write at all those areas, then move closer to Silverado Estates where they can get the point of what we're saying."

"What *do* you want to say?"

"I been thinking on that."

Colon took a square piece of paper from his pants pocket, unfolded it, and handed it to Slic. On it, he had printed, "The wall for the murderer's face. Silverado."

"Silverado?" Slic asked.

"That's the place the murder happened. They'll see that right away," Colon said.

"I think it's too long, but we can find a place for it if that's what you want. We got some things we gotta do first," Slic said. "For one, I need paint. We need to decide color. It should be the same color every time I write, wherever I write. I'm thinking we use red paint, maybe a real deep red like blood, with no other color outlining it."

Colon nodded his approval.

"I'll need some new tips for the paint cans too, depending on what style you want."

Writers seldom used the standard tips that came on the spray paint cans. They interchanged tips from other cans, the way painters changed brushes; each tip creating a different style and width of writing. Good writers, the best ones, scavenged for tips. They took them off cans of shoe polish, perfumes, and household cleaners. And they acquired them the way they acquired their paint; they stole them.

It had been a long time since Colon had talked to anyone about style and he knew Slic's references to style must be quite different than his own.

"Tips?" Colon asked.

"Tips . . . for paint cans . . . they change the style of your painting. There's all kinds of different styles."

Colon's eyebrows pinched together. This was all quite foreign to him. Slic tried again.

"Softball, phantom, basketball. That's what we call the widths of the writing. Softball is five fingers wide, like this." Slic held up his hand, all five fingers pressed tightly together. "The phantom's two fingers wide."

Again he illustrated by holding up two fingers. ". . . and the basketball's the widest, five to ten fingers wide. It's a balloon effect. I think we should use the baseball. The phantom's too hard to read and the basketball's too much like a cartoon for what you want. I don't think I've got the tip for it, though."

"You'll need new tips then," Colon offered. "And paint."

"We can rack 'em this afternoon. If you come with me, they won't watch me too close. You can keep them busy."

"No," Colon said, shaking his head emphatically. "I'll *buy* the paint. We take no chance getting caught thieving paint. That's my decision. For the tips we buy, what?"

"Shoe cleaner. Get two cans of it."

Colon looked at his wristwatch. "It's three o'clock now."

"When do we do the writing?" Slic asked.

"As soon as possible. Tonight I think. If you're ready tonight we do it tonight."

There was silence as Colon looked down at the concrete table.

"You . . . you don't like this kind of writing, do you old man?" Slic asked haltingly. "You don't like me either, do you?"

Colon looked up, startled at the last question. "I like you, toy. I like you just fine. I figure you're going to be okay in a couple of years. But you're right. I don't like what you do. It's not art. It's nothing. It's garbage." He looked down again and whispered. "Garbage."

Slic watched as Colon shrugged his shoulders. He stifled the urge to defend himself against the rantings of an old man.

"Hey, cheer up there Mr. Colon, man. Before you

know it you're going to have this big canvas and you can paint like you want to paint.''

Colon looked up. For the moment, the two had found a common thread of understanding.

8

THE QUARTER-MILE span of the Laurel Street Bridge was designed to give visitors through the west entrance of the 1915 Exposition a breathtaking introduction to the verdant grounds of Balboa Park. It provided passage to El Prado, the glittering exposition avenue, for such luminaries as President William Howard Taft, Henry Ford, and Thomas Edison.

The lily pond and river that once flowed picturesquely beneath the hundred-foot-high Spanish Renaissance bridge were gone. Where they once flowed, Freeway 163 now meandered north and south under its seven ivy-covered arches, arches zealously and righteously regarded as one of San Diego's most important architectural landmarks.

Slic and Colon stood under the arch closest to the southbound traffic lanes and looked reverently up into the dark, awed by the magnificence of the structure. Along Laurel Street above, street lamps glowed, outlining its highest contours. For a fleeting few moments it gave Colon cause to wonder if he had acquiesced too quickly in Slic's desire to defile the structure. He pushed the hesitance from his mind.

"It's not the same driving under it as it is standing here next to it," Colon said, speaking more to himself than the boy next to him. He ran his hand roughly over the concrete.

Slic, agitated with excitement, paced under the archway, and out onto the roadway.

"Under it, over it, man, it doesn't matter. Will you look up there! No writing anywhere. No one's written here before. Look at this man! Look! There's nothing written anywhere."

Slic moved out again from under the arch and looked straight up.

"If I can hang over the top up there I can hit that wide area between the ivy. You'll have to hold me out."

"What do you mean hold you out?"

"I hang over the side. You hold my arm so I don't end up road meat down here. You think your arms are strong enough?" He did not wait for Colon to respond. Choosing instead to leave the old man bewildered at the thought of holding him over the freeway, he pulled a can of spray paint from the waistband of his pants.

In large red letters Slic wrote "Silverado" diagonally on the interior wall of the arch next to them and watched as the paint dripped toward the ground. Drips were not acceptable in good writing. This was a piss-poor job. Even if this was not a job of his own choosing, he still felt the sting of writer's pride. Thankfully, it wasn't his own name he was writing. No one could identify it with him.

There was little time to waste. The freeway was well traveled, even Wednesday at 11 P.M.

Having completed the all-important signature, the two ran to the side of the road and scrambled up the embankment, pushing through thick shrubbery and trees planted decades earlier. They climbed to the crest of the hillside and ran out on the bridge, onto Laurel Street, positioning themselves just short of the midsection of the bridge.

Slic leaned over the side of the bridge and looked down at the freeway below.

"Here's where we separate the writers from the toys, old man."

Slic grabbed the side of the bridge and boosted himself onto the edge, sitting side-saddle facing Colon, who in a reflex reaction lunged for the boy.

"Wait, what the hell are you doing to do?" Colon gasped.

"You want this bridge bombed with your message, right?"

"Yes but not this way."

"There *is* no other way old man. You want to bring a big ladder in and push it against the wall?" He held his hand out to Colon. "Just hold my arm. It'll be fine. I trust you. You're a strong guy."

Colon shook his head. "I'm not so sure I can hold you."

"You'll hold me if you want this done. Now, c'mon we don't have too long here."

Slic maneuvered over the metal railing installed to deter suicides and lowered himself, hanging at first by both hands to steady himself, and, as Colon braced himself and clasped his left hand, Slic let his right arm hang free, leaving him dangling in midair.

Slic felt his weight shift suddenly downward, pulling him toward the ground. One slip, one miscalculation, and he would be a mound of crushed flesh and bone, covered with one of the bright yellow plastic blankets they place over the dead accident victims.

Burning pain shot across his back as he felt his arm pulling from the shoulder socket.

But the pain was overpowered, submerged in the dizzying craziness of his suspension in midair. Twisting ever so slightly, he looked down. For a fraction of an instant he wondered what it would feel like to fall, free form, through the air and hit the asphalt below.

Slic held his breath. His heart raced a thousand miles an hour; every one of his senses was on alert. He had no regard for impending doom, only the sudden uncontrollable yearning to abandon the task at hand and scribble his own initials so they could all see it was he— Slic—who had been here.

"Hurry up!" Colon called from above. "I can't hold you much longer."

Slic's body jolted downward as Colon's sweaty hands on his wrist readjusted to grasp him tighter.

Slic reached into the elastic waistband of his pants and retrieved one of two cans of spray paint. As he did so, a car passed beneath him, its horn blaring a Doppler effect as it sped by. It was always the same. They all honked. And if that was all they did, he was lucky. He had seen motorists actually stop their cars, curse, and even throw things at writers.

He steadied himself again as a second car went by, the sound of its horn dissolving into silence filled with the rush of adrenaline.

Don't look down, he told himself.

The paint can in his hand slipped in his sweaty palm. Enough to jar him back to his task.

Think! Think about anything. The taggers you know. The writing you've done. Just don't look down now. You never look down! Keep your balance and write fast.

Slic tightened his grip on the can. The hiss of the spray pushed yet another surge of adrenaline through him as he wrote, "The Wall For The Murderer's Face." He finished the message in much smaller lettering than he liked to use. But this was a different kind of writing. It needed space, and he couldn't move laterally. He'd have to be content to write as best he could and not worry about the size of the printing. If the police saw "Silverado" below, and they would, they would look at the rest of the bridge pretty closely.

As he finished, Slic heard an approaching vehicle in the distance. A familiar form was moving southbound. He saw the light bar and knew.

It was a police car.

It hurried past under him, at what must have been sixty miles an hour. Above him he could hear Colon yelling, "Shit, it's a police car. Up! You have to come up now!" Slic's thoughts raced.

This is it. I'm going to be arrested. Don't drop me! Just don't let go!

There was a screech of tires. The police officer had seen them. The only question now was how long it would take the car to get back to them. Slic held his breath as Colon began pulling him up. As he struggled to get back to the top of the bridge, he managed to shove the paint can back into his pants. It would take the car several minutes to turn around at the next exit. But, as he pulled his body up and over the concrete edge, he could see the car turning in the southbound lanes and heading back the wrong way against oncoming southbound traffic.

Breathing at a frantic pace, Colon grabbed Slic and pointed to the end of the bridge.

"We need to get into the bushes!"

The two fled over the bridge, away from the southbound lanes. To run across Laurel Street into the city streets would be foolish. They would be easy marks for the police because, while there was one car below, a radio call would quickly bring several to the street.

Slic's knees were rubbery, his head light. To his surprise Colon moved with speed and assurance, running alongside the youth and pushing his shoulder if he started to fall behind.

As the officer's halogen spotlight began sweeping the edge of the bridge, the two jumped onto the hillside, heading north. Slic looked back only once, in time to see a second police unit pull up to the bridge and illuminate "Silverado."

Ahead of him now, Colon urged him onward as they skirted the west edge of Balboa Park.

"Freeze!" Colon whispered.

The police cars had been joined by a motorcycle unit and they were all now shining their lamps onto the hillsides from the roadway below. It had taken only moments for the officers to reach their current location.

The lights moved past them and turned, heading back southward again.

"We need to get away from the freeway," Slic whispered. He turned toward the ten-foot-high chain-link fence behind them, the dividing line between the crest of the freeway embankment and the park's zoo grounds.

"Can you get over?" Colon yelled, pointing toward the fence.

"I can. Can you?" Slic taunted. Then, suddenly realizing where they were, "Hey, man, this is the z-zoo! No way! How do I know what's on the other side?"

"Your choice, toy." Colon leaped onto the fence, and, like an insect climbing a wall, moved upward, disappearing over the top.

Slic looked down onto the freeway in time to see the motorcycle unit begin a second pass along the edge. It was moving northward again toward them.

"Please just don't let it be the bears, not the bears, not the bears," Slic chanted as he jumped upward, clumsily and noisily climbed to the top, and landed with a heavy thud on the other side in several inches of soft powdery soil. The first thing he noticed was the stench. The next was the tall, odd-shaped form standing over him, eyeing him curiously. It was a large bird. An os-

trich. Slic had no time to gauge its degree of friendliness.
Colon was calling from the darkness only a few yards
away.

"We write the same thing up in Silverado now, tonight," Colon insisted. "I won't do this two nights in a
row."

Slic's wide grin was lost in the darkness. He was
giddy with the exhilaration of their near-capture.

Slic and Colon remained in the safety of the ostrich
pen until the police units left, dispatched to other areas
of the city where there was, in Slic's words, "real
crime." Then they leaped back over the fence and continued following the crest of the embankment northward
to the first available freeway exit. They headed east to
Park Boulevard and the tagger's transportation lifeline,
the bus system.

When the bus arrived, there were no passengers. Slic
used his bus pass and carefully replaced it in his wallet.
The two sat next to each other on wide black plastic
seats marked with the initials of taggers who had pre-
ceded them.

"How come you people do this?" Colon inquired,
running his finger over the chiseled initials.

"If you're a writer, you write everywhere all the
time."

"Don't they see you do these things?" Colon whispered, looking at the driver's eyes on them in the large
overhead mirror.

"Naw, man. You travel in twos sometimes and . . .
here. I'll show you."

Slic picked up a sheet of newspaper left on the seat
by a previous rider and opened it wide, creating a barrier
between the driver's line of vision and them. In its open
state, he handed the paper over to Colon.

"Hold this like this."

Colon took the paper by both hands, and as he did

so, Slic reached deep into his pants pocket and retrieved what looked like a small drill bit. With the newspaper as his shield he began to scratch an S into the back of the seat in front of him.

He never finished. Colon mashed the paper noisily into his lap, causing Slic to frantically shove the bit back into his pants pocket. The noise and action had not escaped the bus driver, but the two regained their composure quickly. The driver's suspicions, if there were any, subsided as Colon pulled the stop cord and the two quietly exited.

"Why'd you do that?" Slic asked as they sat on the bus bench waiting for their transfer on the eastbound bus.

"Do what?"

"Pull that shit in there. You could have got us arrested."

"This here isn't done to make you happy, toy. It's being done for me. Remember that. You pulled the shit in there. You do that all the time?"

Slic relaxed.

"That was nothing. Sometimes my homies and I, we go on bus runs. We use our drill bits, rocks, anything that'll mark. If the driver gets real crazy on us, we pull the emergency exit and jump out the windows." He laughed as Colon stared at him, shaking his head in disbelief.

They waited a short time for their transfer to an eastbound bus and in the course of fifteen minutes had traveled the length of Adams Avenue and headed down a canyon onto Montgomery Road. They got off at the corner of Tierra Verde Drive.

"I don't see anywhere I can write," Slic said, looking around at a street without signs.

"How about the bus bench?"

"Maybe we do two smaller ones. One on the bench

here and down south a block on the tractor I saw parked there." Even as he said it, Slic took his spray can from his waistband and quickly wrote their message on the front of the bench back, facing traffic. Like the writing on the arch, it too dripped unacceptably and he cursed the flowing red paint, hoping it would not obliterate the writing. Then he began walking down the street toward the earth-moving equipment parked at the side of the roadway next to the canyon. Colon followed silently, glad the night's work was almost over. It would take but a few minutes to hit the tractor and they would part company. He would wait to see just what kind of reaction they got from police, although how and where they got a reaction was anyone's guess.

When they reached the embankment, Slic pointed to the SKW painted on the shovel.

"The SKW crew was here." He shook his head. "They're bad asses, man. They're wanted by everyone. Me included. They tried to run me over with a car. Not just me, other homies, too. . . . "

He started to say something else but the sudden movement across the street stopped all discussion. Eight youths who looked to be about as old as Slic were walking toward them. Their hands were in the pockets of their baggy pants and jackets, as if simulating holding weapons. They spread out in a loose semicircle, confronting the two directly.

The tallest of the group spoke first.

"Do you write?" he asked pointedly.

He was almost as tall as Slic and his words were spoken directly, menacingly, inches from Slic's face. Slic wanted to spit at him. But he refrained from all but a smile. A closer look at the aggressor's hands and he could see he carried a short club—a hero beater. The club was commonplace among crew members who carried it to beat off members of the public—heroes—who might try to stop them from writing. The hero beater was not the only weapon he could see now. As their hands came out from under jackets, he saw the pellet guns and the rocks.

Slic and Colon were being rushed. It was a common street practice but an increasingly dangerous one. One crew against another or a crew against a single writer. It was a challenge. If you don't write you could say so and they'd leave you alone. But if you declined to admit you were a writer and you were, you risked humiliation, or worse, a physical attack. It went on all the time. No writer was safe from it day or night.

Slic's first reaction was to run. But a successful race against other writers was questionable. He could beat the cops on foot because he knew the streets better than they. He knew where to make the turns and where he could disappear. But other writers knew what he knew. They could follow easily and there were more of them than he cared to try to outrun.

As the confrontation unfolded, Colon tried to move closer to Slic. He was cut off by three of the assailants. The primary challenge was to Slic, not the older man next to him. He knew nothing of rushes and street writing protocol. Perhaps, he even thought at one point, this was some strange ritualistic greeting. He decided to be cautious and see where this took them before he made any moves. He was strong enough to put any one of them, or even two, flat on the ground. But not eight.

One of the group, standing slightly behind Slic, grabbed at his baseball cap. Slic knew that was about to happen. He started to run and they pounced. Three on Colon, five on him. Their fists tore into his face. Hands grabbed and pulled at his pockets. His shoes, socks, hat, anything they could strip from him was taken. The attack was lightning fast. When they disappeared, laughing, into the street and the hillside, Colon was sitting, Slic lying, on the ground. Both were beaten and cut, their clothes—what was left of them—disheveled.

"I think," Colon moaned in exhaustion, "I have written enough for tonight."

"It's okay, old man," Slic whispered, bending forward. "They just wanted my cap. It's blue. Not their color." He felt his pants pockets. "Shit! They got my bus pass." He ran his hands through his hair as he spoke. "It's all part of the action. You write and you get rushed. The only thing that counts is who's up the highest and the most. No one can take that away from you."

Colon wanted to scream out at the boy's cavalier acceptance of this brutality. Instead he simply asked, "You all right?"

"Yeah, I'm gonna survive."

"Has this ever happened to you before?" Colon asked.

"Twice. And worse than this," he said, rubbing his forehead.

"I cannot imagine anything worse than this," Colon said, shaking his head. Then he said, "I have some place we can go that's close to here."

It took them several minutes to completely regain their composure and survey their losses. Colon still had his shoes and his pants and shirt. Slic had lost everything but his pants and shirt. His shoes and socks were gone.

"Oh, man. This is gonna hurt tomorrow," Slic said, slowly and painfully rising to his feet. He followed Colon out onto the street where he stopped to brush the nettles from the bottom of his feet. "Now I gotta get another pair of shoes. The old man's gonna hit the ceiling."

Colon and Slic walked up Tierra Verde toward the canyon side that would lead to the caves. The Silverado security patrol car was not parked in its usual location at the top of the hill. The guard was undoubtedly making his rounds.

Colon motioned for Slic to follow him down into the canyon.

At the entrance to the caves, Slic brushed away the dirt from his clothing as Colon removed the dry shrubbery from the entrance. He entered first and lit the lantern. Slic's eyes widened.

"You like this place?" Colon asked, moving the lantern light around the walls to show the boy the dimensions of the cave. "If you ever need somewhere to hide you can use it . . . I let you use it."

"What is this place?" Slic asked, his voice reverberating. He walked as far into the cavern as he dared without light.

"I'll take you through the rooms back there. It goes a long way back into the mountain, but you can't get out the other side. They blasted it shut years ago."

Colon sat on the ground and offered Slic his sleeping bag. They sat silently, the two of them, for a long time it seemed before Colon, drinking heavily from his vodka bottle, spoke.

"How old are you, Slic? Maybe sixteen, seventeen?"

"Ya. That's close," the boy answered, hesitating to give the man any specific information about himself.

"I like to know, how can you stay out without your mother and father knowing you do this stuff? Knowing you hang on bridges and get beat up like this?"

"They don't know about this stuff. I tell them I'm sleeping over at a friend's house. I can be out all night and they never know. Pop's drunk half the time and my mom don't care as long as I'm not in some gang."

"And when you go out, what do you do all night? This stuff here we did tonight?"

"Sure . . . but tonight was nothing. If I'm out with my friends or even by myself, I write all night. As long as

I have my bus pass I can travel all around.''

"I see. Everyone does this? All your friends?"

"All my friends, yeah. Others work with crews. They can even be a lot more active than that. A crew will party all night, then go out, smash windows, do runs."

"Run where."

"They run into stores, you know the whole crew runs into a store and grabs beer, paint, anything they can get away with. They get drunk and party. And sometimes they look for people to beat up. Maybe someone from another crew wrote on their house . . . they'll go out and get them.''

"Ahhh . . . I see. Those kids who beat us up . . . they were on a party?''

"Maybe . . . maybe not. Maybe they were gangsters. Gangsters aren't writers. They're fighting for territory. We used to get along okay with them. Now word's out they got us all targeted. They want us off their turfs. So they hit us with anything. Like I said, one tried to run me over. Some homies got shot at too."

"That doesn't scare you?"

"No," Slic said, smiling widely. "We just try to stay out of their way if we can. Sometimes we can't—like when they go out tag banging, shooting at each other's houses. I don't do that shit.''

"This is going on all the time?"

"All the time. Everywhere. Every night. You have no idea. Every other kid's out there doing it. I tried to stop once. I couldn't though. I don't like the violence part of it. But down here at least we don't jump in like they do up in Los Angeles, where you have to be beaten up by your crew before you can become a member.''

"Don't you go on dates, go to the movies?"

Slic laughed. "That's fifties shit old man, where you been?"

"I don't know but after tonight I think in some other

world. Your world is like an animal world. If I didn't see it tonight with my own eyes, I couldn't believe what you tell me now. But I believe you.''

Slic found himself growing defensive.

''What do you mean, animal world?''

''Animals. Dog eat dog. Living day to day like that. A person gets beat up, maybe killed because he wears a color, or puts his baseball hat on with the bill on the wrong side of his head. That's the way you live your life? That's the way you want to live? You kids you think life's a color, a hat, a scribble. That's not respect for life. You tell me every kid does this and you know, I worry. I worry there's not much left in life. My life's over. It's you . . . your life has nothing in it. No honesty. No respect. To me, you and your friends, you're animals . . . all of you.'' He took a long drink from his vodka bottle as the boy studied his face.

Slic searched for the weapon to respond and found a ready tool.

''And how about you, old man. You're the one who held me out over the bridge tonight. You're the one who wants to cover that wall a block away with paint. Not me. What makes you any better than me?''

Colon's response was immediate and razor sharp. ''I have a *reason* to do it. That's why. You have no reason at all.''

9

"DON'T DO THAT mommy!" Elizabeth scolded. "You're not supposed to put food back on the serving plate!"

"You're right," Judith said, returning the bread to the side of her breakfast plate. She had taken the piece of French bread from the serving plate and found she could not eat it. French bread was her mother's favorite but she could no longer chew it or swallow it.

In the back wing of the house the day nurse was yelling directions to Judith's mother. They had long since adjusted to voices raised not in anger but to overcome her mother's hearing loss.

Elizabeth ate her toast and pushed her scrambled eggs around the plate, the "polite" way to make them "disappear." Judith knew something was on her mind.

"Mommy?" she asked, without looking up.

"Uh-huh."

"Is grandma going to get well?"

"She's holding steady, honey. All we can do is hold her steady and keep her comfortable."

On the surface, Judith's answer seemed to satisfy the child. But it was a lie and they both knew it. The truth

103

was, her grandmother was getting sicker. But Judith was simply not prepared to tell Elizabeth her grandmother was slowly dying. The word dying hadn't yet entered their discussions. Dying meant death was imminent. Death wasn't imminent for her mother. It wasn't the right word. How could a child, or anyone for that matter, understand how someone could be dying over several years. Instead, Judith sought comfort in the rubric of "holding steady."

The phone rang, interrupting a conversation that was searching for an end. Elizabeth answered it.

"It's for you, mom," she yelled from the kitchen.

It was Farrell. His voice had a slightly breathless quality, unusual for a man whose voice seldom revealed emotion.

"Judith. We've had a break of sorts in the Threadgill case. Can you meet me at that little coffee shop off Washington Street near 163? I have something interesting to show you. And on the way, you might want to take a look at the bus bench on Montgomery Road just down the street from the intersection of Tierra Verde."

Judith was puzzled. Farrell seldom became personally involved in a pending case. Yet he had interjected himself into this one, clearly wanting to see it to a successful completion.

"Larry . . . you don't have to invest your time in this. Pike and I can handle it."

"I want to help on this one, Judith. It's important to me. If it gets to be too much I'll let you know. It's just that a police report on this crossed my desk this morning as a possible connection to the Threadgill murder. I'd like to follow up on it."

"I need to wait until Elizabeth's friend picks her up for school, and I'll see you there let's say in thirty minutes?"

Judith quickly dressed, checked on her mother, and

said goodbye to Elizabeth when the carpool arrived.

The bus stop Farrell had referred to was only a minute from the house.

Judith turned right at the corner of Tierra Verde and drove down Montgomery Road, slowing at the bus stop and pulling over to the curb. "The Wall For The Murderer's Face. Silverado." There was no mistaking it. Someone was referring to the murder at Silverado. But what did they mean by the wall?

Judith reached into her glove compartment and grabbed the camera she kept there for times like this, when an immediate need to memorialize evidence arose unexpectedly. She did not want this writing to disappear by the hand of some other writer before their investigators could come take a look at it. Judith checked the camera window. Twenty-two shots were left. She took seven.

Farrell was already at the restaurant when she arrived, his breakfast, black coffee and dry toast, untouched.

"I saw it on the bus bench," she said, sitting across from him.

"You haven't seen anything yet. It's on the Laurel Street Bridge too. So far those are the only two places. A police officer almost had them last night at the bridge but they got away."

"They? There's more than one?"

"There's at least two. The police are positive of that. A young kid and someone who looked older. They didn't get any kind of good close look but they're pretty sure one is older."

"What's the message mean? It's the same in both places?"

"We're not sure yet."

"Can we take a look at the bridge?" Judith asked.

"Sure. I'll drive."

It took less than five minutes to get to the bridge. They

parked in the grassy divider looking up at the arch. Judith, who had brought her camera, snapped shots of the "Silverado" at every angle. A telephoto lens would be needed to capture the smaller print on the bridge span a hundred feet above them.

"How did they write that stuff?" she asked, pointing to the writing on the upper level of the bridge.

"The officer who saw them first said one was actually holding the other out over the traffic and he was writing like that, just hanging by one arm."

Judith shook her head.

"Larry, I know these messages are referring to the Threadgill murder, but what's the meaning of wanting the wall? What wall?"

"It's got to be the retaining wall where Threadgill was killed. Let's think about this. We know someone was up there the night Threadgill was killed. Whoever it was wrote on the wall that they saw it. This Slic person. He had to have been up there to paint the wall and got interrupted. That's my theory, anyway. And now he's prepared to tell us or show us who did it if we let him paint the wall."

"It looks like he, or they, want that wall in Silverado real bad. Bad enough to agree to paint the killer's face on it. Have you ever seen anything like this, Larry?"

"Not in all of my twenty years prosecuting murders. Never. It's not some kind of game he's playing. He's being very direct about this. 'Give me the wall and I'll paint him.' That's what he's saying. I tell you I think he saw it. I think he was up at the wall to do his own thing and he saw something he wants to bargain with now. But to paint a wall? That's all he wants. Why?"

"Who knows. Maybe he wants something he hasn't told us about yet. That isn't going to go over too well," Judith added. "We've never bargained away case investigations this way."

"We've never had a case like this before. I say we've got nothing to lose. The pressure's turning up on finding Threadgill's murderer. People in high places are getting antsy and we don't have a thing yet. What do we do if this guy really saw it and we lose him? I'm thinking we use him as our police artist. Let him paint. Only we give him two weeks. No longer. I'm willing to participate in this exercise but we'll find out pretty quickly if it's a hoax or some kind of game by some pervert."

"How many people are going to be in on this?" Judith asked.

"I suggest as few as possible. Me. You. Pike. Others on a need to know basis only."

"Okay and we need to tell this person or persons to do it in a set time. How are we going to do that?" Judith asked.

"We'll write back to him. I'll get you back to your car. I need to contact Pike."

10

PIKE FOLLOWED THE foot trail along the retaining wall. He had been against it from the beginning.

"Foolish. A waste of time. Nonsense. You get two notes scrawled on a bridge and bus stop and all the sudden you have a letter from someone who saw the Threadgill murder? Ridiculous!"

"That's the point," Farrell had said. "We don't know if this is for real. But more preposterous things than this have happened. It can't hurt. We give him some time to paint the wall and then see what happens."

Pike resisted, then offered the obvious. "How about we set a trap. Post the wall area and arrest them when they show up."

"On what charge? Vandalism's all we have at this point. And it's a misdemeanor. That's not enough to hold him but it is enough to make him—or them—nice and mad. And, if we do that, we get nothing. Look, I got two calls from a *Trib* reporter yesterday. They want to know what we've got on the Threadgill murder. The Silverado Estates Homeowners Association has posted a five-thousand-dollar reward for the capture of the killer. It was all over the news. And this morning . . . this is the best so far . . . 'Crime Today' called. The national crime television mag-rag. They're doing a bit for next week on our unsolved murder. They want to interview me. I've declined the invitation, but you can be sure they're going to mention our lack of evidence in the case. In short, the heat's on us. We need to let whoever it is that left these notes regale us with his artistic abilities. But we give him a short period of time. Two weeks from today.''

Pike was still not persuaded. He had sought support from Judith and found none. He chided her, gently of course, about how, as between Farrell and him, he was always the loser.

So here he was in broad daylight, a can of red Krylon spray paint in his hand; his thinning hair blowing wild in the wind coming off the canyon. He felt silly holding the can, and worse, what he was about to do ran counter to everything he believed in.

He'd been made a common vandal, and a clumsy one at that. His large index finger smothered the tiny spray tip. As he sprayed the red paint at the wall, his finger felt the cold liquid cover it. He rubbed it off and only made the mess worse, smearing it unevenly on the palms of his hands, leaving them a light shade of pink. He cursed and stepped back from the wall. Then he cocked his head to one side, amused at his sudden pride of authorship. It actually didn't look half bad: ''You have two weeks.''

''What good's this going to do?'' he mumbled to himself. ''An ultimatum like this has no meaning to him. He can do whatever the hell he wants whenever he wants. Wherever he wants.'' Pike gingerly replaced the can in its brown plastic bag and walked to Tierra Verde Drive to his car. Within five minutes he had left the same message on the bus stop next to Slic's message. They had decided not to try to respond to the note on the

Laurel Street Bridge. They would have to obtain the consent of the Balboa Park Subcommittee of the parks and recreation department and in the process they would have to completely divulge why they wanted to paint on the bridge.

Amazingly, no one had tried to stop Pike. Few people made any move to even acknowledge his criminal conduct. Only a man in a white Volvo, a young boy in tow, had pointed at him and honked his car horn to express his outrage.

He also got several threatening looks from Cal Trans workers trimming the sycamore trees along Montgomery Drive. He had but to flash his pocket badge at them and they did not bother him again, although they did huddle briefly to cast stern looks of disapproval his way.

He was glad to be done with it all.

11

TWO WEEKS WAS not enough time to paint a mural, particularly when the painting periods were limited to daybreak. But Colon's overall concept for the mural was firm. He'd been over the prepaint sketches hundreds of times and knew every detail, every line, down to the number of brush strokes it would take for each figure.

Late at night, in the recesses of the caves beneath Silverado Estates, Colon worked by lantern light, sketching a final pencil drawing of the mural, then recreating it as a grid drawing that would eventually be transferred to the wall. During these drawing sessions, Slic looked on. Sometimes bored, he paced about. At other times, overcome by curiosity, he nudged close to the older man, looking over his shoulder or peeking around the corner of the page Colon was working on. Although pretending not to notice, Colon was amused by the boy's confusion.

"Murals . . . art . . . it takes more than a can of paint you steal," Colon chided. "It's not just the painter who decides what gets painted. The materials you choose to work with, they also decide for you what kind of painting you are going to get. Me, I like seeing the little things in a picture. Many colors. I pick paints and brushes that help get me what I want. Those paint cans you use . . . whoosh . . . whoosh,'' he waved his arms wildly in the air, ''no faces, no eyes.''

"Yeah, you're some new breed of painter, old man. Keep this up and I can get you a real job somewhere," Slic jabbed back.

Colon laughed, enjoying the repartee.

"I'm no different than artists from hundreds of years ago. My own favorites, the mural painters from the Renaissance in Italy . . . you ever hear of that place? . . . They each had their own special recipes—they didn't let anyone in on their secrets. . . . They even ground up precious gems to get bright colors. When they died, their paint recipes died with them. I'd like to be a person like that, sometime maybe, but there's no time now. I'm out of time, eh? Just give me a pigment for color and something to mix it in. Those are the only two things I need. And some brushes . . . good ones. Like these.''

Colon, sitting with his legs crossed on the floor of the cave, carefully lined up ten or twelve new brushes on the ground. Slic sat across from him and ran his index finger over several of them.

"Go ahead, you can touch them, pick them up.'' Colon gently prodded. ''These are nothing special. Acrylic. Some of the animal fur bristles, now they can be very expensive. Not these. I like these for murals. The acrylics don't fill with water as fast as the animal fur does. Animal furs go limp in . . . oh . . . a half hour. Acrylics let you paint longer at one time.''

"Where'd you learn about painting like this?'' Slic asked.

"In school, I took some art classes. But mostly I learned from doing. I've painted a few murals here and there. Mostly to get money for meals. I got murals on restaurant walls right here in San Diego."

Slic squinted in disbelief.

"Yeah . . . right here in this city. Down in Little Italy. Go look sometime if you don't believe me. Small restaurants. La Casa Mia and Lopardo's. Little murals, but good ones."

He looked at Slic and winked.

"I know a thing or two about painting."

Colon put the brushes and paints in a plastic carrying case and placed the case next to a small pile of newspaper clippings he had collected over the last week. At the top of the pile a picture of a somber Judith Thornton stared out, framed by the headline, PROSECUTOR ADMITS NO NEW LEADS IN THREADGILL MURDER. Of the faces of all the actors in the unfolding drama, the only face not included in Colon's materials was that of the murderer. That face, Colon kept in his head for the time being. It would be the last face he painted on the mural.

"Take a look at this, Slic."

Colon handed the boy his final sketch of the mural. "What do you think of this?"

"It looks good. What is it?"

"You can't tell? You come with me later. You'll see how an artist paints a mural."

"Judith!"

The voice at the other end of the phone was excited.

"It's me, Laura Schultz." Laura was her immediate neighbor to the west.

"Judith! My gawd . . . you're up on the wall!"

"What wall?"

"That murder wall at the Thuli's house, that's what wall! And my gawd . . . Judith it's really good, it looks just like you. I called Barbara and Ellen and they're on their way to see it now. I saw a police car . . . okay I think another one's going up the . . . Yes, it's another police car . . . I've got to go. I want to see it before someone takes it down . . . see you later.''

Judith hadn't replaced the receiver more than a minute when the doorbell rang. It was Pike.

"You heard yet?" he asked, stepping into the marble-floored entry.

"Just something about my face being painted on the wall? Why my face? I thought the murderer's face was supposed to go up?"

"I haven't seen it yet Judith. I'm on my way over now—come on with me."

Minutes later Judith was standing before the wall. Her eyes swept left to right.

It was a magnificent chalk sketch. She recognized the scene immediately. It was a courtroom. The judge's bench with the outline of a white chalk figure, towered next to a witness stand, also occupied by the chalked outline of a figure. To the right, the jury box sat, as yet empty. A chalked figure lay prone on the courtroom floor, the victim Threadgill no doubt. Standing over him was the figure of a man, his face blank, holding a large rectangular object in the air as if about to throw it down. The murderer loomed the largest figure on the mural. Behind him, furthest to the right, was the figure of a woman holding a scale. It was the only finished figure. It was unmistakably her.

Pike whistled, long and low.

Judith, eyes glued to the wall, could only murmur in response. "I'm flattered."

12

IT WAS MONDAY morning. Judith had just settled into reviewing the day's superior court calendar when Pike appeared in her doorway. It had been just over a week since Threadgill's murder. Over the weekend, the mural's primary figures had been painted, although the faces of the judge and the murderer still remained blank. Pike had carefully photographed each step, chronicling the mural's development, waiting anxiously for that one face, hoping the investigation stayed under wraps long enough to arrest the murderer.

She could tell something was wrong as soon as Pike entered. His face was red and sweat had begun to drip downward from his forehead onto his jawline.

"The city litter control office got a bunch of calls this morning from people who're angry about the mural," he said, falling onto one of Judith's two small linen-covered sofas. "Most of them are people seeing it from the freeway down in the Valley. They want it down— now." They had known the Monday morning commuters would be the first to see the painting. But they had not anticipated widespread objection to it.

Pike pulled a wrinkled handkerchief from his pants pocket and wiped the back of his neck. "They've got two citizens action groups ready to go out this minute and blast it away. I called the Silverado Estates Home-owners Association a few minutes ago. I just told them I was a concerned citizen. They know about the mural but don't know what to do about it. The guy I spoke to thinks the whole thing's going to be taken care of by the city at the council's nuisance abatement committee meeting tomorrow night."

"Has anyone else called?" Judith asked.

"Just some print jockey. He wanted to know if we're going to prosecute whoever's painting it. When the PR folks called Farrell, he called me and told me to come over. He's on his way over here now."

Farrell was glum-faced by the time he reached Ju-dith's office.

He dropped a three-inch pile of pink telephone slips on the corner of Judith's desk.

"That bad?" she asked as the pile flattened into a mound.

"That bad." Farrell's reply was terse, flat.

"Who's complaining about it?"

"Who isn't?" he said, taking a seat next to Pike. "Mostly people driving on Freeway 8. They can see it as soon as they get to the Fairmount exit. A few people do like it. We're not the right agency to be handling the calls but we're not referring anyone over to the city. We need to control this thing for now. That's not going to happen if we shunt the complaints off to the city. I think we need to get Pike out there to the wall. We need to make sure one of our graffiti vigilante groups out there doesn't cover the painting. They've threatened!" Farrell was referring to the private citizen groups that had sprung up over the last year. In morning and evening patrols they scoured the city and covered, gratis, any graffiti they found on public or private property.

Pike had winced when Farrell suggested he stand guard. "Can't we get the property owners of the wall to be sure no one trespasses?" he asked.

"Can't. They'll be in Europe for two more weeks. Of course," he added, "Pike can't stay out there indefinitely. Just long enough to stabilize things. Meanwhile we need to get to someone at the city level who can help us. We need to be on top of this council subcommittee meeting set for tomorrow night. I don't want to deal with the mayor's office unless, and until, I have to."

"I think we should go to the meeting and just listen," Judith said. "We can't let there be a vote to remove it. We can't allow it."

"We can't let this investigation out of the bag either," Pike added emphatically. "Once that happens, we lose our artist and our case."

"So, what do you suggest?" Farrell asked, looking directly at Judith.

"As much as I hate to do it, we're going to have to take this outside the three of us if we're going to guarantee the mural gets done," Judith said.

Judith reached for the phone and pressed her secretary's call number. "Mary, get me Councilman Valdez on the phone."

Roberto "Bobby" Valdez was living the American dream. Born in San Diego, he spent his youth traveling with his father and mother, migrant farm workers who followed whatever crop was being harvested. He studied hard and, against all odds, won a scholarship to Stanford University followed by Hastings Law School for his JD degree. He passed the California bar exam on his first attempt and spent two years with O'Dell, McCauley, and Habinger in Los Angeles, where he specialized in plaintiff's insurance litigation.

At the firm, he did what all promising associates did.

He carried around the partners' briefcases and wrote trial briefs. There was, in the world of high-pressure law firms, no chance of his making a solo appearance in court until he'd reached his third anniversary as an associate. But despite his promising career, he was unable to settle comfortably into wood-paneled offices and a life run by billable hours and punitive damage awards. His enthusiasm waned. The 7 A.M. to 10 P.M. workday suited some, not him. He turned his back on the mahogany panels and partnership track, and settled in the San Diego barrio community he had come from, quickly establishing himself as the community liaison to the city chamber of commerce.

When the incumbent in the Seventh District council seat decided not to seek reelection, Valdez ran in an open race and won a grass-roots come-from-behind victory in a field of eleven challengers.

The Seventh Council District was one of extremes in economics and race. Straddling Freeway 8, the northern half of the district included the suburban communities of Tierra Santa and Del Cerro; the southern half incorporated the black and Chicano populations as well as the burgeoning Southeast Asian immigrant populations. The problems of the district were equally diverse—rising crime, economic decline, cultural diversity. What Bobby Valdez promised was a vision for the entire district beginning with the elimination of gangs and their graffiti.

It was Valdez that Judith turned to for help.

Her first conversation with him was short but cordial. There had been little likelihood he would turn down the request to talk with the chief deputy from the district attorney's office. Although the jurisdictions of city and county almost never overlapped, there was always a need to maintain cooperation. And for a young politician on the way up, the councilman was anxious to meet new friends with big problems to solve. Within a minute or two he had shuffled his afternoon appointments. He would be available at 3 P.M.

Judith arrived ten minutes early. It was an office filled with an eclectic assortment of Valdez's own personal belongings and inheritances of his predecessor. Liberally sprinkled throughout the furnishings were photographs of his wife and two young children, papier mâché animals that were obviously the product of the children's school projects, and a wall covered with his own black-framed diplomas and civic awards.

No sooner had Judith relaxed when the door to the office opened and a handsome young man with black hair and brown eyes greeted her.

"No, please, stay seated Mrs. Thornton," he said as Judith stood to shake hands. He took her extended hand in both of his. "It's good to finally meet you. I've been reading a great deal about you."

"All good I hope," Judith laughed.

"Oh, yes . . . all good."

He sat in the armchair next to her instead of taking the seat behind his desk.

"You brought no files with you, Mrs. Thornton. Our visit's either social or very confidential."

"For now, confidential. Extremely so."

"You're investigating someone in our office?"

"No, not at all. I'm here on a matter affecting a murder investigation our office is handling."

"Is this something our office here has a role in?"

"Not exactly . . . but maybe."

A mixture of a smile and a perplexed look spread across his face.

"I'm sorry," Judith said, "I didn't intend our meeting to take the shape of a TV game show." She glanced at the open office door. "Can we close the door?"

"Of course," he said, his tone suddenly intense. He

rose, shut the door, and returned to his chair next to Judith.

"This is difficult for me," she began, "because the case is very sensitive and the investigation is proceeding . . . having to proceed, in ways neither I nor any of my colleagues would have ever expected. How can I say this . . . it is *imperative* the details of the investigation remain confidential. In fact only three members of my office, at the very highest levels, know what is occurring and why. To divulge the details of our work would undoubtedly destroy the investigation and result in the loss of significant evidence, maybe even the loss of the murderer. Our ability to continue the investigation and catch the murderer depends on the continuation of something the city might actually be wanting to discontinue."

Valdez followed what she was saying and the significance of it as well. Beyond this, he realized one bad step in a case like this, one improvident move, and the result would be political embarrassment; at worst a loss of public confidence and political damage that could last a long time, even into the next election.

"Reduced to the bottom line, you want us here at council to do something or keep doing something, or you lose a murderer?"

"That's correct, and . . . I'm not meaning to be evasive or coy about this . . . I just can't give many of the details."

"Can you tell me what it is you need us to do or not do?"

"Of course, if you can be patient while I sort this out. It's an issue of graffiti, a mural actually that's being painted on a wall in your district."

"Ahh," he said, his eyebrows rising in sudden recognition, "has this anything to do with that mural over in Silverado Estates?"

"How many calls have you received?"

"Probably twenty or so in my own office, mostly from cellular phones in cars. People saying they were offended by what they saw. Enough for me to set the issue on the agenda of our nuisance abatement subcommittee meeting tomorrow night. . . . You realize of course that I head that committee?"

"I realize more than that. If I recall your campaign platform last year, and the major focus in your district for the last four months, has been fighting gangs. And eliminating graffiti."

"This isn't just council inaction you want, Mrs. Thornton. You want something from me. What is it you want?"

"Time. We need two weeks," she whispered. "The wall with the mural is in your district. We want the mural on that wall to be completed, and it may take another week. After that, the wall is immaterial. We don't really care what happens to the mural. Before that, what we need is your personal cooperation without your divulging any of this to anyone; not your colleagues, staff, or anyone else."

"You understand that if your investigation is not successful and gets bungled somehow and my help to you proves improvidently granted, the press will have a field day with me. The public perception is going to be less than favorable. To me Mrs. Thornton. Not you. My constituents, my own people, will say I violated my oath to them. . . . I violated my own beliefs. Any help I give you is based on blind trust."

"I know that. We wouldn't be asking for this kind of help if a homicide wasn't involved. I just want to say . . . my own office is in an untenable position too. The artist of the mural is unknown to us. He's blackmailing us. If the mural doesn't go up, he doesn't tell us who he saw kill someone. In a way we're acting on blind trust too."

She carefully avoided telling him the artist was going to incorporate the face of the murderer into the mural.

"I don't know the details or the murder victim . . . although I read the papers and I think I can guess. You understand I don't want to violate my word to my district . . . it's a big district. The poorest of the poor live in my district and some of the richest live there too. The freeway splits them apart but they have lots of things in common and their children and the safety of their neighborhoods are two of those things. You're asking me to violate something I feel very strongly about and to do it based on . . . on nothing really but your word that there's an important investigation underway and you're going to be successful. What do I tell them if you don't succeed?"

"Tell them you tried to catch a murderer. I'm sure your constituents are as interested in catching murderers as they are in wiping some guy's version of art off their walls and freeway signs."

The councilman sighed and rubbed his hands together. "If I help you I need two things from your office. First, I need some assurance in writing that there is an important murder investigation underway and my help is needed. I don't want anything detailed. Just something. Second, and this is going to be harder for you . . . I need a hook. Something I can hang my hat on if I get backed into a corner tomorrow night. You know what I mean?"

"A big part of the way I make my living, Mr. Valdez, is finding hooks for judges and juries. All I'm asking for is a chance to gain some time."

His mood softened. "I won't promise anything but if there's some way to help you without compromising my own office . . . well . . . we'll see. That abatement meeting is tomorrow night at the College Park Community Center."

"I'll be there. I'll sit in the back and I won't be saying much unless I have to."

"It's at 7 P.M. I want to warn you, if you haven't been to one of these public meetings before, it can turn ugly very fast. There are a lot of very angry people out there."

"Is there any background information I can look at that might help?"

The councilman rose and turned his back to Judith momentarily while he fingered through the files in the lower drawer of his credenza. When he turned back to her, he held five or six thick manila files.

"Information. Lots of it. It's not in any particular order, just background I've been throwing in here for the last year or so." He handed the files to Judith.

"Just send them back when you're done. I genuinely hope there's something in there that will simplify all of this."

Judith skimmed through the top file. It contained mostly memos from one city agency to another.

"Thanks. I'll get them back to you. And I'll see you at the meeting tomorrow night."

Immersed in the research materials, Judith decided the best approach would be to read everything she could and hope a pattern developed and the important facts stuck with her. That night in the silence of her office at home, Judith pored over the memos Valdez had given her. They addressed the causes of graffiti, the costs and the remedies. None of them provided a clear disposition of her problem. None provided the hook the councilman invited. They got her no closer to keeping the mural intact.

After the memos were read, she reviewed what seemed like hundreds of cases and local regulations; everything she'd been able to collect in the last twenty-four hours that had anything to do with graffiti laws and municipal ordinances. Most discussed the elimination of graffiti and the punishment for the crime. None provided for the retention of an illegally painted mural.

This was not her specialty. Hers was a criminal law background. Some knowledge of county laws and administrative regulations were necessary to do her job, to be a good county prosecutor. But she'd had no occasion in her career to deal with purely city matters. That was the domain of the city attorney. Seldom had there been any overlap for her to deal with. On those few occasions when it did happen, the case was transferred to the city attorney. If it was absolutely necessary for the DA to handle the matter, it was assigned to a junior attorney in the office.

At midnight, Judith closed the last casebook and quickly skimmed over the eight pages of notes she'd taken during the evening. It wasn't much for four hours of work. She checked on Elizabeth and walked quietly into her mother's room. Even with the glow of only one night light Judith could tell she was awake. Her eyes darted to Judith as soon as she entered the room. Judith turned on the small light next to the bed.

"Hi there, Mom. You been up long?" The questions still came, even though her mother could not answer.

Long ago, Judith had determined to treat her mother as though she still understood every word she said. Judith noticed immediately that her mother's nose was running. She grabbed a tissue and gently squeezed it around her nostrils. "Let's see, do you need a change?" Judith turned back the flannel coverlet. An acrid odor filled the room. A bright blue line ran up her mother's disposable plastic diaper, signaling visually that she needed a change. "No wonder you're not asleep. You're soaked." More than soaked. When the diaper wasn't on just right it could be a minor catastrophe. This diaper hadn't been put on tightly enough. Urine had leaked out, and the wetness ran the length of her mother's back, soaking the entire underside of the nightgown. Luckily, the plastic liner was under her and the sheet was dry.

God, she hated plastic now. Especially blue plastic. Everything was blue plastic.

Judith removed and carried the wet clothing into the laundry room, and threw the diaper into the small plastic diaper pail in the bathroom. Then she returned and took a pair of disposable plastic gloves from the box of plastic gloves that sat next to the bed. She washed and powdered, pushing her mother one way then the other until the new diaper was as "in place" as she could arrange it. A warm flannel nightgown she heated in the dryer, a quick bowl of microwave cream of wheat and applesauce, and her mother was ready to go back to sleep. Judith took the washcloths out of the woman's tightly clenched fists and rubbed the inside of her palms, moving each finger gently back and forth the way the nurses had showed her, replacing the washcloths with new, lightly powdered ones.

As her mother lay on her side, eyes still wide open, Judith reached for the small log cabin on the dresser next to the bed. She flipped open the roof. "Lara's Theme," from the movie *Doctor Zhivago*, filled the room. She had given the music box to her mother for Christmas a decade earlier. It played to the end of the theme and Judith rewound it, letting it play through a second time. Before it wound down, her mother's eyes had closed. She was asleep. Judith closed the roof and replaced the music box on the dresser.

It was one o'clock. Judith's exhaustion was compounded by a sad, empty feeling as she covered her mother, tucking the blanket up over the woman's shoulders.

Judith sat a few minutes on the bed beside her, resting her hand briefly on the woman's head. Her white hair had thinned so. Judith made a mental note to ask the day nurse to wash her hair and keep the room extra warm while she changed and bathed her. That running nose could be the start of a cold. A cold could mean the start of something worse, like pneumonia. And that, Judith had been warned, could mean sure death. Judith rose, and being close to her mother's ear, gave her a half-hug, whispering goodnight.

After one last stop in her office to gather her research into a pile, Judith set her radio alarm for 6 A.M. and fell into bed. Her life was certainly the top and the bottom with no end in sight for either extreme. The most she could say was that everything was as complete and comfortable as it could be for the moment.

13

ONE OF THE hallmarks of Valdez's term in office
had been to take the council into the community. Whenever he could, he called his meetings in the town halls
and community churches. The people loved it. They
came, yelled, vented their frustrations, and left feeling
as though someone had actually listened to them. And
it was not a show for him. It was for real. He meant for
them to vent. He meant to listen to them. And after he
listened he took action. Win or lose, he did what he
wanted to do and what seemed right.

Tonight, as he had done on numerous occasions all
over the district, he called a meeting to discuss the gang
and graffiti problems throughout the area. The clanging
of metal folding chairs attested to an overflow crowd.

Judith sat at the back of the cold, austere recreation
room and hoped no one walked in who recognized her.
She hadn't signed in. She was certain Valdez would not
introduce her.

Judith surveyed the audience of perhaps sixty—men,
women, and several children. They were a cross section
of cultures—black, Hispanic, white—and most were
dressed informally. Several members of the group, how-

ever, stood out. Seated against the wall to her right was a woman in her late sixties, in formal black attire, accompanied by a younger woman also formally dressed, who looked and acted as if she was her daughter. Another sitting front row, center, tapped her fingernails noisily against the back rim of the empty chair next to her. Remembering the manicured woman she had encountered at Melody Harmon's office, Judith fully expected the woman would be the one to launch an attack.

At five minutes to seven there was a flurry of activity at the back door. Valdez had arrived. As he entered he glanced toward Judith, smiled, and nodded in acknowledgment. He spent five minutes shaking hands and talking freely to anyone who approached him. Eventually, he made his way to the front of the room where an eight-foot-long table had been set up and covered with a white linen tablecloth.

Several minutes were consumed as Valdez shuffled his files and set a pen and pad of yellow-lined paper before him. Finally, he stood and raised his hands slightly to silence the chatter and bring the meeting to order.

"Good evening, my friends. For those of you I've not yet met, I am Councilman Valdez. I'd like to introduce the members of our council subcommittee who are here tonight to address several problems of mutual concern. After I've introduced them, I'd like to give a brief report on the most controversial matter on our agenda this evening—the mural that's been painted on the wall in Silverado Estates. I know we have a member of the Silverado Estates Homeowners Association here to answer any questions you might have."

One by one the six subcommittee members, who by this time had taken seats at the table facing the audience, were introduced and their professions and businesses revealed to the silent group. They sat at the white-clothed table with Valdez, willing members of the discussion group but content to let the councilman lead and shape the format of the evening.

"Can I ask first how many of you are here because of the mural going up in Silverado Estates, that's the mural some of you may have seen from the freeway?"

Three-fourths of the people in the room raised their hands. The councilman looked at Judith in the back of the room.

"Well, let me begin by giving you all an update on the situation." He paused. Judith wondered what kind of update he was going to be giving. He couldn't possibly have any information other than what she had supplied, and that was not much.

"We've had an on-site examination of the mural." That was news to Judith. "It's on private property and so it's not that easy. We can't simply take our own paint and white it out. I've been told the owners of the property are out of the country on vacation and it may be that we have to await their return before something is done about the art. We estimate that might be several weeks."

A woman in the audience, indeed the lady sitting front and center, raised her hand. The councilman acknowledged her.

"It's not art. It's an abomination. Art makes you feel good. Have you seen that body being painted on it? The person painting it should be arrested." There were voices from around the room humming in agreement. "I'd like," she continued, "to see some action taken to stop the person."

"Well," spoke up a young woman from the back of the room, "something can be art even if it makes you feel awful. I don't think we ought to be judging the artistic quality of the piece of work going up there."

Another voice, a man, added, "I'm a professor at San

Diego State, very near that wall. To tell you the truth, I'm not offended by the mural itself, I mean the idea of a mural being there. I just think the subject matter's in very poor taste. I had to explain to my five-year-old what the hell a picture clearly depicting a murder was doing on the wall.''

A woman was called on by Valdez. ''I don't think this is art. I don't think anything should be up there where I'm forced to look at it. I don't really care what it is. To me it's just no different than the tripe I see every day on the freeway signs. No different at all. And I resent anyone telling me this is somehow art. You've all lost your senses if you think people should be forced to look at that.'' Her comments drew random, noisy responses around the room. It was clear the crowd was split in agreement on her comments.

A man seated at the table spoke up.

''Ladies and gentlemen, I've been introduced already. I'm Duncan Gallo, the assistant to Melody Harmon at the graffiti abatement department. I serve as a public member on the councilman's subcommittee. Some of you know I am dedicated to the immediate removal of any unauthorized graffiti or murals. We can debate the differences between art and graffiti, there are some, but the point is, whatever's on the wall is not authorized in any way by the city or the owner of the retaining wall. I think it must come down and as fast as we can get it down. That's rule one. Remove graffiti as fast as you can. Otherwise, we are sending a message to the community that some forms of vandalism are okay. And this is vandalism. It's the destruction of property. And, if I am correct, Councilman, it's still a misdemeanor, maybe even a felony if it costs over five thousand dollars to correct the problem or remove it.''

''That's correct,'' the councilman added. ''It's still a crime. I'd like to remind you all that our city's municipal

code Section 95.0127 states, and I'm going to read
this . . .'' He picked up a piece of paper and read. '' 'The
city finds and determines that graffiti is obnoxious and
constitutes a public nuisance . . . and must be abated to
avoid the detrimental impact of such graffiti on the city
and its residents and prevent the further spread of graffiti. The ordinance further states the city shall issue a
notice to abate the nuisance, or initiate a prosecution
against the responsible person violating this section, or
both.' The question is whether we need to wait for the
owners to return before we enter onto their property. The
Thulis are legally responsible for removing it. But they
don't even know it's on their property yet.''

Judith could see the councilman was trying to find the
hook. His colleague was complicating matters. Gallo,
now standing, spoke again.

"There are several other provisions in the municipal
code allowing us to enter private property to abate nui-
sances. We'd need to get the city attorney involved and
get a court order. It might take a day or two, but it can
be done."

A man spoke up in a loud voice.

"I think you just go in and sandblast this thing away.
It'll take an hour, maybe two, but there won't be no trace
of it left."

The man's comments jarred Judith's memory. Where
had she read about the blasting process? She quickly
pulled out the notes she'd taken during her prior night's
research, locating the page dealing with graffiti removal.
Her inclination was to speak up right then and offer what
knowledge she had. But something told her to wait. A
tactical instinct perhaps. She wanted to see where the
discussion was going.

"I would suggest," Gallo stated, "that we request the
city attorney's office explore sandblasting the mural
away. I think we have a representative from that office

here. It will leave the wall virtually spotless and we won't have to worry about dealing with a property owner returning to find large blotches of paint on his wall.''

A woman dressed in a suit rose and identified herself as Kathy Wickham, deputy city attorney. She informed the audience that an order might be obtained but it would take a day or so and it would be best to seek the approval of the city council itself. Consensus was quickly reached within the subcommittee. An order for sandblasting would be sought by the full council the following morning.

Judith left as soon as the meeting was adjourned. She needed to review her notes more closely and examine the state administrative code.

If she could execute her plan just right, she might just have her hook.

14

JUDITH SAT AT the glass table in the kitchen looking out over the swimming pool and beyond it to the small guest house. Despite the beauty of the acre of lawn and garden surrounding the house, she spent little time in the backyard. In fact, she couldn't remember the last time she'd sat outside and had a cup of coffee. It had to have been over a week ago.

To the right of the guest house, her rose bushes, all twenty-five of them, were in full pink, yellow, and salmon bloom. She had missed their first budding. The first buds yielded perfect flowers, especially in the tea roses. She so looked forward to it every year. This year it had happened before she thought to look.

Increasingly, it seemed, the simple, colorful things she had enjoyed in her life were slipping away from her. She hadn't noticed the creeping malaise until it was suddenly there, and she felt powerless to stop it. Maybe the truth was that she just didn't have the energy. Certainly there was precious little time to relax; not with the economic pressure of keeping the house running smoothly. And not with the emotional burdens of a mother needing full-time attention, Elizabeth's busy schedule, and her own high-pressure job.

Judith looked around the yard. Nothing out there seemed exciting anymore.

There was no joy. Happiness perhaps, but not joy. And not even the happiness she'd known in the past; the happiness of getting up in the morning . . . *feeling* the day happening around her. Perhaps there lay the truth of it all. She didn't want to *feel* what was happening around her now. It was far easier to feel nothing. It was far easier to just *deal with the day*.

Well into her second cup of coffee, Elizabeth emerged from her room for breakfast and the day began.

As soon as Elizabeth was packed into the neighbor's car for the carpool to school, Judith took out her files and reviewed them. The night before, she had carefully tabbed several passages with yellow Post-Its. Now, in the freshness of the morning, she realized she had within her grasp a means to hand the councilman the hook he might be willing to take.

Judith could hear the nurse in her mother's room. She emerged with a worried look on her face.

"I think your mother has a bad cold, Mrs. Thornton. Maybe the flu."

The flu. Judith lived in constant dread of the flu season. The flu was the beginning of the end at the end. That's what the doctor had told her. He had been medicinally blunt. Her mother was undoubtedly going to die of pneumonia. Judith had had to decide then, tell him right then, if she wanted any "heroic steps" to be taken when the pneumonia came—paramedics, hitting the emergency button on the house security system, dialing 911. Judith had said no. No heroic steps. No antibiotics. It had sounded so simple and so humane at the time. So brave. Now, perhaps, here was the flu and she felt anything but brave.

Judith reassembled her files and quickly walked to the bedroom where she found her mother in bed, in an upright position, slumped to one side. Her eyes were blank, her mouth ajar.

"Have you taken her temperature?" Judith asked, holding her hand on her mother's forehead.

"It's 99.8. Just barely anything. I'll call you at work if it gets any worse."

"I'm going to give a call to the doctor, Jean, and see if we can get someone to see her today." The minute she said it, however, Judith knew calling the doctor was useless. Getting a doctor, even the doctor who had been treating her mother for a decade, to make a house call was impossible. No doctor had visited the house in a year. Since her mother couldn't make doctor's office visits anymore, that was that with the doctors. Her care had been relegated to aides and nurses.

"I'll talk with Mom's doctor and see if we can get something to make her comfortable. You call the supervising RN, Jean, and see if she can come over from the agency this morning." If they pressed the issue and sounded panicked enough, the agency Jean worked for would send the roving RN over. If they were facing an emergency, she'd be able to tell them.

Judith glanced at her watch. The city council meeting was scheduled to begin at 9 A.M. It was 8:10. She had to be out of the house at 8:30. She walked to her mother's side and gave her a hug.

"Mom."

There was no visual response from her. She was concerned, but she'd seen her worse than this before; times so bad Judith knew in her heart she was about to die. And she hadn't. She'd bounced back in hours.

"Mom? I'll be back this evening. Jean will take good care of you."

Judith held her mother's face in her hands and gave

her a kiss on the cheek. Her face was warm.

"Call me if anything . . . anything . . . gets worse, Jean. Okay?"

"I promise Mrs. Thornton. But if you don't hear from me it means everything's holding steady. I'm not going to drag you back here unless I need to."

On her way through the kitchen, Judith pulled a sticker from the telephone drawer. On it was the twenty-four-hour hotline telephone number for the San Diego Hospice. The hospice had signed on to care for her mother the month before. It treated patients and families of the terminally ill, those who have been diagnosed as having less than a year to live. Judith's mother had been "diagnosed" as qualified for the program by her doctor. Judith had found the hospice nurses and support staff to be of immeasurable help. Within two hours of Judith's initial interview with the hospice nurse, every need of her mother's that had gone unfilled and unknown the previous year had been met, from a wheelchair pad to the ordering of an adjustable hospital bed. More than any other agency that had entered her house, they had seemed to know what to do, when, and precisely how.

Judith pulled the sticker from its backing and placed it directly on the kitchen phone. She'd had the sticker for weeks but somehow she couldn't bring herself to attach it to anything. Now, maybe just for this one time, she needed it immediately accessible.

It was 8:25. Judith glanced into the bedroom at her mother, dozing now, peacefully, with Jean at her side reading the morning paper. She had set in motion the medical support system she had constructed around her in the past year. She allowed herself to indulge in the belief that between Jean, the roving RN, and hospice, someone would be available to reach her and respond to a crisis. She was free to go.

*   *   *

The city council committee room was packed with members of the public. Judith saw several people she recognized from the evening meeting. The councilman was there, as was Duncan Gallo.

At precisely nine o'clock, Councilman Valdez called the meeting to order.

"We're here to decide this morning what kind of recommendation, if any, we'd like to make to the full council concerning the mural that went up in Silverado Estates. I don't need to tell you about the number of calls we've received. They're running eight to one to take it down. I'd like to take the next hour and let those of you here in the room who want, speak."

The venom and intensity of ill will rose even above that which Judith had witnessed the preceding night. One after another, twenty people in all approached the microphone and used their three-minute allotment of time. They threatened everything from stealth removal in the middle of the night to lawsuits against the city for allowing it to stay up.

Finally, Councilman Valdez asked for testimony by those who wished to speak in favor of waiting and exploring the possibility of leaving the mural up, with the consent, of course, of the owner of the wall. One man, age seventy or so, wearing a brown beret and a long black coat, approached the microphone.

"Honorable council," he began, in a voice trembling with the nervousness of a lay person who had never spoken at a public meeting, "I am here because I am a lover of art. Art is a . . . a reflection of what is true." He faltered, grasping for words, dealing as best he could with the hush that had fallen on the room. "Have you ever wanted to say something, really say something, important? I have. You see, I think . . . no . . . I know whoever has painted this mural sees what none of us can see. Maybe he has seen something in his life that he wants to tell the world about, maybe how it has affected him. I say, let him speak. I plead with you to let him speak. Let his truth stand.''

Judith held her breath. How close he himself was to the truth! How frighteningly close. She glanced around the room, hoping he had not struck too responsive a note with the crowd. He had not.

Judith felt a combination of joy and sadness. The silence that had fallen upon the room was respect for him, for his age, not agreement with his expression of support for the muralist. He had persuaded no one. Most of the audience frowned in disdain; no one, no matter how sympathetic, would prevail on this issue. Judith could see it on their faces, in their eyes. He could have his say but the painting must go.

When he had finished his speech he turned and walked slowly back to his seat. He sat, shoulders slumped, head bent slightly forward.

"Thank you, sir," Valdez said. "I think your words of support for the mural are heartfelt. But, I think it is clear we have a consensus in the room against retention of the mural. Frankly, we must proceed with caution on the issue of removal. I propose we request staff explore the removal and the legal issues surrounding mandatory removal—without the owner's consent—and report back to us next week.''

The room buzzed with a sudden infusion of angry energy.

"Hell, no!" a man yelled, rising from the middle of the room. "No one-week wait. By that time this mural's going to be done and we'll never get it off. Frankly, I'm damned sick of my life and the lives of my neighbors being dictated by vandals. Sick of it!" The crowd burst into applause.

Valdez raised his hands to silence the audience. "I— I cannot stress how important it is that we proceed with caution, this is going to have to take a little time. This mural—graffiti—is on someone's property. The city just can't go onto someone's property and sandblast his wall. It's not done like that. The city could be subject to substantial liability.''

Whether or not the councilman was trying to find a way to legitimately delay the proceedings, he was correct in his legal assessment. Maybe this was the time to give his assistance a little push.

Judith rose and was motioned by the councilman.

"My name is Judith Thornton. I'm a resident of Silverado Estates and I'm on the district attorney's legal staff.'' She sounded so impressive. The several rows of people at the front of the room turned to look back at her. "I want the painting removed as badly as the rest of you do. But I agree with the councilman. We need to be very careful what we do. And not just because the owner of the wall is away or because there might be liability if the city goes in and erases or sandblasts without permission.'' Judith waited a moment, sorting in her mind those facts she could remember from her reading.

"We need to be very concerned about the environmental consequences of hydroblasting. The biggest concern I can see is what happens with storm water runoff. If I recall correctly, the state environmental quality laws only allow storm water to be discharged into storm drains. It's illegal to put anything else in them. I believe I've seen a city or state report indicating that the city could lose state environmental funding if the law is violated. That could mean millions of dollars lost to San Diego. For example, we need to be certain whoever sandblasts is going to be using a self-contained unit. That means whoever removes the graffiti has to be able to carry away all the water they use.''

The councilman became animated. "This is just the kind of concern I have about rushing into a forced removal. Whether the mural is up one more week or even a month is immaterial. We can examine the law and then proceed on the best course. I want to assure you that your concerns will not be dropped. In fact, I'm going to reset this matter for . . ." He turned to the staff member who was taking notes of the proceedings. "What's a good estimate of time needed for a complete report-back on this issue?"

The staffer replied confidently. "Three weeks if state ordinances are involved and if the city attorney needs to look at it."

"There is no question the city attorney must examine the issue if there's a potential for loss of city revenues. We will set our next meeting for three weeks from today, here at 9 A.M."

There was not a sound from the now-hushed room.

Judith breathed a sigh of relief. She had the time she needed.

It had been a long, tiring day. The delay set in motion by Valdez would give Judith more than the amount of time she needed to see the mural to completion. They had given the muralist two weeks. He was making true his promise. The painting had proceeded at a rapid rate. The two significant faces yet remaining were those of the judge and murderer. She fully expected the painter might take his time, play it close to the time limit.

At mid-afternoon, Judith had called home to see how her mother was doing. Jean reported she was holding her own and had napped most of the day.

By the time Judith had picked Elizabeth up from school and stopped by the grocery store it was five-thirty. Something, a now-cultivated intuition about such things, told her to plan a quick dinner and have Elizabeth in bed by seven-thirty. She needed the evening free in case any steps were needed to be taken to care for her mother. Jean would not be able to spend the night.

Her mother was still asleep when Judith reached home. Jean had changed her and made her comfortable. She hadn't had anything to eat though and had had the bare minimum of water. Jean did not need to remind Judith that the intake of liquid was crucial, especially since her mother was sick. Jean had forced sips of liquid into her throughout the day, but that would have to continue throughout the evening as well. By the time Elizabeth had dinner and was tucked into bed, Judith knew her evening was just beginning.

Everything was well under control until eight-thirty. On a routine visit to her mother's room, Judith felt her forehead. Her fever had spiked. Worse, Judith heard a raspish breathing. She felt her mother's legs. Macabre though it was, the nurses had told Judith that when her mother did begin the dying process, her extremities, her legs and feet especially, might begin to feel much cooler than the rest of her body. From that time, Judith, in times of real and apparent crisis, had reached for her mother's feet. Her legs and feet were warm. She wasn't dying.

This is irrational, Judith thought. It was beyond the irrational. Feeling to see if her mother was dying? She felt helplessly silly.

But having dealt with that matter, the illness consuming her remained. It was certainly pneumonia. And it was 9 P.M. Who could she possibly call on to get her through the mounting panic? Pneumonia could claim her in a matter of hours.

Judith fixed herself a cup of coffee, and debated whether she should try to deal with this on her own. She glanced at the hospice sticker on the telephone. If she was going to call, she needed to call now while it was still reasonably early.

Within minutes of dialing the number, Judith was

talking directly to the supervising hospice nurse. Yes, there was a field nurse in the area and they could have the nurse at the house in approximately thirty minutes. And, the nurse asked, hospice always asked, how she—Judith—was doing.

Judith could choke out only a few well-chosen words. "I'm fine. But if you can, send someone quickly because my mother's . . . very ill."

The nurse assured her someone would be there soon. Judith looked at the kitchen clock. It was 9:20. There was a sudden relief in knowing she would not have to deal with this alone.

Judith settled uneasily into a living room chair and waited. When car headlights shone on the wall she rose and looked toward the street. An older model Chevy had pulled up in front of the house. Relief turned to dismay as Judith saw the person who she could only assume was the hospice nurse. A man, a huge, rotund man, was waddling toward her house.

Judith had always requested female nurses for her mother. In fact she had once had a substitute nurse sent from the agency and when she learned it was a male nurse she sent him away before he even had a chance to look at her mother. Her mother would have been mortified to be seen by a male nurse she had never met before. Judith after all was the guardian of her mother's dignity, what was left of it, as well as her health. The male nurse, despite his pleas, and the pleas of the supervising nurse over the phone, did not get near her mother.

And now here, on the eve of a crisis of possibly monumental proportion, was a male nurse. But she was desperate. She would reserve judgment; her mother was so out of it, so unresponsive to the world and perhaps so near death that a male nurse would have to be okay. If necessary . . . if she felt at all uncomfortable, she would just have to send the man away and call hospice again.

The doorbell rang.

"Mrs. Thornton? I'm from hospice. I was sent over to see your mother."

Judith's stomach churned. Before her stood a grossly overweight man carrying a beat-up black medical bag. He was wearing a white nurse's jacket with a name tag. Roger Pruett. His eyes were red-rimmed and tired. The man, she thought, needs sleep.

"Come in, please. I'm Judith Thornton."

He stepped into the entry and then turned into the dining room.

Judith poured out the day's events beginning with her observations in the morning. She quickly recited her mother's intake of food and water, which weren't much.

"The worst thing though is Mom's lack of response. There's just nothing. No nods, no response at all to anything. I'm afraid she's got pneumonia and I know that could mean just a few days or even hours."

He smiled. "Let's go see Mom."

Judith led Roger down the hallway to her mother's bedroom. He listened to the horrible rattle that had scared Judith into calling him. Then he took his stethoscope from his ragged bag and placed it on her mother's chest. Then he did the most remarkable thing Judith had seen in all the times anyone had ever treated her mother. He turned to Judith.

"Is your mother hard of hearing?"

"Yes . . . she wears a hearing aid."

He bent down until his mouth was right up next to her mother's right ear. In a loud, low voice he half-yelled, "Mom, hello! I'm Roger. I'm your nurse. I know you're not feeling well. I have hold of your hand here." He picked up her right hand and held it in both of his and continued to speak into her ear. "If you hear me, Mom, squeeze my hand."

There was no pause, not a hint of hesitation. Her mother squeezed his hands. Hard.

He smiled. "I knew you were there, Mom. I'm going to give you some water. It has aspirin in it. Will you take them for me?" She squeezed again. "Good girl."

Roger left the room and returned with a full glass of water, tinted white with aspirin. By this time her mother's eyes had opened. The nurse fussed with her pillows until she was sitting almost upright. He took a large syringe from his bag. Then he filled it with the water and spoke again.

"You're going to have to take the whole thing, Mom. Okay?"

A syringe at a time she drank the entire glass of water. He paused, letting her catch her breath between gulps of water. His timing was such that after she had drunk the entire glass she was barely out of breath.

"There!" he yelled into her ear. "That'll keep you until tomorrow morning when I come back to see you. Okay? You get a good night's sleep." With this he pulled the covers over her and turned to Judith. "Can we talk?"

Judith, unable to think of anything but her own ignorance, led him out of the bedroom into the dining room.

"Your mom's going to be fine. She doesn't have pneumonia. What you were hearing was just phlegm at the base of her throat. From what I can tell her lungs are fine. Perfectly clear."

"She's not . . ."

"Dying? Oh, no. In fact she'll be around a long time. Her fever is very slight. It should disappear overnight. I'll be by at nine tomorrow morning and we can see if she needs anything else."

"Can I get you a cup of coffee or tea?" Judith asked.

"Actually, yes, if you don't mind I'd love of cup of coffee. Even instant's okay. I drink a lot of instant coffee," he said, smiling.

Together they drank half a pot of coffee. His eyes were red-rimmed and pink because he had been up for twelve hours straight. That's what he had told her. He was the person who set things right in the houses he went to. Told the truth. Laughed with the people like her, who had panicked at nothing. And cried with the families who he had to tell that death was there before they knew it was on them. His presence was a comfort, this man, who had such a firm grasp on life and death. He knew its coming and goings. When to panic, when to relax. There was so much comfort and power in that.

Eventually the phone rang. It was the hospice nurse for Roger. When he returned to the dining room he announced he had to leave quickly.

Before leaving, he checked on her mother and Judith made him promise he and only he would return in the morning.

Then she waved to him as he waddled down the driveway and she watched his car leave the curb and slowly drive down the street.

How could she have been so wrong. About everything. Her mother. That man. What was happening right in front of her eyes.

15

JUDITH HAD THE reprieve she needed. Three weeks to study the environmental impact of removing the mural had assured that. As she pulled her car into the small parking lot next to the courthouse, a lot reserved for the district attorney's top officials, she noticed Farrell had arrived before her. His black 500SEL Mercedes, usually parked straight-arrow in its space, was straddling two reserved spots, not only impermissible etiquette, but highly uncharacteristic. Something was wrong.

When she'd called Farrell the night before to tell him about the three-week continuance, he was elated. There had been no hint of anything amiss. But something was amiss now. It was confirmed by the look the receptionist gave her as she stopped by the front desk to pick up her phone messages. There were other signs. Mike Timkin's office door was closed. Timkin was Farrell's PR man. She could hear him inside his office, engrossed in animated conversation. Not once did it cross her mind that the cause of general concern was the mural.

Farrell's office door was also closed. She knocked and Farrell yelled for her to come in.

"Your car's in violation of several office ordinances, Larry."

"Are you ready for this?" he asked, ignoring her humor and motioning for her to come in and sit down.

"That muralist of ours has done it big time."

"What are you talking about?" Judith asked, confused by the unexpected nature of Farrell's comment.

"You don't know." It was an observation, not a question.

"Know *what*? All I know is we've got the time we need to get that painting on the wall."

"Well hell's broken loose all up and down the courthouse and the phone is ringing off the hook. Your artist it seems, has finally gotten around to painting the murderer's face."

His pause underscored the strain in his voice. "I've had three calls . . . from reliable people. His murderer is Marcus Steele. *Judge* Marcus Steele."

"No." That was all she could think to say. No. It couldn't be.

Marcus Steele was a sixty-year-old, well-respected member of the San Diego Superior Court. A senior member with impeccable credentials. Past president of the San Diego County Bar Association, past assistant district attorney, named "Judge of the Year" in 1988 and 1990. Lion's Club member, devout Catholic, husband to the same wife for thirty-six years, children . . . grandchildren.

"There's some mistake," Judith said. "I've got to go out and see it now," She headed back for the door.

"Go ahead," he called after her. "I hope it's just a slight resemblance. Some kind of coincidental resemblance. Because Judith," she turned back toward him at the door, "if there isn't, we have one hell of a mess."

* * *

Even approaching the mural from a distance, Judith knew it was no mistake. No coincidence. The face of the man holding the large, vaguely brick-shaped object above his head was no other than Judge Marcus Steele. The piercing eyes and aristocratic face were undeniably his. The only unusual thing about his face were his eyes. Steele's eyes were blue. But they had been painted a grayish-white. Judith attached no special significance to the discrepancy.

Pike arrived to find Judith staring at the newest addition to the mural.

"It's really him," Pike said, obviously more amused than concerned. "Do you think this painter really saw Judge Steele?"

"No way," Judith said. "The man's everyone's idol, mine too. Judge Perfect. I can't think of a person who dislikes the man, nor can I imagine him killing anyone. No way, Pike. I've been in his court. I've seen him sentence people. The worst ones. He's so passive he's disqualified himself from sitting on death penalty cases. He must have picked up Steele's picture from the paper. Like he did me. Or maybe he's just confused and put Steele's face on the murderer instead of the figure of the judge."

"Well, before you leap to any conclusions one way or the other, I gotta tell you I ran Judge Steele through the computer and interesting . . . he lives just across the canyon from our victim. They share the property line. . . . Interesting angle, eh?"

Judith was visibly stunned. The area to the north of Silverado Estates, Del Norte, shared a common boundary.

"You . . . you mean Steele lives in Del Norte?"

"Right at the edge. Three acres . . . including the canyon up to the Threadgill property line."

Judith did not respond because she couldn't.

"Changes the complexion of things a little, doesn't it?" Pike said.

Judith's beeper sounded, startling them both. She pulled it from her purse and read the caller's number. It was Farrell's office phone number.

Judith returned Farrell's call from her car phone.

She was never one to blunt the blows of bad news.

"It's a God-honest portrait of Steele, Larry. There's no mistake."

His tone had softened since the morning discussion, emotion giving way to reason. "Well, you need to get back here pretty quickly," he said. "Steele's going to be in at eight-thirty tomorrow morning to talk about our muralist. I need to figure out what in the hell I'm going to tell him."

PART THREE

DISSING THE KINGS

16

IT WAS 3:57 when Pike swaggered down the hallway toward Farrell's office.

Farrell had set the meeting with Judith and Pike for 4 P.M. and this had given Pike the afternoon for his investigation. It wasn't much time to do any meaningful snooping. But even while his two colleagues had been recovering from the shock of Steele's face appearing in the mural, and were struggling emotionally against casting the man as a murder suspect, Pike had been looking for reasons why Steele might have been painted on the wall.

Pike allowed himself to be guided by his intuition about Steele, an intuition acquired from years of confronting the unexpected coincidence and analyzing evidence just under the surface of the obvious. In his opinion, it was too much of a coincidence having Steele's face painted as the murder suspect and then have him turn up as a neighbor of the man murdered. Pike was determined to dispel his concerns once and for all. He had begun at the most logical and, thus, least fruitful, of places. As expected, the interviews with

Threadgill's widow and neighbors of the two men yielded only glowing accounts of each man.

If by some irrational chance Steele did kill his neighbor, why? Some business deal gone sour? An unfaithful wife? None of these simple explanations seemed to fit. The men knew each other but had no mutual business interests Pike could find. Their wives barely spoke and they did not mix socially.

Pike had had no time for plot maps and surveyors. On hunch alone, he had walked the perimeter of Threadgill's property. Whatever it was, he believed it was right there operating on the law of averages. Neighbors fought over the mundane: tree limbs carving up views and boundaries, boundary disputes, rowdy kids playing music too loud.

Pike had stopped at what he estimated to be the boundary between the two properties. It was marked by row on row of rose bushes, obliterating any other natural or artificial boundary that might exist, obliterating the boundary itself. Why, he thought, would the boundary of two concededly distant neighbors be obscure?

Now, as Pike arrived at Farrell's office, he realized Judith and Farrell were already engaged in heated discussion about just how Steele should be handled the next morning. He grabbed a quick cup of black coffee at the secretarial message station and lost no time expressing his views.

"He's guilty. When he comes in tomorrow we shouldn't give an inch. Not yet."

"What makes you think he did it, Pike?" Farrell was more conciliatory than he had been earlier in the day. But while his shock had worn off, his concern had not.

"The whole neighborhood's open," Judith said. "It's all one-acre minimum lots."

"I know the acreage up there. It's not the size of the

lots I'm talking about. It's the boundary lines between Threadgill's lot and Steele's.''

"So, what's so unusual about it?" Farrell asked.

"It's got rose bushes on it."

"It's got what?" Farrell asked.

"What's so unusual about rose bushes, Pike? I mean, I've got more than twenty of them lined up in my yard," Judith said.

"It's where they are that I think's interesting."

"And that is . . ." Farrell left the sentence unfinished.

"They're all along the border between the two properties."

"They do make a nice border," Judith said.

"Look, you two can think what you want but the fact of the matter is the border between the two properties is hard to find. I went out and walked the perimeter of the Threadgill land. I couldn't get through to the Steele property. The line's somewhere in the middle of a field of roses. Now, what does that tell you?''

"They both like roses?" Farrell was being sarcastic.

"Laugh if you like but tell me how many homicides you've worked where the murderer's some irate neighbor who couldn't control his temper anymore. You know as well as I do. They're the worst calls for the police; the most vicious. No one goes to them without a backup unit in place.''

Neither Judith nor Farrell contradicted him. "I'm telling you," Pike continued, "I've personally worked fifty, maybe fifty-five in the last couple decades." He was blinking rapid-fire at Farrell, a sure sign his emotions had reached a fever pitch. "Just, let's not cave in yet. That's all I'm saying. I just have this feeling in my gut that there's something out there we haven't found. It's there. I know it is. Give me a chance to find it.''

Farrell could dismiss explanations that didn't make sense. He could discount the significance of the rose bushes and Pike's walk around the properties. What he dared not dismiss was the man's intuition.

"What do we tell Steele when he comes in? We can't tell him the truth."

"We tell him there's a murder investigation going on. And that we need the wall to remain intact because the person who painted it might be a suspect," Judith offered.

"That ought to satisfy him short term," Farrell said, "but I don't think he's going to go for the idea of leaving it up there for any lengthy period of time."

"Let's take stock of where we are now," Judith said. "The wall's been painted. The face we've been waiting for is up. It's just not a face we expected to see. Maybe if it had been someone else we could track them down. But it's not just anybody. It's Steele. We have to find our muralist. If he's on the level, he's telling us a superior court judge is the murderer. We need this out of the guy's mouth. No mural's going to be enough. I want him to see the judge up close and tell us he's the guy."

"But we promised . . ."

Judith cut Pike short. "We promised only that the man would get to paint the mural. He promised to paint the murderer. All parts of the bargain have been met. We never said we wouldn't try to contact him about the painting. Now we have a strong obligation to do just that. A man's entire reputation and career are in jeopardy."

"So tomorrow we tell Steele what?" Farrell asked.

"We tell Steele we understand his concerns," Judith responded, "and we tell him we need to contact this muralist and find out if he saw anything out there. We play it close to the vest. I don't think we want to give the impression for now that Steele's a suspect in anything. We tell him we're as surprised as he is that his face popped up out there." She turned to Pike for support. "And that's the truth, isn't it? It's time we need. Time to find the guy who did the painting. Does that satisfy you, Pike?"

"As long as I get a little more time, that's all I need. How do you think we go about contacting the guy? We're almost back to square one."

"Not quite," Judith said. "There's something about the wall I'm finding interesting. We know every face that's up there in the painting except one. The judge's. I'm holding the scales. Threadgill's on the ground and Steele's standing over him. Whose face belongs to the judge?"

"Do you think the painter added someone he knew?" Farrell asked.

"Yeah. Like maybe he added himself. Or maybe that's Slic's face up there. Muralists often do that from what I understand. It's a signature of sorts."

Pike stood and started moving about the room.

"How about I get a good close-up photo of the face and pass it around on the streets. We'll see if we come up with a better ID. This Slic's still active out there. Someone'll recognize him."

"Do it fast, Pike," Farrell said, ending the meeting by reaching for a stack of files on the corner of his desk. "It's going to be a tough meeting with Steele tomorrow morning."

17

JUDITH AND FARRELL expected Steele might arrive upset the next morning. They did not expect he would arrive with an attorney. Nor could they ever have expected the attorney would be Alan Larson. Larson was the epitome of winning by courtroom shenanigans. Steele was the epitome of propriety. The duo made no sense.

Larson and Judith had tangled before. And, while Judith respected his abilities in trial, she harbored a seething resentment of his ethical conduct.

Larson was one of the new breed of criminal attorneys for whom courtroom etiquette was an obstacle to winning. Thus he did the only thing he knew to overcome it. He ignored it.

Although it had never been proved, Judith was sure it was Larson who had put a pinhole through the bottom of a stack of paper cups during the Bobby Engle trial. The embarrassing result was that during her opening argument to the jury, Pike, who was seated at her counsel table as investigator, had water dripping down his arm, much to the delight of the spectators and the jury. It was Larson too who had needlessly ripped apart Niki Craw-

ford, the chief witness against Engle. And he had known
what he was doing.

Gimmicks.

That's what Larson used to win.

Deep down, though, what irritated Judith most was
that the gimmicks won Larson's cases for him, and he
was not disparaged because of it. In fact, he was re-
warded. Criminal Defense Lawyer of the Year, Golden
Gavel Awards. The list seemed endless.

When Larson entered Farrell's office behind Steele,
his eyes met Judith's very briefly. It was strange how
one could work so closely in the courtroom with people
in case after case, the way she had opposing Larson, and
still know nothing about what they were really like. Judith had nothing on which to judge the man but his
conduct in court—and what she had seen and experi-
enced she did not like. So she did not like him.

With introductions out of the way, Farrell invited the
group to take a seat at the circular wood conference table
nearest the window.

As they settled into their high-back chairs, Steele was
the first to speak. "I must emphasize how terribly embarrassing this is for me, Mr. Farrell." He might have
continued had Larson not placed his hand on the jurist's
arm.

"Judge, I'll be the first to state *I* am dismayed with
this state of events," Farrell responded, noticing Larson's cue.

"The issue for me," Steele continued, "is whether
you are going to do something about it. I have had Mr.
Larson call the city attorney's office, thinking that is the
appropriate agency to bring my complaint to, inasmuch
as this is vandalism and graffiti, and that agency and the
city nuisance abatement department are the people responsible for removing it." Larson again placed his
hand on Steele's arm. Steele stopped and motioned to-

ward Larson. "I'll let Alan here explain what happened when he called them."

Larson took over. "When I called the nuisance abatement I learned the mural had become a district attorney matter. That in itself is not a problem. However, your office routinely appears before Judge Steele on criminal matters. It's, let's say, uncomfortable . . . to have the district attorney's office 'protecting' a mural which is at its best libelous. I mean here is the district attorney's office handling a mural depicting one of the judges of this court as a murderer."

Farrell broke in. "I completely understand your discomfort."

"Then do I take your concern to mean you're going to see that the painting, or at least the judge's face, is promptly removed?" Larson asked, the inflection in his voice rising ever so slightly.

"Not at this time," Farrell responded crisply.

Up to this point neither Larson nor Steele had asked why the mural was going to stay put. Or why the district attorney's office was handling what most would consider a minor city matter. Now, with conversation at a stalemate, the questions loomed.

"Up to now," Larson said, "we've been making a couple of pretty big assumptions. We've been assuming that there is a reason for the painting remaining on the wall. I need to ask, on behalf of Judge Steele, whether that assumption is correct."

"It is," Farrell stated.

"Then can we further assume the reason that the painting will remain is because of the murder that occurred at the foot of the wall?"

Larson had done his homework.

"That's also a correct assumption." Farrell stopped, then offered, "We're conducting an investigation of the murder and the mural is an integral part of that investigation. Mrs. Thornton is directing that."

It was not an invitation for Judith to speak. And she remained silent, allowing Farrell and Larson to find a common ground of agreement as to just how much information about the murder and the connection to the mural was going to be revealed.

"And I am correct in assuming there are no plans to remove the painting?"

"That's right, we are not in a position to remove the painting at this time."

Judith looked at Steele. His face had flushed red at Farrell's statement. She had seen that happen before, in court, when Steele was angry. There was no hiding his anger now and despite Larson's renewed placement of his hand on the man's arm, Steele's anger burst forth.

"Are you saying that I'm a suspect in this murder?"

"Not at all, Judge," Farrell said. "*All* we are saying is that there is a major development in the investigation that involves that mural and we can't remove it until the investigation is complete."

It was odd, Judith noted, that not once had Steele, or Larson for that matter, mentioned that the murder victim was a neighbor of Steele.

The judge shifted about angrily in his chair.

"Then you are permitting this . . . this accusation against me? Because that's what it is. It's an accusation that I have done something wrong; good God, that I killed someone! *You* may know I didn't kill anyone, but what is the public to think?"

"Well, Judge," Farrell soothed, "we look at it as if it's someone's interpretation of the event. Not that it happened the way it's depicted."

"That's about the stupidest thing I've . . . I go to court every day and hear murder cases. A murderer hearing murder cases?" Steele was enraged.

"Is there any way we can change your mind about this?" Larson asked, attempting to bring his client's anger under control by moving the discussion to a more optimistic note.

"I wish there was," Farrell said.

"Then my client and I have to discuss what course of action we need to take." It was the first time Larson had referred to Steele as his client.

"We're willing to wait a reasonable amount of time on this, maybe a few days. But anything beyond that is too long. Unless, of course, you're willing, Larry, to make a public statement exonerating Judge Steele of any wrongdoing and assure us he is in no way the subject of the investigation. Then we can roll with this a bit longer and allow this investigation of yours to wind down. But we have to have a visible and public statement."

"We can't make any public statements about this, Alan. Not right now. We're not sure . . ."

"You're not sure of what?" thundered the judge, his face again reddened. "Not sure I'm guilty of this murder?"

Farrell was keeping admirable control of his own temper. "The only thing I can say is that the city is referring the public's concerns about the mural to us. But I want to assure you that the mural's removal is still being studied by the city council. No conclusion is due on that for several weeks."

"And in the meantime what do I tell people who call me up and tell me they've just seen me on a wall killing someone? Do I tell them the district attorney is studying it? I think not," said Steele, pursing his lips, indignation replacing anger.

"I don't think anything productive's going to be served by discussing this further," Larson stated. "I can understand the need to conduct an investigation, but if the judge's face is still on that wall three days from now, we're going to consider it harassment of him by this office and we're going to do whatever it takes to stop it. I don't think I need to remind you that Judge Steele is currently engaged in trying a criminal case that's been ongoing for several months now. If he were to file allegations of harassment against your office or seek an injunction, there would be an appearance of conflict with your office. He would have to disqualify himself from hearing all cases tried by your deputies. He might have to declare a mistrial in the case now before him and it would have to be retried before another judge. That would be an awful waste of taxpayer money. I'm sure you'd agree. Let's think on this for a day or two and I'll get back to you . . . or shall I get back to Mrs. Thornton? I'm assuming her presence here means she is conducting the investigation.''

The backhanded slap at Judith was clear; she listened, took notes, and took over when told to.

Judith's jaw set in physical response. Farrell, however, was on his feet.

"I think, Mr. Larson, that our conversation is over. I'm not attributing to Judge Steele any of your statements concerning pending cases. But I find it an affront to insinuate any criminal cases might be held hostage or improperly handled by your client or my office. And you are indeed correct. If you need to discuss any matter related to the Threadgill murder, it is Mrs. Thornton you want to talk to,'' Farrell said.

While Judith might maintain a cool, silent demeanor in the face of Larson's challenge, Farrell felt no such constraints. He might have concluded silence was the better approach had the attack been only on Judith. It was, however, a power play intimating the Threadgill investigation might compromise his office. That was untenable.

Larson turned to face Judith. "I'm sure we'll be talking, Mrs. Thornton."

"It's always a pleasure to discuss legal ethics with you, Alan," Judith said.

Steele was silent as the two left the office.

"You were a little feisty there, maybe?" Judith asked. Farrell walked over to the small coffeemaker he kept in the corner of his office and poured himself a cup.

"The meeting stopped being productive," he said flatly.

"Larson?"

"Uh-huh."

"Why would Steele engage Larson? He's the only judge I know of who's brought him up short in trial for his antics and cited him for contempt. Granted, the court of appeal reversed it on a technicality."

Farrell carried his cup of coffee back to his desk and sat down.

"Well, look at it this way, Judith. If you were really in trouble, criminal trouble, who'd you get to represent *you*?"

There was a silence.

"I'd resist the temptation," she said.

Farrell leaned back, coffee mug in hand, "Maybe Steele needs a trick or two."

"Maybe," she said, under her breath.

"We don't have a lot of time on this, Judith. I think Larson will wait a few days, but I'm not sure what he's got up his sleeve. You know, I actually feel sorry for Steele. There's no evidence he's anything but a completely innocent person whose mug's gotten plastered up on a wall by someone who just might be a lunatic."

"We're not jumping to any conclusions on this yet, Larry, remember. I've got Pike doing some preliminary checks on Judge Steele."

"Larson's going to play hardball. And he's already

thrown the first pitch. Steele's quite capable of causing havoc with our calendars. If he's looking to file some kind of suit and then disqualify himself in the Slenger robbery trial he's on now, we're going to start that case all over again. At a loss of what, two months of trial work? That's thousands of dollars, and hundreds of wasted man-hours. We can't afford it. We can't risk that unless we have some evidence he's involved in the Threadgill murder; more evidence than some mural painted by someone who's obviously interested in one thing—getting his way. Getting his painting. Let's give Pike three days to poke around for something, anything.''

Pike had sequestered himself in the basement of the newspaper for the better part of the morning. In high-profile cases, he liked to run through the press clippings in the paper's morgue. The editors were always cooperative, and gave him access at any time he found convenient. For the most part the process yielded background information. Occasionally, however, something more substantial appeared.

With each click of the computer button, the newspaper articles shuffled on and then off the screen from right to left. Pike had begun his search in the local section of the daily news. That was where he expected to find the articles dealing with politics and judicial appointments. He had started with 1976, the year Steele became president of the county bar. He moved forward in time to Steele's appointment to municipal, then superior court. He watched the esteemed judge's hair thin and his face mature. There was the usual in the articles. His childhood in Escondido, California. A full scholarship to Princeton, then Harvard Law School. He'd belonged to a small law firm that handled exclusively civil rather than criminal cases. All of the partners were now on the state and federal benches, esteemed veterans of the law. There was not a blemish on his record, nothing that would indicate he was capable of a violent murder.

By 11 A.M., Pike's eyes were beginning to ache. He'd been at the screen too long. He needed to be back at the station by noon. On a hunch, he decided to move into the society section of the paper. It was in the Currents section that he expected he might find some material on Steele's social activities. It wouldn't take more than fifteen minutes, he was sure.

Surprisingly, there were more references to Steele's social activities and contributions to charitable causes than there were articles about him in the political section of the paper: photo after photo of him appearing at black-tie events for children, the elderly, homeless, and terminally ill. He built facilities, chaired fund-raisers, and to read the accounts, was one of the principal benefactors of theater and music in San Diego.

According to one personal profile, Steele's hobbies included gardening, and to this end, it was noted that he had cultivated an impressive garden of tea roses at his residence. Clearly, he was an expert horticulturist. Indeed, several color photos showed him in uncharacteristically casual attire, clipper in hand or surrounded by the flowers he loved.

In every article he was ever the judicious, elegant man with the warm, engaging smile. A man of immense and obvious likability.

There was only one article that seemed slightly out of place. It was a short note, almost sketchy in detail, reciting an incident at the Torrey Pines golf course a year earlier. Two lines of the article stuck in Pike's mind:

At the ninth hole, unable to make the putt, and clearly angry at his caddy's club selection, an irate Marcus Steele swung the iron at the young man, barely missing his head. He later apologized for the outburst.

Pike's eyes narrowed as he read the article again. "Perhaps," he wrote in his notebook, "there is a complexity here we've overlooked. It seems our icon might just have a few human flaws."

The discovery of Steele's previous outburst made Pike all the more determined to leave no stone unturned. He had spoken to every one of Threadgill's employees, every one of his business associates. His wife had been subjected to two days of questioning. Aside from the one newspaper reference to an outburst of temper by Steele, he had found nothing pointing the finger at the judge and there was not a clue as to who would kill Threadgill, or why. Pike had walked every foot of the Threadgill property, and along the border between the Threadgill and the Steele land. Still nothing.

The only thing Pike had not yet done was canvas the neighborhood. The afternoon had been spent walking and talking to neighbors, interviewing those who would consent to light questioning. After four hours all he had to show for his labor was a bag of Tiny Tea Donuts one neighbor insisted he take with him after her interview.

Pike had walked the length of Tierra Verde Drive and now he walked southward toward his car. A bright pink sun was setting behind him when he saw her. He'd noticed her earlier in the day, a small, frail old woman with long stiff white hair that was thin and combed straight back, giving her a resemblance to a windblown Albert Einstein. She walked stiffly and slowly in her heavy gray coat. A mixed golden longhaired dog on a leash traced her footsteps and walked slightly astride, intuitively understanding any uncontrolled pulling might topple the woman.

Pike approached slowly.

"Good evening, ma'am."

She stared at him and pulled back, frightened. He tried to assuage her concerns by showing her his police department badge.

"I've been interviewing people in the neighborhood to see if anyone saw or heard anything strange or unusual a week or so ago when one of your neighbors up here was murdered."

She was staring blankly at him.

"Did you know ma'am that a man was murdered up here?"

"Y—yes. I knew that." Her voice was as frail as she. She pulled gently on the dog's leash.

"Great dog," Pike said, bending to stroke the animal's head. Its fur was matted. It needed a bath. He disliked dogs. Undoubtedly his hands now carried an ugly doggie odor. "What's your dog's name?"

"I don't know. He . . . he doesn't have a name. I'm just taking care of him while his owner's away."

"Are you staying near here?" Pike asked, suddenly worried the woman really was lost. She turned around and pointed aimlessly down the side street.

"Ah—ah I live down there. But I'm only staying in the house for a couple of days."

Pike had seen her walking several hours earlier. She seemed to know where she was. He decided to hang back and see if she actually made it home.

"Okay, ma'am. I hope you and your dog have a good walk."

As Pike started to walk a safe distance away, to a position of observation, the woman called after him.

"I saw a man coming from that canyon where they found him."

Pike turned and walked back to the woman.

"Found who, ma'm?"

"Found . . . him. The man who got killed."

Pike pulled a pen and small notebook from the inside pocket of his coat and began to take notes.

"When did you see this man coming from the canyon?"

"That night, I think."

"The night Mr. Threadgill was killed?"

She stared blankly at him.

"I didn't know the dead man's name."

"Do you know the man who you saw coming from the canyon?"

She pulled gently on the dog's leash, staring at Pike's feet.

"No. But I'm only . . ."

"I know ma'am. You're only staying a few days."

"That's right."

"Can you describe anything about this man you saw coming from the canyon?"

"He was, let's see, tall. He had white hair and he had a thing in his hands."

Pike shifted nervously from side to side as the old woman stared at his rapidly blinking eyes, her mouth slightly ajar.

"What was the thing he was carrying?"

"It looked like a brick."

"What color brick was it?"

"I don't know. I just know the shape. You see I was out at night with my dog and it was very dark up there." She nodded west and up Tierra Verde, toward the Thulis' house. "That's all I know. What I saw." The dog tugged anxiously on the leash.

"I have to go now because it's time for the dog to eat."

"Ma'am, I'm going to need to get your name and your address because this sounds like very important information you have."

"Oh, well now . . . I'm not allowed to give out my name to strangers."

"Well, do you know Mrs. Thornton? The lady who lives in the big gray house on the corner down the street just a bit?"

She stared silently at Pike before uttering an emphatic, "No."

"She's a neighbor of yours. A very nice lady. Can we come talk to you together?"

The woman looked furtively around them, her wrinkled face expressionless.

"I . . . I don't know . . . I'll have to check with the people who own the house I live in."

"Can you do that, ma'am? I'd like to come see you tomorrow."

She started walking away, allowing the dog to pull her fragile frame a few steps.

My God, he thought. She's our witness. She'd seen something; he was certain of that. A tall man with white hair. Brick in hand. It all fit. Steele's height and hair color. A blunt weapon. He needed to show her a photo of Steele. Pike had a small photo of Steele in his jacket pocket. He always carried photos of his investigative targets, just so he could be sure he and potential witnesses were talking about the same people.

"Have you ever seen this man before, ma'am?" Pike asked, offering the picture to the woman. She looked at it, but did not remove it from his extended hand.

"That's certainly looking like him. But when I saw him you see he was very scared and running but that's him."

The dog pulled, jolting her balance.

Pike was beside himself.

"I'll be coming to see you, ma'am. I promise. Can I walk you home?"

The woman didn't respond. She walked away, without looking back.

He watched the woman for fifteen minutes as she walked slowly and stiffly up the street then back down. She slowed at Talon Drive and allowed the dog to pull, quickening her pace into the ranch-style home on the corner.

As Pike walked back to his car, intent on speaking with Judith first thing in the morning, he crossed paths with a man and a woman who looked to be in their mid-fifties.

"Excuse me," Pike said, again flashing his badge. "I'm Pike Martin, a detective with the San Diego Police Department. I'm investigating the murder of William Threadgill several weeks ago."

"Oh, wasn't that just awful," the woman said. "We knew Mr. Threadgill . . . and . . ."

Pike wasn't interested in their expressions of sympathy.

"I just talked with the lady who lives there on the corner."

"Mrs. Carpenter? The lady who walks her dog?"

"Yes. She said she was just visiting."

"She tells everyone she's visiting up here."

"She's not visiting?"

"Oh, heavens, no. She's lived in the same house in Silverado Estates for thirty years. Her husband died several years ago. She lives alone with her dog and seems to do okay."

The man added, "We all try to look after her. She has some thought process problems."

"What kind of thought process problems?" Pike asked.

He did not want to hear the answer.

"Oh . . . she's quite senile, Detective Martin, quite senile."

*   *   *

Pike had a headache. He'd spent the better part of the morning gathering information on Mrs. Ida Carpenter. According to the county tax records, she had indeed lived in Silverado Estates in the same small house, for thirty-three years. The house was now in an irrevocable trust administered by a daughter, Pamela Norquest, who lived in Newport Beach, ninety miles to the north. By telephone conversation, she assisted Pike as best she could.

According to Pamela, her mother was still able to care for herself, her house, and her dog, who it turned out did have a name, Queenie. She was not, therefore, legally within the category of persons needing the appointment of a conservator. Pamela telephoned her mother nightly and visited every other weekend if she could.

Pamela was certain her mother was quite capable of accurate observations. She was also certain her mother was on the precipice of senility, perhaps even a mild case of Alzheimer's disease that would eventually require closer supervision or even nursing home care.

Judith could offer no help. She had seen Ida Carpenter on numerous occasions and said hello, but that was all.

Now Pike sat preparing a police report detailing his observations and conclusions. He succinctly concluded a possible star witness might well be incompetent to testify in any case against Steele.

18

"IT'S STARTING JUDITH."

"What's starting?" she asked, not lifting her eyes from the file she was reading.

Farrell circled around her desk and sat on the edge, close to her.

"The pressure. I just got a call from someone in the governor's judicial advisory group."

Judith put the file down and leaned back in her chair.

"I won't ask who it was. But I can guess what it was about. Someone wants to know what I'm doing to a certain well-known judge. Of course there's an undercurrent of concern about me . . . a very subtle one . . . that goes something like 'this could really jeopardize her judicial application.' Am I close?"

"Oh, you're close. Not quite those words but the message was there."

"What did you tell him?"

"I told him you'd do anything for an appointment."

"Very funny."

"Actually I told him I wouldn't be part of any pressure. In fact . . . I think I might have gotten a little rude with him, but you know me and besides, that's the DA's prerogative when faced with improper political pressure. Unfortunately, he got the result he intended since I'm in effect here delivering his message."

"Did they really think I want a judicial appointment so badly that I'd sacrifice a homicide investigation? A murder? Who do these people think they are?"

"Rich and powerful," Farrell said, standing. "You know, Judith, we can shift the investigation to someone else. It's a hot investigation. Maybe one person shouldn't take all the heat it's going to give off. I'm willing to take it. Absorbing political heat is a big part of what I get paid to do. It's what the public expects."

"Thanks, Larry, but I'm not going to let anyone dictate to me how I'm going to conduct a case. You can't let the office be dictated to either."

"I have no intention of doing any such thing. But we could put together a small group to handle the initial steps in the investigation of Steele; give you a little insulation until we know how we're moving on Steele or whether we're moving at all."

"You know I don't do well in groups, Larry. Groups lower the standard of attention to detail . . . automatically."

"Okay . . . I offered. I don't want to see this needlessly jeopardize your chances."

"Larry, if I get an appointment I get an appointment. I don't want it contingent on my being a good girl. If he calls me . . ."

"He won't call you. No one will call you directly. They'll call me again and they'll call your friends." He pointed his index finger at her in mock humor. "Beware of friends who you haven't seen in years calling to have lunch with you."

"I'll bring my lunch till this is over. I don't know where this thing with Steele is going but I'll tell you, the fact he thinks he has to bring so much pressure on us makes me pretty suspicious. Pass *that* back the next time someone calls you. Tell 'em I wasn't suspicious but now I am.''

''I think I laid it out pretty well to them. They might not press it again. It depends on how strong they perceive your interest in being a judge really is. You know these people have very long institutional memories. This could hurt you long term if Steele is dragged through the mud and then comes out smelling like a rose. Anyway, Judith, if it all gets to you, come on in and talk. Promise?''

She ignored the question. ''You know, Larry, it's not beyond the realm of reason that Steele's involved in this some way. Pike's done a superficial check and it turns out Steele's property borders along the Threadgill property. Even though Threadgill was more into social scenes up in Rancho Santa Fe, and didn't do much socializing with the folks down here near the city, I'm guessing he knew the Steeles. What bothers me is that he never once mentioned it here. Not once said he knew him, or that they were neighbors.''

''I'll do the best I can to keep them all at a distance til we're done with the preliminary investigation. You know the big assumption this all rests on is that this artist of ours is on the level. If he's playing footsie with us, or has a screw loose upstairs, we're all going to pay for it.''

''I don't know, Larry. I just have this bad feeling about Steele.''

''Like he's guilty?''

''Like he's guilty.''

What Judith had told Farrell was true. She would never jeopardize an investigation for a judicial position. What was happening to her judicial evaluation was unconscionable and it bristled to her very core. It only made her all the more curious about what Steele had to hide.

But the fact remained that her dream of being on the court was surely in the balance.

She'd wanted to be a judge for as long as she'd been an attorney. She knew full well what she was up against. The old-boy network was too loose a term. It had more to do with money, power, and longevity. In the back of her mind was the realization that appointments to the bench were in the laps of the gods. Timing was everything: your own political party in power when you have the connections to move quickly through the system, not being too young to be perceived as inexperienced or too old to be regarded as lacking energy. Her timing right now was the best it could be. And despite her vehement denunciation of the tactics being used against her, a thought, a very small one, lurked embarrassing and troublesome in the back of her mind. If she was wrong about this artist, or even if the artist had made a good faith mistake in plastering the face of this influential judge on the mural, her time for a judicial appointment might pass. As Farrell had intimated, the judicial institution has a long memory. It translates into the evaluation forms as "qualified" rather than "well qualified." And it stays there on paper for years.

When Elizabeth had settled into her pajamas and nestled down in the family room to watch television, Judith said goodnight to Jean. The aide had fed and changed her mother's clothing, and Judith found her room filled with the clean, comforting odor of baby powder. Her mother was propped straight up in bed, wide awake, watching the nineteen-inch color television Judith had given her as a Christmas gift. She was wearing the long-sleeved pink flannel nightgown with the lace ruffle color and cuffs Judith's aunt had sent for Christmas. Her mother's focus shifted from the television screen to Judith as soon as she entered the room.

"Hi there, Mom. You're looking beautiful." Judith sat next to her on the bed, facing the television. She noticed her mother's gaze shift back to the screen. A John Wayne western was on. A shootout was underway, all guns trained on the lone hero, bodies falling to the left and right of the screen. Wayne was still standing tall in the center of the screen when the action was over. There was a time Judith's mother would have turned the channel immediately, setting the dial on a cooking program or talk show. Now, action movies were the ones she enjoyed and could become engrossed in. Judith found herself combing the TV guides for the blood and guts action films she would never let Elizabeth watch.

Judith sat with her mother until the movie was over. Now and then Judith commented on the action, or noted the actors who had died years before. She wondered if her mother recognized any of the old actors walking on and off the screen. When the credits rolled, Judith patiently flipped the channels, looking for another movie whose level of violence looked promising. Judith settled momentarily on the Classics Channel where *Step Lively*, an old Frank Sinatra musical, was playing. She recognized the music immediately. She hadn't seen it in maybe twenty years but as a child she'd watched it hundreds of times. There was a youthful Sinatra again tonight singing "Some Other Time, Not Now," but Judith didn't want to watch it. Finally, she asked the question that had been on her mind all evening.

"Mom, what would you think if I never became a judge?"

As Sinatra crooned melodically, Judith turned to her mother. Her head had tilted sideways on the pillow.

She'd fallen asleep.

19

THE CAVE WAS growing cold now that the sun was about to go down. Slic and Colon were sitting together on the ground, each with a sketchbook in hand. Occasionally the older man looked over the top of his companion's sketch pad and nodded with approval or pointed out some line or perspective that in his opinion needed correcting. The sketch sessions had become an evening ritual with the two. At first Slic had had difficulty straying from the balloon figures he had been using in his writing. Colon however had encouraged him to try other types of line drawings, and had even brought some of his chalks to encourage the boy to experiment with other mediums.

Gui Colon sketched, unaware of the legal processes his mural had unleashed. He had no idea the face of his murderer was a renowned judge. There were no newspaper articles to tell him of the accusation he had made against one of San Diego's most respected jurists. And Colon couldn't have cared less. As far as he knew, Steele was a nobody. In painting the face of the man, he had discharged his duty. The murderer had been delivered. The police could certainly find the killer now.

Indeed, given the general tone of the argument he had overheard before witnessing the killing, Colon had been led to believe the murderer lived nearby or knew the victim. No, he was certain the police got their part of the bargain.

And he had his mural. That was his part of the deal. Colon could not have known of the firestorm controversy surrounding the propriety of his art. He had never thought beyond completing the project. Now that it was done, he was unwilling to give up his hilltop cave or the friendship he had established with Slic.

"You like this one, old man?" Slic asked, handing Colon a sketch of a hand, his hand. The fingers were outstretched as if reaching for something. Every knuckle, every wrinkle was perfectly placed.

"This here is good. Very good! You ever see any of Leonardo da Vinci's sketches?"

"Yeah, I've seen some of them in an art magazine. They look like this don't they?"

"It's a pretty close match here. We move you next into some painting, eh?"

"Maybe . . . I might like to try it sometime. You think you can show me how to use the paints?"

"Oh, I think so," Colon said, a serious look covering his happiness. "I think I still have some of my old brushes and maybe even some paints. You'll need a canvas . . . just a small one at first. Painting's expensive. Maybe you can find some way to work and get some supplies. If you really want to paint, you're going to have to think of some way to finance your work . . . that is, until you sell one."

"You think I might be able to sell paintings?"

"I don't see why not. You must be good though. At least good enough for a starving artist sale, you know, 'No painting over $39.99?' "

"Maybe I'll try something like that some day. But I

don't know . . . it's not the kind of stuff I can do . . . I mean it don't matter, even if I'm good there's no way I'm gonna do anything big that's gonna sell like that."

Slic extended his hand and Colon gave the sketch back to him.

"Don't you have no dreams, Slic?"

The boy shrugged. "Sure I do. I dream all the time, mostly about these guys with guns like, chasing me."

"No . . . no . . . not those dreams during the night. Dreams about your life. What you want to do. What you want to be and make out of yourself."

The boy reflected in silence, a quizzical look spreading across his face.

"I want to write on the highest thing in this whole damned city."

"Ah, and what would that be?"

"The overpass on Freeway 805, the one that curves a couple of hundred feet up over the San Diego River. That would really be painting the sky, man, they'd be falling at my feet from here to Los Angeles."

"Hah . . . that's not a dream! You can do that any time you want to. All you need is a can of your stolen spray paint and a couple of those . . . how do you say your friends? Homies? To hold your rear end out over the traffic. If you fall maybe you get lucky and fall in the river instead of into the roof of a car."

"I paint good, old man," Slic responded defensively.

"You do! You have talent. You can draw what you see . . . what you are feeling. Not everyone can do that. Not even every artist can do that. I see that . . . there on the sketch pad. You could be even better if you let yourself do some real art, not just big cartoons. You have to try. Just once in your life."

Slic was silenced. Colon had struck a sensitive chord and surprisingly, had wounded the young man's feelings.

Colon waived his hand toward the cave entrance. "A dream, you see, is something that can't be seen yet. It might not even exist yet."

"Oh you mean like Martin Luther King had a dream?"

"Yeah, that's the kind ... something that's deep down inside you."

"I ... I don't have no dreams like that," the boy said haltingly.

"A pity. Everyone needs a dream. Even if it won't ever come true."

"I don't have no *time* for dreams." He lingered in contemptuous inflection over the word "time." I sure as hell don't have time for dreams that won't ever come true. I live in City Heights. You ever been there? People leave their houses only when they have to. The little kids, they see gang fights every day. They get shot because someone missed the person they were aiming at. You can hear guns firing in the middle of the night and police helicopters. You know, old man, sometimes when I go out I look back at the house and I think, you know, maybe it's the last time I'm going to see it. And in my house it's a battle zone just like the outside. The old man's throwing dishes or yelling or slamming doors. I keep my dreaming short and hanging over the freeways." Slic stopped, slightly embarrassed at having laid bare a small part of his emotions, then continued in a mellow monotone. "So don't preach to me about your grand dreams, old man."

Colon suddenly bristled. He had been trying hard to shape the boy's thoughts and understand his motivations. But the "I'm a poor kid" excuse had pushed a button. Colon stood, towering over Slic.

"Do you think you're the only person in the world who had it bad when they were young?" he snapped. "My mother scrubbed other people's floors until her knees were raw and she limped. I see my little brother die, *die,* in my own mother's arms. I saw pain in her face that has never, never gone away from my memory. I saw days with no food on the table; days when she opened a can of peas and give me the vegetable and she drinks the juice from the can for dinner. Eh? That's poor. I taped the soles of my shoes when they came apart and they flapped all day long with teachers and other kids staring at me. Laughing at me. You want to hear some more? We compare more notes? So don't whine to me. How do you say . . . 'Go get a life.' Go think about what you're going to do when you get too big to hang from bridges.''

Colon sat again, sorry he had been so rough on the boy. Slic, however, had not been as bruised as the man thought.

"You were that poor, eh, old man?"

Perhaps some perspective had been good for the boy.

"Yeah," Colon said, a smile spreading impishly across his face. "And I was bad. Really bad. I was what you call a delinquent. I spent my days down on the pier watching the tuna boats unload their catches. But I had this dream . . . all the way through the bad times. Deep down inside I wanted to fly like a big bird, an eagle. I could never do that but I could paint it. I wanted to paint it someday, way up high."

"You still have that dream?"

"It's not my dream now."

"What is?"

"I'll show you what is, come with me."

Colon led Slic out of the cave, up to Tierra Verde Drive and across the street onto the Thuli property. They walked quickly down the pathway to the wall and stood silently before the mural. The moonlight reflected off it.

"Here it is . . . the end of my dream. To be known." He turned and faced the boy. "And to be respected. The things an artist wants all his life. Isn't that the same thing you want, toy, eh? To be known? Why don't you look for a better way to get yourself known? Instead of being on a wanted poster? How do you like the painting?''

"It's good, old man. I like it. I like it a lot."

"Tell me what you see in it, Slic. What do you see in the face of that murderer?''

"I don't know . . . it's a face."

"But what is it you *see?*''

The boy stood silently, staring blankly at the wall.

"Let me ask it this way. What do you think I was trying to paint?''

"Well, I can see the fear on the murderer's face. You painted it like it was an accident, didn't you? It's the murderer who looks afraid."

"It wasn't an accident. It was done in anger. That's what I saw on his face. He was blind with anger. He was confused. See his eyes? Look closely.''

Slic stepped closer to the figure of the murderer.

"They're kinda white."

"See . . . I painted him a blind man.''

"That's cool, yeah, I see that.''

"Art sees things different ways and it can say the truth in different ways. That man acted in blindness. That's what I have to say.''

"People down there on the freeway aren't going to see that," Slic said.

"Maybe not the people down there . . . but the people who want the man's face on the wall . . . they might notice it.''

"Maybe you can be a witness in court.''

"Oh they will come looking for me. They've probably been watching me all the time.''

Slic was suddenly aware of his surroundings, his survival senses automatically taking over. He glanced nervously toward the footpath at his right.

"Don't worry, toy. They won't stop me. They don't want to stop me."

But Slic, fidgeting and unable to shake the growing nervousness, had made up his mind to leave.

"I . . . I got to go now. I got some homework to do."

Colon smiled broadly. "You go home, toy, and work hard. Get up and go to school tomorrow. You come back tomorrow night and I'll bring you some of my really good brushes and maybe some paint."

Slic relaxed and spoke slowly and deliberately. "Okay. I think I can be back. I know I can. I'll be here at eight o'clock. It's Friday night so I can stay late. You want me to bring something to eat?"

"It would be good, yes. You bring some bread and I'll bring some cheese. We can talk artist talk and eat like Italian painters!" He laughed loudly.

"Goodnight old . . . goodnight, Colon."

Colon nodded. "Goodnight, Antonio."

"You can call me Tony."

"Tony, then."

Slic took several steps and paused. "Did your mom really drink the water from the can of peas for dinner?"

"She did, Tony. She really did. More than once."

Slic's face was downcast, visibly saddened at the picture Colon's words created.

"It's okay, Tony. Times got better for us. They did. There was a time we never ate another can of peas, really." He smiled gently at the boy and nodded.

"See you tomorrow morning, Colon. I want to see whose face goes up on the judge on that mural."

"What time?"

"About 8 A.M.?"

"I look forward to it."

When Slic left, Colon gathered up his sketches and placed them in a pile near the cave entrance. He would sleep in the cave tonight and paint the last portrait on the wall in the morning. Only the judge's face remained to be painted. That face, he had decided, would be his own.

Colon walked to the cave entrance and stood outside looking northward over the canyon. The lights of Mission Valley shimmered below in crisp rows of white and gold. The kid had changed. He could see it in his face. He heard it when he asked about his mother.

Colon felt a sadness well up in him that he had not felt in years. His poor mother. What had she lived through? He suddenly missed her, terribly. Maybe a little of that pain though had touched the boy. Made him want to do more with his life than paint scribbling. With more time, maybe he would give up the craziness out on the streets. Colon breathed deeply. He hadn't been able to do everything he'd wanted to do. But he had done enough. The mural was still up and that meant something. Now maybe he could help this kid.

Judith was awakened by a sudden, sharp movement of her bed followed by a rolling motion. The wood pillars on the canopy bed were creaking and the door was rattling. An earthquake. It was a familiar experience for anyone who had spent any appreciable period of time in Southern California. Before the wood in the bed frame had stopped creaking, she was up and checking Elizabeth. It had been a big one but Elizabeth had slept through it.

Judith quickly walked the long hallway to her mother's bedroom at the other end of the house and found her asleep as well. The green digits on her mother's clock radio blinked four-thirty.

On her way back to her bedroom, Judith stopped in the family room. The chandelier above the breakfast table was swaying. She flipped the light switch to the backyard lights. Outside, the water in the swimming pool was still sloshing back and forth. Judging from experience, the quake had, indeed, been big.

Judith retreated to her bedroom and adjusted her radio to the all-news channel. It had been a 5.5; moderately strong by southern California standards, centered in the Hemet region of the San Bernardino Mountains. She pulled the sheets up over her shoulders and for a long time lay awake, waiting for the aftershocks.

20

THE MORNING AFTER the earthquake, flashing red lights racing across the living room wall summoned Judith to her front door. A white and orange paramedic truck was winding its way up Tierra Verde, its overhead emergency light circling on its roof. Judith walked outside to the street and looked westward. The truck had stopped at the curb across the street from the Thuli house. Several police cars and a fire truck were also parked at the curb. The coincidence too much to restrain her curiosity, Judith began walking toward the site of the commotion.

As Judith reached the bend in the street, she noticed two men in white jackets disappear over the side of the embankment. They were in no hurry. If someone was down the canyon, they were either not hurt seriously, or they were dead.

"Excuse me, ma'am, we need to keep everyone back," the police officer nearest her shouted, waving her away from the scene as a second officer began stringing yellow plastic caution tape across the shrubs bordering the hillside.

"I'm chief assistant DA Thornton, Officer . . ."—she looked at his name tag—". . . Thomas."

His mood softened noticeably. "Sorry, ma'am. There's been a landslide and some guy down in one of the caves on the hillside was killed."

"Was it someone who lived up here?" Judith asked.

"We're not certain just yet. We don't think so but the investigation's not completed."

"Is it a homicide?"

"We're pretty sure it isn't. The coroner's preliminary observations are that it was an accident. We suspect the earthquake last night loosened up the dirt and a major piece of the mountain fell in. The guy probably suffocated when a part of the hill came down on him."

"You have a name on him?"

"Colon. First name G-U-I."

Judith's attention was drawn to the figure of a boy sitting alone on the curb about twenty feet from where they were standing. His face was buried in his hands, his body bent forward. Judith noticed his clothing was caked with mud, especially at the knees of his blue Levi's. His hands and face were dirty.

"Who's the kid?" she asked. "A friend?"

"He says his name is Antonio. He apparently knows the man who was killed. As far as he's been able to tell us, he came up here to visit with the guy and found the cave-in. He tried to dig him out but couldn't. It was his yelling that caused a couple of the neighbors along the canyon to call us and when we got here, we found him. Still digging."

"Did he say what they were doing down there?"

"No. Just that the man liked to go down there and draw sketches."

"What kind of sketches?"

"He didn't say."

"Mind if I talk to him?"

"Go ahead. We're not holding him for anything."

"By the way, Officer, did you find anything down there in the way of drawings?" she asked.

"Yes, ma'am. At least three. And sketch pads, pencils, brushes. He had a regular little art shop going."

Judith's heart was pounding, racing in sudden recognition of the connection between victim and location.

"Officer, don't touch or move anything in that cave, please. Not a pencil, not a brush . . . *nothing*. I've got to make a call to our homicide investigator. It's possible the man who died may be involved in a previous homicide." She turned toward the boy sitting on the curb. "And don't let that kid go *anywhere*. Post an officer *next* to him if you have to. He may be a witness." She wasn't really sure what the boy might be witness to, but he knew this man Colon's connection to the case and for now, that was enough.

Judith could have summoned Pike through the officer's radio phone but she wanted privacy for her conversation. Pike was at his desk. He could be there in fifteen minutes. After talking with him, Judith hurried back to the site of the cave-in. This time she drove.

The boy was still sitting on the curb.

"Is he a relative of the guy who was killed?" Judith asked the officer.

"No. He says he was a good friend. The old guy didn't have any relatives. He was about sixty-five, sixty-six years old. At least that's what the kid said."

Judith walked over to the boy and sat down next to him.

"You knew the man down there?" she asked. He turned away from her. His eyes were red and his dirty cheeks were tear-streaked. She tried again, this time more direct.

"Do you know the man who was killed down in that cave?"

Judith didn't notice the police officer until he was standing next to her.

"Mrs. Thornton, I gave the order not to touch anything in the cave, but this was pulled out before the order was given."

In the officer's extended hand were two sheets of white paper. On one was a pencil line-drawing of a face. Judge Steele's face. On the second sheet of paper, there was a rough sketch of the mural. Judith stood and edged closer to the officer.

"You're certain these came from down there?"

"I personally took them from the officer at the cave entrance."

"And you say there are other papers down there?"

"From what I could see there were a lot of papers."

"Officer, can you place these back in the cave where they came from or as close to that as you can? Is the cave going to be sealed off? I am requesting it be, because there does appear to be a connection with the homicide that occurred up here a couple of weeks ago."

"I'll be sure it's sealed, Mrs. Thornton."

Judith turned back to the young man sitting on the curb and sat down on the other side of him.

"Antonio, I need to talk to you. I know about the pictures. I think I know what this man Colon was doing down there. He was drawing a scene of a murder on the wall across the street. If you were down there and had anything to do with this you're a witness and maybe an accomplice if he was involved in the murder that's happened down at the wall."

At the word "accomplice," Slic raised his head from his hands.

"He didn't kill nobody."

"You want to tell us who did?"

"I don't know who killed no one. He was my friend. That's all I know."

"Can you tell us what his name is?"

"Gui Colon. He lives somewhere over on India Street." The boy looked past Judith at the steel gray county car that had parked several yards from them. On seeing it, Judith rose again and greeted Pike.

"What do we have, Judith? Sounded like a hell of a big break."

"I'm not so sure, Pike. We have a guy dead down there in a cave and he had sketches of the mural and of Steele down there with him. We need to get into the cave to see what's there. The coroner's there now. As soon as they get the man's body out, I'd like to take a look around."

"I've called for our photographer to come over. You've frozen it all down there?"

"The officers have cordoned it off."

"Who's the kid?" Pike asked, nodding toward Slic.

"He says his name's Antonio and he knew the man who died down there, a Gui Colon. I had the police tell him to stay put, but there's really no reason to hold him. I'd like to get the basics from him and let him get out of here."

Pike walked closer to the boy.

"Antonio, I'm Pike Martin, an investigator with the San Diego Police Department. We need to get your address and a phone number where we can reach you in case there's anything we need to follow up on." He took a small notepad from his pocket as Slic stood.

Slic stood and recited his name. "I live at 6450 Moreno, Apartment E. We ain't got no phone. They took it out."

"You enrolled in school?"

"Hoover. I bus in."

"Antonio, I'd like to ask you about this Mr. Colon. Do you know what he was doing down there in the cave?"

Slic remained silent, wondering if he should tell the officer about Colon's dream for the wall. They had his sketches and would certainly figure it out, if they hadn't already.

"Antonio," Judith added, "we know the sketches here are the same ones painted on the mural across the street. I think . . . I'm thinking right now that Mr. Colon is the artist who painted the mural up here. Am I right?"

Slic remained silent.

"That was kind of a broad question, Antonio. Before you answer it I want you to understand we don't think you're involved with the wall painting in any way. I think," Pike quickly added, "that just to be absolutely safe I'd like to read you what we call a *Miranda* warning. It lets you know your rights and that anytime you want you can tell us you don't want to talk anymore, okay? We read it to suspects, but like Mrs. Thornton said, you're not a suspect in *anything*. Okay?"

"Yeah. Okay."

Pike took a small white card from his wallet and began to read the rights to Slic. At the conclusion, Slic said "I'll tell you what I know. It's really not too much. This guy . . . Mr. Colon . . . he *was* painting the mural."

"Was he painting it by himself?" Judith asked.

"Yeah. I wasn't helping. He knew what he wanted to paint."

"And why? Why did he want to paint it, Antonio?" Pike asked.

It took Slic a few moments to formulate his answer, but it was one, he was sure, that Colon would have approved of.

"He wanted to make a statement about something he saw."

Pike began blinking. Nervous energy had overtaken him.

Judith put her hand on Slic's shoulder. "Antonio, did

he tell you what it was he saw?'' She drew in her breath and held it.

"He saw someone get murdered across the street there near the wall."

Pike's head tilted back. Judith exhaled and continued.

"Antonio. This is very important. Did he ever tell you he knew who the murderer was? His name or . . . or what kind of work he did?"

"He didn't know the guy at all. He just remembered his face. He never said no name and he never said nothin' about where the man worked. All's he knew was the guy's face. He sketched it a lot of times."

Judith held out the sketch of Steele's face.

"Is this the man?" she asked.

"That's the guy," Slic said. "Do you know who that is?"

"That's not important right now," Judith answered, definitively brushing aside his curiosity. "Did Mr. Colon tell you exactly what he saw the man do?"

"Said he saw him club a man with something."

"Club him? He said the murderer used a club?" Pike asked.

"No . . . no, not a club. I didn't mean to say that. Something heavy . . . he never knew what it was."

"He wrote 'I saw this. Slic'?" Judith continued.

Here, Slic paused before answering.

"He wrote it. B-but . . . he w-wasn't Slic. That . . . was a kind of a . . . accident. He never wrote that name. He's not Slic."

There was too much hesitation, too much anxiety and conclusiveness in the boy's voice. He was talking like he was uncomfortable defending Colon but compelled by something to do so.

Judith and Pike's eyes met. They both knew at about the same time.

"You're Slic. Aren't you?" Judith asked, lowering

her voice. Pike was relieved he'd had the foresight to Mirandize the kid. He was as aware as Judith of Slic's record.

A pained expression crossed his face. "You going to arrest me?"

"Is there something we should arrest you for?" Pike asked.

"Well, *I* wrote that note you mentioned on the wall."

Pike's voice rose. "You wrote a hell of a lot more than that. Every agency in the city wants to get their hooks into you, boy!"

Judith raised her hand motioning for Pike to ease up. The situation confronting them was suddenly far more complicated than a simple note scribbled on a wall.

"How old are you?" Judith asked.

"Seventeen."

"This is *not* an easy matter, Slic. We're somewhat aware of, shall we say, your history, especially along the freeways. We can't guarantee anything to you. But . . . we're not going to arrest you. . . . "

"Judith. Can we talk?" Pike asked Judith. They walked to the far side of the street.

"I say we arrest him. You realize who he is, don't you?"

"I know darned well who he is, Pike. But I'm not about to jeopardize a murder investigation by blowing the whole thing open. And that's just what'll happen if we take this kid in. He's a juvenile. He automatically gets an attorney. Think about it for a minute. If we get him an attorney, the lid's blown on this whole thing. Are we ready for that right now? The truth of the matter is, the kid doesn't know what a powder keg he's sitting on and I'd just as soon leave it that way. At most he's a witness. He's not a murderer. We start linking him up and we could lose him and let the cat out of the bag for good. We need to check this out more carefully and keep everything status quo. All we've got right now is a kid who's heard some statements from this Colon, and a mural with Steele's face on it. That's not a lot.''

"That's damned near nothing," Pike added. "Okay. We let the kid go but I personally don't want him writing his name on *nothing* til this is over.''

The two walked back across the street to where Slic was standing, looking over the embankment.

"Antonio, we want you to go home. Detective Martin here will drive you. We'll be contacting you in a couple of days to talk again after . . . after we've had a chance to piece everything together. Detective Martin will give you his number and mine. Call if you have any questions or if you remember something you haven't told us. Do not . . . for your own good . . . do *not* do any tagging. Promise me that.''

"Promise. But . . . how about him?'' Slic motioned toward the area of the road nearest the cave.

"Don't worry. I'll stay here until Mr. Colon is out,'' Judith said.

"Just remember, if you tag and you're caught I'm not going to be able to do anything to help you.''

"Mrs. Thornton?''

"Um-hummm . . .''

"If that man . . . Mr. Colon, didn't have no relatives, what happens to his things?''

"The coroner will pick up everything down there in the cave and they can be claimed by anyone who thinks there's a claim to make.''

"Oh . . .'' He was choking back tears.

Judith put her hand on his shoulder.

"He was special to you, Antonio.'' She said it as a statement.

The boy shrugged his shoulders.

"He was . . . kind to me. He was . . .'' The boy

brushed his cheek, smearing a trail of tears over the dirt on his face. ". . . teaching me to draw."

Judith looked at the boy's dirty, disheveled clothes.

"Do you have some things down in that cave you'd like to have?"

He nodded and bent his head forward.

"Maybe some of the art equipment, brushes, stuff like that?"

He nodded again.

"I think we can see they get to you if they're not involved in any kind of crime. We'll have to keep the sketches for now."

"I don't want the sketches," Slic said, recovering his composure. "The brushes. He was going to teach me to paint with brushes."

"We'll let you know when it's ready for release."

Pike put his own hand on the boy's shoulder and began leading him toward the car when Judith called to him.

"I want to go through the cave tomorrow morning, Pike. About eight."

Judith stayed at the site until she was assured the area was secure and all items in the cave tagged and removed.

She watched in silence as Colon's body, wrapped in a bright yellow plastic body bag, was lifted up over the side of the road and placed onto a gurney and into the waiting white coroner's van. Judith watched until the van disappeared down the street. What kind of man, she thought, could have such devotion to a concrete wall? Inexplicably, she was drawn back to the other side of the road, to the Thuli home and the pathway leading down to Colon's mural.

Judith stood staring at the mural. It was odd. In the painting Steele's eyes were a whitish-silver. Had Colon painted what he'd seen?

Judith looked at her wristwatch. Eight-thirty. She

needed to call Farrell right away. This couldn't wait until later.

The mural had been so important to any case against Steele. Now it *was* the case against Steele.

A cold, silent witness against him.

Farrell was at his desk, reviewing case files when Judith called.

"Are you certain this man Colon is the artist?" he asked.

"It's him. Slic, the kid he befriended, has given us some of the details."

"Slic? Isn't that the name on the wall?"

"The same one. He was here, at the cave site. It seems he and this man Colon were holed up part time in a cave up here. I live just down the street and the cave's news to me. Anyway, Colon painted the mural and there's no doubt in the kid's mind, or mine now, that Colon believed he was painting the murderer he saw. That's what he told Slic. Slic says he never saw anything. His moniker's up there on the wall by accident."

"What're your feelings about that?" Farrell asked, hesitant to release the boy from liability just yet.

"I believe him. Colon was the one with the knowledge."

"We have to tell Larson this, you know?" Farrell said, with just enough question in his voice to avoid a flat statement.

"What do you mean tell Larson? We don't have to tell him anything."

"Good God, Judith, the only man fingering his client is dead. The only evidence you have so far against his client is Colon's hearsay to the kid and a painting. The kid's information isn't admissible because it's all hearsay and the wall's worthless to us."

"Look, Larry, maybe strictly speaking you're right.

In any other case I'd call the attorney. But this isn't any other case. And there's not a shred of exculpatory evidence in this for Steele. We have to turn over the evidence that exonerates Steele. That's all the law requires. If anything, the evidence, especially what Slic has to say, implicates Steele even more. The kid says Colon knew what he was doing; he knew what it was he wanted to say.''

"I'm just glad the judicial evaluation committee isn't listening to you now, Judith.''

"Please, Larry, I need a couple of days more. We'll need a search warrant for Colon's house.''

"That shouldn't be too hard. You want it going through our typing pool?''

"No. I'll have Pike type it himself. This is still under wraps.''

"How about this Slic?''

"All he knows is Colon is dead. He doesn't know how important the mural is and from what I can tell, he hasn't the slightest idea the murderer's face belongs to a judge.''

"Okay, Judith. Let's talk this afternoon. We'll take a few more days to wrap up the investigation on Colon's death. Then we talk again. You, me, and Pike.''

When Judith was through talking with Farrell, she telephoned Leon McLarety, the president of the Silverado Homeowners Association. What, she asked, did he know of a cave in the hillside north of Tierra Verde Drive. As it turned out, he knew only what the written history of the Estates told him. Within ten minutes he had delivered to Judith a thirty-page summary of newspaper articles and reminiscences of people who had lived in the Estates and were familiar with Young's caves and the tunnels that honeycombed the area. The document, entitled "The Secret Past of Silverado Estates," came complete with hand-drawn maps of the tunnels and locations of the various rooms dug out decades earlier by Young. The rooms carried strange names, Queen's Room, Treasure Room, Satan's Den, and Angel's Circle. After studying the three eight-by-ten maps attached to the history, Judith retrieved her own map of the Estates lots and placed it roughly over the map of the tunnels and rooms.

While neither map was drawn to scale, it was apparent that one of the tunnels might run under Threadgill's property to a room which, if it did not border Steele's land, surely continued on underneath it.

had already removed the items in the cave when Colon

21

"COM'ON, BECKY!" Pike drawled to Judith, in sarcastic reference to Tom Sawyer's companion-girlfriend with whom he had found himself lost in the blackness of Injun Joe's caves.

"I'm coming, Tom," she quipped back in a squeaky, high voice.

After finding Colon's sketches in the cave the day before, and locating maps to the underground tunnels, Judith was set on exploring them. If Colon had gathered any evidence of what he'd seen, he might have stashed it in one of the tunnels or caves. It had taken all morning to get approval from the city to enter the cave. After Colon's death, it had been officially sealed to minimize the risk of further cave-ins and injury.

The kidding stopped not far into the cave. Judith unrolled the maps she'd shown Pike that morning. The two casually dressed explorers examined them again by the light of the camping lantern Judith had brought along. This cave, where Colon died, had no name on the map.

There was no sign of death there. No blood anywhere. Only a dirt slide blocked what the map said should be the first in a series of tunnels. The evidence technicians had already removed the items in the cave when Colon died. Before their search, Judith and Pike had reviewed the report on the nature of the items found.

At the edge of the cave, near the door, a stack of paper was found. There were ten sketches, six of the same picture depicted on the mural. The remaining four were close-ups of Steele's face. Three old newspapers from the days immediately following Threadgill's death, one containing a large picture of Judith, rested close by.

The evidence technician had carefully compiled a list of every piece of paper found and had numbered and initialed them. Each was potentially an item of evidence to be accounted for in open court. The list was not long. A sleeping bag. Two bottles of vodka. Three sketch pads. Seven large paint brushes. Seven containers of tempera. Six tubes of oil paint. Three smaller oil painting brushes and one small, unblemished canvas.

"There's no doubt this is the guy who painted the mural. And there's no doubt he's fingered Steele as the murderer probably without knowing who the guy is," Judith commented following their inventory of the cave.

"You want to keep going? Through there?" Pike asked, pointing to the cave-in that stood between them and the mountainside.

"After you, sir."

Pike's mouth twisted in a mock snarl. "That's what I thought you were going to say."

Pike left the cave and returned several minutes later with a shovel he had thrown into the trunk of his car as an afterthought. Twenty minutes later, sweat dripping from his cheeks and down his neck, he had cleared a hole into the blackness of what the map labeled Young's Passage.

According to Judith's map, they were headed in the direction of the Queen's Room, where they found a six-foot square chamber.

It was clean. Nothing littered the dirt floor. Not a piece of paper or piece of cloth.

"My best guess is that Colon never came back this far," Pike said, continuing on into the adjacent tunnel.

According to the map, the room they entered next was Satan's Den. Thus far, they had seen nothing unusual.

"It's so cold," Judith said, wrapping her arms around her chest. "I'll bet this is close to the center of the hill."

"Do you really want to go all the way to the other side of the mountain, Judith? There's no need. I don't think there's any indication anywhere that . . ."

Pike's thought was frozen as they entered the Angel's Circle. The lantern light waved across the cave walls to the ground. Strewn about were the remains of clay pots, maybe a dozen of them. Several bricklike objects, which on closer examination appeared to be primitive statues, rested against the cave wall.

"Look at this, will you?" Pike exclaimed. "Do you recognize any of these things?"

"I've never seen anything like them. Take some photos, will you Pike? Close-ups."

Despite the fact that the police photographers had taken photos of the cave and everything in it, Pike had brought his own thirty-five millimeter along with him and began taking his own pictures. Then, with only a lantern to write by, Pike attempted as best he could to diagram the cave and where the various items were laying. Judith pointed out the objects she wanted him to add to the diagram or photograph. She always refrained from participating in the actual collection of potential evidence so as to keep herself out of the "chain of custody." Only her investigators handled evidence since they would be testifying about where and how it was found. If she entered the chain, she would have to testify, and that would require she remove herself from her role of prosecutor. She could not ask, and answer, questions about how and why evidence was collected.

When the photography and diagramming were complete, Judith selected three of the statues and Pike labeled them with yellow tags that carried his initials. Pike would return later with plastic bags and boxes to package them for removal.

It was the shape of the statues that intrigued Judith. She retrieved one and carefully noted it had a tapered end and a heavily squared blunt end. Rough facial features could be made out on the larger end, which she assumed was the top. At the tapered end were roughly carved talons, giving the statue a part-man, part-bird appearance.

Following the discoveries in Angel's Circle, Pike and Judith pressed onward, no longer questioning the need to follow the tunnels through to the far side. In only one other cave did they find any evidence of human habitation.

Rays of light finally broke the darkness at the end of their tunnel. When they reached the opening, Judith was able to squeeze through the three-foot chasm between the slab of concrete and dirt that had been placed there years earlier to block entrance into the tunnels.

Pike's girth did not allow him to pass through the narrow entrance. Unwilling to risk pushing the heavy slab outward and causing another landslide, they doubled back, retracing their path, marveling at the accuracy of the maps Judith carried.

Outside the tunnel again, Judith found a patch of sun and stood, warming herself.

"Can you get those sketches checked into evidence, Pike, and please get those photos developed right away. I'd like to take them down to the Museum of Man this afternoon and see if anyone can help me identify them. I figure we found them pretty close to the edge of the hill, near the Threadgill property."

22

━◆━

JUDITH'S ARMS LOCKED around the cardboard box as she jostled it into a comfortable position. She waited for the buzzer and the click of the lock release before using her hip to push the heavy metal bar across the door, forcing it open. The hallway that led to the second floor of the Museum of Man was enormous and empty. An imposing series of concrete steps twisting first to the left then the right lay before her. At the top of the stairway a door opened and a gaunt, thin man appeared.

"Is that you, Mrs. Thornton? I'm Henry Tegler," he said, "curator of the museum. I've been expecting you. My secretary informs me you have several relics you need some help identifying. Come on in and we'll take a look."

He held the door open for her to enter, then led her into a huge, brightly lit room, illuminated principally by the floor-to-ceiling wood-paned windows that lined the far wall. The room had the distinctively sterile look of a college research laboratory. Judith set the box on one of a series of gray tile counters that lined the walls and crossed the length of the room. Underneath the counters were drawers, each labeled alphabetically. Above the counters lining the walls, glass-faced cabinets held an assortment of clay pots and straw baskets.

"This is where we do our research and piece together our finds. As you can see, it's quiet and out of the way of the public. Normally, you'd find two or three of us back here working but my staff's out at a dig site this morning. Is this the material you collected?" he asked, motioning to the box.

"Yes, I hope I brought the right ones for you to look at. There were a number of items and photos. I brought six pictures and two of the items that look like statues. If you need additional items I can bring them in."

"Well, let's have a look."

Tegler gently cut away the tape Judith had placed across the top flaps of the box and removed the photos resting on top of the statues. He set the photos out in a row on the countertop and reached into the box with both hands, removing the first item wrapped carefully in a plastic bag.

Tegler studied the object for several minutes, then uttered a long, slow whistle.

"Where'd you say you got these?" he asked.

"In a tunnel system under an area called Silverado Estates. It's over near State College. My office is investigating a crime and in the process of doing that discovered these things. I've never seen anything like them and thought maybe you could give us an idea what it is we have here."

"Steatite," Tegler said, turning the rectangular object over in his hands. There was enough inflection in his voice to indicate he was interested. Very interested.

"Steatite?" Judith asked.

"It's a kind of soapstone, talc. It's heat resistant. And it's easily carved. On a scale of one to ten with ten as the hardest, it's a one. It was used by the Indians for making smoking pipes and cooking implements. Rectangular slabs of it with holes at one end were often suspended in a watertight basket to cook acorn mush or even boil water. They were called comals. Sometimes the comal was used like a griddle. A piece like this here,'' he said, picking up the more flat of the two statues, ''could be carved into an ornamental statue. It was soft enough for that, and the Indians grew quite adept at carving pretty intricate pieces.'' He continued turning the statue over in his hands and then set it down and began silently studying each of the photographs.

''Then it's not that unusual.''

''Well, that depends on where you are in California. If you found these items in the wild here in San Diego, and not placed there by someone, it would be *very* unusual. These are not implements made by local San Diego Indians. These, if I am correct . . . And I believe I am . . . are Chumash.''

''That name sounds familiar.''

''The Chumash were one of the principal Indian cultures in early California. If you spend any time in the Santa Barbara area just north of Los Angeles, you know the name well. Archeologists have found evidence of their settlements throughout the modern Santa Barbara region and the Channel Islands just off the Santa Barbara coast. Some of the more complex Chumash relics have been carbon-dated at one thousand years old, although the culture itself dates back perhaps as long ago as thirty-five thousand years.''

''Could they have come this far south?''

''Not as far as we have any evidence. Their dialects have been seen as far south as Malibu but that's it. When the five Los Angeles region missions were established, the Chumash had a pretty hard time keeping their culture together. Like most of the Indians who were subjugated to the missions, they eventually left mission control and became domestic servants and cowboys on the big ranchos. Most of the others lived in extreme poverty. I personally can't imagine any part of the organized Chumash culture this far south.''

''What does it mean if these are Chumash relics?''

''It means you've got quite a valuable find on your hands. If I could give you some advice, I'd say don't touch another thing in the caves where you got these implements and statues. Make an official request and we, or some other historical association, come in and do some documentation. I personally find this extremely exciting. Any archeologist would. There's of course always the chance that someone put these things in the cave, but judging from the photos and scattering of these objects that we see in the photos, it would have to be someone who didn't understand their significance.''

Tegler carefully studied the photos a second time.

''You say you didn't move any of these items around before the photographs were taken?''

''No, nothing was moved. And we'll leave it where it is until someone can look more closely at it and confirm what it is. We really don't know what, if any, significance this has to our murder investigation. It's like I said, it's all there, in a very unusual position in relationship to where the murder took place, so we're dotting all the i's and crossing the t's.''

''Let me know if there's anything we can do for you. We've gotten pretty good at excavation these past five years.''

''Mr. Tegler, can I ask you if this kind of collection would have a very substantial monetary value?''

''Depends. It could be extremely valuable to a private collector. I've seen these kinds of items auctioned for thousands of dollars. It's hard to say. The items would have to be studied closely. Anyone who has even a remote interest in this kind of item or has even the slightest knowledge of their potential significance is going to understand the monetary potential to collectors and museums.''

"Thanks, Mr. Tegler. This has been a tremendous help. I can't speak for the homeowners association or whoever it is that owns this stuff. It was found underground so if it has value, there might be a battle over it. I'd love to leave these with you . . .''

"No, no . . . I understand completely. I'd never expect these to be left here.''

Tegler carefully wrapped the statue again in the plastic bag and placed it cautiously in the cardboard box.

"Don't drop this, Mrs. Thornton," he laughed. "You'll break my heart, you will!''

Tegler followed Judith through the doors, holding them open for her and accompanying her to her car where he held the box as she unlocked the trunk and placed the box inside. As a final formality they exchanged business cards and Judith promised to keep him apprised of what action was taken.

During the short five-minute drive back to her office, Judith reflected on the statues. Their shape intrigued her. She recalled the forensic reports on Threadgill and the opinion of the coroner with respect to the shape of the murder implement. It had been both blunt and sharp. Like the statue she was carrying in her car trunk. It was just a hunch.

In her office again, Judith telephoned Pike and requested the complete forensic report on Threadgill, including any tests conducted on the tissue at and near the head wounds.

The written forensic reports reached Judith by mid-afternoon, and they were enough to cause an immediate conference between Judith, Pike, and Farrell. At the bottom of the last page of the six-page report was the notation Judith had half-expected would be there. Traces of talc were detected in and around Threadgill's head wounds. More interesting still, the report indicated that "the talc was found in the wounds caused by both blunt and sharp objects, or object."

As happened more times than she could count, they had stumbled on a break in the case. An extraordinary break. They had, perhaps, a clear picture of just what the murder implement might look like. But where they should begin looking for it was quite another matter.

23

JUDITH WALKED THE five long blocks from the courthouse to the Chapman Building on Ash Street. The building was one of the oldest remaining brick structures in San Diego, at various times housing the city chamber of commerce, county public defender's office, and a variety of state and federal representatives who had need of reasonable accommodations at the lower end of the rental spectrum.

Alan Larson had invited Judith to come to his office and discuss what he had called the phantom case against Judge Steele. It was an unusual request. Prosecutors seldom paid personal visits to defense counsel. But this was an unusual case. Steele was not officially a suspect in anything and no one felt comfortable viewing his involvement by way of traditional charging processes. More interesting was Larson's invitation to discuss the matter. It had arrived in the form of a surprisingly conciliatory letter. Larson was never conciliatory. He was a pit bull. Always as ruthless as the system would allow him to be.

Judith had no need to debate the pros and cons of meeting with Larson on his own territory. She wanted to hear from him as badly as he wanted to hear from her.

Despite its age, the interior of the Chapman Building had held up remarkably well. Black and gray marbled flooring and deep brown walnut wood-paneled walls in the lobby maintained the original feeling of distance and austerity. Three ceiling fans, no doubt replicas of the originals, circled in unsynchronized monotony.

Judith checked the slightly uneven white lettering of the black marquee. Larson's office was on the fifth floor. Judith's choices were two: the wide, uncarpeted concrete stairway, or an elevator controlled by the only elevator operator still at work in the city. She chose the stairs, watching as the walnut panels in the lobby gave way to the thickly painted gray walls.

Larson's office was at the end of the hallway to the left of the elevator. She stopped outside the door. At eye-level, ALAN LARSON, ATTORNEY-AT-LAW, faced her in large brass letters.

Had she walked into the office without knowing whose it was, Alan Larson would not have been on the list of possible occupants. She stepped onto the royal blue carpeting. High-backed armchairs covered in burgundy brocade sat side-by-side against a wall of silver and blue brocade wallpaper. On the dark cherrywood end table between the chairs sat a small bowl of mixed hard candies.

A middle-aged, well-dressed secretary greeted Judith, explaining Larson would be with her in a moment. He was, Judith assumed, behind the walnut wood door his secretary was standing guard next to.

Within a few minutes the door to Larson's office flew open and he emerged, a bundle of kinetic energy, dressed in a gray warm-up suit.

"Judith, come in, please," he said, extending his hand and giving her proffered hand a shake. "Pardon my informal dress, I've got a conference in Orange County beginning later this afternoon and I'm driving up there right after our meeting.''

She searched awkwardly for words. Larson was an adversary with whom she had no common ground. ''No problem . . . I like your office.''

''Bet you're surprised. You expected jail-issued furniture, right?''

Judith could feel her cheeks flush red.

''That's okay. I enjoy the prison mantle, cultivate that aura. This furniture is all pretty new, actually. My practice used to be almost exclusively off the appointment list from municipal and superior courts. I've added some privately retained clients since the beginning of the year, and I've had to cut back on the court appointments.''

''You're not giving up the appointments lists?''

''No way. I can't take one hundred percent refined air for too long. Give me that recirculated stuff in the jail, right?''

Protestations of his vows of poverty aside, Larson was obviously in transition. This representative of the destitute, the downtrodden, the forgotten, was edging into the big time. He was still professing his love for fighting the big fight for the honor of law and justice, but the seeds of luxury had been sown. They were all around him in blues, silvers, and gem tones. If he could stay out of the business of representing the drug lords, he might do okay and retire into the world of the three-piece wool suit.

Larson closed the door behind her as she came in.

''Have a seat,'' he said, pointing to one of the two matching brocade chairs across from his desk. She sat silently for the several moments it took Larson to sit at his desk.

''Well,'' Larson began, ''I guess it's kind of up to me to get the ball rolling here since I'm the one who initiated this meeting. As you could tell from our first meeting, Judge Steele is quite upset. So far the feedback to him has all been positive. And there have been lots of expressions of concern and even sympathy. But I need to know two things on his behalf . . . assuming you can tell me."

"I'll do what I can. There's an ongoing investigation and some things can't be made public yet . . ."

"I know that . . . I know that . . ." Larson interrupted, shifting energetically in his chair.

"But I'll tell you what I can."

"Okay, that's all I'm asking. Here's the problem. There's a wall with the judge's face on it. It's not a flattering picture. He's clearly depicted as a murderer . . . or at least someone who is assaulting another person. Now, this person is someone we know is dead . . . he's been murdered. I guess the issue is . . . how long is that mural going to be allowed to stay up?"

"I can't really disclose that."

"Well, are we talking in terms of days, weeks, months? Forever?"

"Not forever."

He wagged his index finger at her. "You're being cute." Judith bristled at his choice of words.

"Not intentionally. We have no need to keep the mural up indefinitely. We're talking weeks."

"Okay. I can at least carry that back to the judge."

"I see no reason why not."

"Good, good. I have a second question. It's far more serious. So I'll be as direct as I can. Is Judge Steele a suspect in the case involving the death of William Threadgill?"

Judith took a short breath before she answered.

"All I can say is that the investigation is ongoing. I'd be misleading you if I said yes or no. You know prosecuting offices. Anything is possible."

"I was hoping for some shred of information that

might make Steele feel a little more at ease. He's taking a couple of weeks off to get out of the limelight.''

"Why?" she asked. She was surprised. No one had brought charges. No one was talking about bringing charges. Even Judith, as close as she was to the investigation, had no idea where the investigation might end up.

"It's too uncomfortable for him hearing criminal cases. With the publicity hanging over him he just thought it would be a good time to do a little relaxing with his wife and grandkids. He'll be around in case anyone needs to talk with him. You can always reach him through me.''

"Doesn't he have a big murder case pending?" Judith asked, recalling the veiled threats made when they last met in Farrell's office.

"He's clear. The case he's on finishes up today. The defense attorney in the capital case scheduled two weeks from now asked he disqualify himself because of his potential involvement with the district attorney's office. He respects that. He of course would never do anything to create an uncomfortable situation with your office or the defense bar in a serious case, so he's disqualified himself.''

"Well, I wish I could have helped you . . ." Judith's last words hung suspended in her mouth. "What's that?" She pointed to the bookshelves behind Larson. On the third shelf from the top sat a statue, a slab of stone cut roughly into the shape of a bird. She had seen one like it before. It was still sitting in a cardboard box in the trunk of her car.

Larson looked over his shoulder.

"You like that?" he asked, standing and putting his hand on the stone.

Judith stood and, although uninvited, circled behind the desk.

"It's one of the most unusual pieces of sculpture I've ever seen."

"It's an early California piece. It's made of soap-stone."

Judith needed to be cautious, to extract information and give nothing away while she was doing it.

"What Indian culture did you say this is from?"

He pulled back, surprised. "I didn't, but it's Chumash I'm told, from up near Santa Barbara. Are you familiar with Indian artifacts?"

"Somewhat, yes," she said. "Do you mind if I pick it up?"

"No, please feel free. It's a beaut, isn't it?"

"It really is. It . . . caught my eye."

Judith slowly picked up the smooth slab of stone and turned it over in her hands.

"It's discolored," she remarked, running her hand over it. "See, it's a brownish color."

"Yes. That's what makes it so damned unique. We think it was used at some point as a weapon."

Judith's stomach churned as she asked the question.

"Who's 'we'?"

"Judge Steele and I. This was a gift from him. Isn't that extraordinary? You know he's on the historical site board for the city. This artifact fell into his hands. Call it a retainer," Larson laughed.

Judith placed the statue back on the bookcase.

"Have you had this very long?"

"Maybe a week. I got it just after the judge came in to see me about the mural. He came in and presented it to me."

"Don't let this one go, Counselor. It's a real collector's item." Judith looked at her wristwatch in mock anxiety. "I need to get going. I have another appointment in my office in twenty minutes."

"We'll talk again?"

"I'll keep you posted every step to the degree I can."

Judith was shaking as she got into her car. Every once in a while, not often, a prosecutor stumbles on the big clue. Sometimes it's in the paperwork somewhere. A witness that didn't get looked at. A piece of evidence that slipped past and surfaces at trial. It's never like this. The murder weapon never lands in your hands via defense counsel. It was almost too incredible. But what better way to dispose of a murder weapon? Hand it off to your attorney. She considered her dilemma and her options.

There had been cases, a rash of them in recent memory, testing the ethical standards a criminal defense attorney would be held to if he came into possession of evidence, particularly evidence that would incriminate his own client. The area was a minefield for the unwary. If you ended up with evidence, and you knew it was evidence, within a reasonable amount of time it had to be turned over to the prosecutor.

The lesson: If you end up with what looked like evidence, don't ask about it. If you did, you might end up hanging your own client.

But what do you do if you're the prosecutor and you're the only one that knows an item in defense counsel's hands might be evidence?

Judith had seen and heard Larson's reactions to her examination of the statue. He hadn't given the impression he knew a bizarre relationship might exist between it and the artifacts she and Pike had found underneath Silverado Estates.

Judith was in a tight spot. The statue was stained with something. But how could she have it tested? Ask Larson for it? He'd surely deny the request. He would never become a witness against his own client. And Larson had no need or ethical obligation to verify the nature of the statue. Even if Larson knew the statue could not have been the weapon, he might dump it.

The thought of obtaining a search warrant for it crossed her mind. But what would the warrant be based on? She would need to demonstrate there was probable cause to believe it was an instrument of the Threadgill murder. What evidence was there that would establish that? That things appearing to be Chumash artifacts were found under Silverado Estates and something that *looked* like one of the artifacts had a stain on it and was seen by her in Larson's office. Not enough. Even with the most pro-prosecution judge, they'd never get past even a preliminary judicial review.

And finally, oddly enough, there was *him*. She had knowledge that, if used in just the right way, could destroy his career.

If Larson was accused, even inferentially, of aiding and abetting his client in concealing a murder weapon, he could face disciplinary proceedings, or even face defending his license to practice law.

This was powerful information in her hands.

Powerful.

24

IT WAS MIDMORNING the day after Judith's visit to Larson's office and the excitement Pike felt in her finding a statue so similar to those they had found in the cave had not diminished. It was not, however, contagious excitement. Neither Farrell nor Judith, with whom he was meeting in her office, were prepared to take any action to secure the artifact.

"I don't think we have enough," Judith said. "Steele's not going anywhere and I'd hate to see us jump the gun and be wrong on this. We're going to have to wait for the right moment to get our hands on it."

"It's there though, Judith," Pike implored. "You saw it. It had the stains on it. If we test it we're going to find blood."

"You may be right, Pike," she fought back, "but how in the heck are we going to get our hands on it? There's no probable cause to believe that statue is the murder weapon. Not that I can see. Do you really see any probable cause?" He was silent. "You're too anxious on this one, Pike. We can afford to wait it out," she said.

Pike sat, his hands folded before him as he leaned

forward on his chair, staring at the floor. It was always like this with Pike. Holding him back, keeping him contained so that he didn't cause more damage to an already fragile situation.

"Can we talk motive?" Judith asked.

The intent underlying a crime must be shown by the prosecution because it describes the mental state of the perpetrator, and thus the mental element required for a crime. Motive, however, describes why a person commits a crime. The motive for a crime need never be proved by the prosecution. You could have the most evil motive imaginable in committing a crime. If you didn't have the requisite criminal intent, there's no crime. Still, as irrelevant as motive might be to proving a crime, if you can find a motive, you might be led to the perpetrator.

One by one the duo voiced the factors that could influence a motive for Threadgill's death. Judith spoke of them in no particular order, hoping a pattern would develop. Patterns. Always looking for patterns leading to evidence. Leading to explanations.

An explanation lay right on the surface of the facts in Steele's case. Rare artifacts found in tunnels and caves that crossed the boundaries of the lots in the Estates. There could possibly have been a dispute over the objects.

"I'd like to take a closer look at the lot maps for the Estates," Pike said, "and see exactly where it is these tunnels lead. I don't know who owns them or who's responsible for maintaining them. When Pike and I were down there in the cave that had the artifacts in it, I could have sworn we were close to the Threadgill property. I want to nail down the boundaries."

"Have we blocked the tunnels off?" Judith asked Pike.

"They're blocked. No one can get in. Nothing in them has been moved."

"I have several of the articles we found, including one statue that's similar to the one I saw in Larson's office. I'd like to drop them off with Tegler down at the museum and have him take a closer look. We need an anthropologist's report on it. Once we get that, we'll have an idea what we're dealing with."

"How about the statue in Larson's office?" Pike asked, unwilling to give up on immediate pursuit of the statue.

"We have to leave it where it is for now," Judith said. "I'm sorry, Pike, there's just no probable cause to seize it. And I don't want to tip our hand too early. It's safe where it is so long as Larson isn't aware we've focused on it."

As Pike stood up, preparing to leave, Judith called after him. "Pike, you're right; at some point, we need to shake the statue loose from him and see what that discoloration is. If he voluntarily gives it up, all the better. But we need to be sure he doesn't get wind of our suspicions about it or I'm worried he'll dump it and there'll go our case."

"What we need," Pike said, "is something or someone that'll tie this all together for us."

"How about that kid, Judith? The one who knew our muralist?" Pike asked. "I think it's time to bring him in."

25

SLIC LOOKED AWKWARD and out of place sitting at the polished cherrywood conference table in the spacious office. He still sported the baggy plaid pants and the loose flannel shirt, but the black beret was new, an addition to his wardrobe since Colon's death. His hair was longer, too, and while Judith didn't want to ask, she surmised he had gone to bed late and gotten up too early. He was here now to talk about whether he could receive immunity in return for assisting in the prosecution of Steele.

Immunity was a tricky thing to work with as a prosecutor. It was a tool and a sword. If you have a key witness in a felony case, you use it to induce them to testify for you, and you forgive the crimes the witness will confess to on the stand. You guarantee the witness's freedom in return for your win. But you don't just grant it in your office over a cup of coffee. You have to ask the superior court to grant it. And you may have to negotiate through a witness's lawyers. Even if it's granted, the witness isn't off the hook completely. He can be prosecuted if he commits perjury in the process. And you still have opposing counsel to deal with. If there's anything a good defense attorney relishes, it's a chance to go toe to toe with a star prosecution witness who's also a criminal.

Granting Slic immunity from his crimes was on Judith's mind when she asked him to come in to the district attorney's office to talk about Colon. Pike had presented her with a fifteen-page report on his painting sprees, most of it a compilation of previous reports filed in the various agencies. She had been assured by Pike that since Colon's death, Slic had indeed stopped, or at least temporarily suspended, the business of painting the heavens with his spray cans.

They had decided to avoid discussion of Slic's conduct. Still, the discussions with him were sensitive. The city attorney had not agreed to refrain from prosecuting him for misdemeanor charges. She shuddered to think about the reaction she would get from Nick Margolis down at the city transit office if she told him Slic was sitting here in her office.

"Hi, Slic. I'm Judith Thornton and this is Pike Martin, one of our investigators. We haven't had a chance to talk since we met out near the wall several nights ago. I need to talk with you now, about Colon and what he was doing up there during the time you got to know him. It's important because we're investigating a homicide . . . that's a murder. Can I tape this discussion on my recorder?"

The boy grew restless, rubbing his hands together and leaning forward, eyes cast down to the table. He wants to leave, Judith thought.

"Don't worry, you're not a suspect in the killing. We just want to know what you know about Colon. You want some coffee or a Coke maybe?"

"Yeah, thanks. Go ahead and start that thing if you want," he said, pointing to the machine she had placed slightly to the right of him.

Judith pressed the button on her phone, summoning her secretary, and asked her to bring Slic a soda, and a cup of coffee for her. Then she pressed the start button on the recorder. She stated the time and place, then began her discussion.

"Maybe," Judith began, "you can tell me what you know about Gui Colon. I'm not going to ask you anything right now about your own involvement with the mural. Please stop me at any time."

"He was my friend, all right?" Slic asked, soft defiance in his voice.

"I realize that. He was also painting a mural on a wall up in the area where he was killed."

"Yeah, like he wanted to finish it in the worst way. Look, I didn't kill no one!"

"No one's said you did."

"I just want to be sure you understand that all I did at the wall was to put my initials on it the first night I went up there when no one else was there. That's all I did. And that was way before Colon painted that mural."

"I want to be very clear that we are only talking today about Mr. Colon. We know he is the person who painted the mural. We want to know about how and why he painted it, if you know."

"He painted it because he saw this man kill this other man. He painted what he saw."

"He told you that?"

"Yeah! I was with him when he was painting it."

"Did he ever seem confused or unsure that the person he painted on the mural was the actual murderer?"

"No way! He said he saw the person and he . . ." Slic stopped.

"He what?" Judith asked.

"He was going to get back at everyone by making them give him time to paint the mural. You see, like, he wanted to paint a big bird . . . like . . . an eagle. But then he saw this thing happen up at the wall and he said, wow, I can't do my bird but I can do this other thing . . . I can paint that killing I saw.''

"Did Mr. Colon ever say any names . . . did he know any of these people?''

"Naw. He never said any names. None of them. Only . . . you . . . he took a picture of you from the paper. I saw him doing that so he could paint you up there as the prosecutor in the case. I never heard him say anyone else's name. He painted the murderer from memory, from sketches he made.''

Judith handed Slic a small pile of papers.

"Yeah! These look like the sketches he made.''

"Can you think of anything else you want to tell me about Mr. Colon or the mural?''

"I can't think of anything. I just went along with him . . .''

Judith interrupted. ''No, don't talk about what you did or didn't do right now. All of this is just preliminary, we're only starting to look at this and your input is very important. You have all kinds of other problems with the law that involve your activities around the city. You might want to talk with an attorney about them at some point but this is not about you, here. We want to know about Colon.''

Earnestness swept Slic's face.

"It's like this, see. I just wanted to be with the man. At first I didn't wanna be there but he like, made me help him. Then after I got to know the guy, I liked him. He showed me . . . how to paint . . . what a real artist does. . . . He promised . . .'' Here, the boy stopped, moved by a sudden surge of loss, and of pity for himself.

"If you can remember anything he said or did that might help us, will you call?''

"Yeah . . . I suppose.''

Judith reached into the long, deep drawer of her desk and removed a large clear plastic bag holding an assortment of oil paints and brushes.

"Before you leave, Antonio, do you want these? They were in the cave with Colon when he died. There's no family. I think he'd want you to have them." She held the bag out to the boy. Slic reached for them, his face showing no emotion. "Paint something really good with them," Judith said, holding onto the bag a moment longer than she needed to.

After Slic left, Judith turned to Pike.

"It was Steele. I know it was. The question is, do we file murder now or do we wait?"

"Not much has changed in the past three days," Pike continued.

"We have a possible motive and we have Slic," Judith followed quickly.

"And Slic, right."

"He says Colon wasn't confused. He painted what he saw."

"He also says Colon wanted to get the system. Who better to go after than a sitting judge? And he could have taken Steele's face out of the paper just like he took your face out. I'm just playing devil's advocate here, Judith. That statue in Larson's office is the key. We have to get it into testing."

"There's no charge against Steele. There's a mural and a kid whose truth and veracity is somewhat shaky, let's say. And Larson's going to just laugh if we ask him to turn over that statue so we can see if his client's guilty of murder. I'd sure laugh if I were him! Then I'd dump that relic as fast as I could."

"We may not have probable cause right now to search the office or seize his statue," Pike said, "but do we have probable cause to arrest Steele? Right now, do we have facts and circumstances in our knowledge sufficient to warrant a prudent person believing Steele committed an offense?''

Pike's approach was methodical. ''Let's focus on evidence here. We have a motive. Rare artifacts under both properties. They fight over them. We know that under that timid exterior is a temper that's capable of harming someone. He almost bashed his caddy's head in.''

''That's not much,'' Judith said.

Pike continued. ''We also have a woman who saw Steele come out of the canyon Threadgill was killed in.''

''But she's senile, Pike. I won't even be able to qualify her as a witness. Larson will rip apart her capacity to testify.''

''The kid. Slic. He says he saw Colon paint Steele's face and Colon told him he was painting the killer. That's Steele.''

''That's all hearsay, Pike. It'll never come in. It's not admissible evidence.''

Pike persisted, ''We have the mural.''

''The mural. Right. The artist's dead. Who's going to explain the mural to a jury?'' Judith asked.

''We have the statue in Larson's office. It's got the stains on it.''

''You know as well as I do it's going to be tough to get the blood into evidence or get a DNA test into evidence even if it matches Steele's blood DNA. So far the courts have had problems with the testing and we can't count on it here.''

Pike and Judith reflected on their point-counterpoint. Pike spoke first.

''Well, do you think a prudent person would think Steele committed the offense?''

''I think so,'' Judith said.

Pike smiled. ''I think so too.''

Farrell interrupted, ''It might get you an arrest warrant. It's going to be tougher in front of a jury.''

26

JUDITH HEARD THE heavy thump and leaped to her feet. In her haste, the Saturday newspaper she was reading fell clumsily from the kitchen table to the floor. The noise had come from her mother's bedroom. The weekend aide had left early; her mother was in the room alone.

At the door of her mother's room Judith found the caretaker's nightmare. Her mother had fallen to the floor, and was lying on her side in the two-foot-wide space between the bed and the six-foot-long wood dresser. How it could have happened was of no moment. She would deal with it later, deal later with the aide who had just bathed her mother. For now, the need was to make her mother comfortable, then figure out how to get her back up and on the bed.

Judith, her own body trembling, crawled across the bed from the opposite side and stood at her mother's head. She turned her, leaning her mother's back against the bed.

''Trying to get away again, weren't you?'' Judith said, fighting to keep her own composure in the face of overwhelming helplessness and vulnerability.

Her mother made no sound. Her eyes alone showed the fear that had overtaken her. They were open wide, as clear an expression of surprise as was possible for her.

In all of the everyday struggles to maintain her mother's care, Judith had achieved the necessary control. The lifting and pulling and forcing of water down her throat, the cajoling down of the pureed food. She could stay in control of what was happening or at least give an order to someone to help do something or tell someone else to get the help it took to do it, whatever *it* was. But this . . . this falling and not being able to get her mother back up again. It was in these moments that she knew defeat, complete humiliation; that she knew for all the struggling, the war was lost and the paralyzed body and broken mind could never be made whole again.

"We've got to get you back in the bed again, Mom. I'll lift, you just smile."

Her mother's eyes relaxed and softened, in them a deep sadness, and something else. An apology. She was sorry. For the pain. For the trouble she was causing. How like her mother.

Judith choked back tears, fighting for control of herself. If she broke down now, there would be no way to stop the flood of despair sweeping over her. This was life's final humiliation, a moment when, for all her strength, she could so clearly see how utterly expendable they were.

The emotion of the moment, however, had to give way to the physical problem at hand as Judith calculated just how she was going to raise her mother from the floor onto the bed. She could call someone to help but it seemed so drastic. Her mother was okay. Maybe, Judith thought, she could accomplish the task quickly.

In her best health Judith's mother had weighed somewhere between 150 and 170 pounds. She had been bottom heavy, a hereditary characteristic Judith observed in all three of her mother's sisters and one of her mother's two brothers. Since the onset of her illness, her mother had lost a substantial amount of weight, perhaps as much as forty pounds. But the reduction in weight had not lessened the problem facing Judith. A 170-pound person who was able to help a little was far easier to deal with than a 140-pound person who could not move at all. Her mother was as good as a 140-pound weight.

Judith gently pushed and pulled until her mother was sitting up. From behind her, Judith reached her own arms under the armpits of her mother and pulled up, trying to remember what all the aides had told her about lifting from her hips and not from the lower back. She imagined she and her mother were a humorous sight, Judith lifting . . . breathing heavily as her mother's body hung limp against her own. She tried twice to lift her mother high enough to maneuver her onto the bed.

"This is hysterical, Mom!" she said as loudly as she could without yelling. "I've become a . . . hum . . . man . . . shovel." And with the last word, she lifted and pushed her mother face-first onto the mattress.

"Are you okay?" Judith asked, quickly recovering and rolling her mother over so that her face was sideways on the bed.

Judith was breathing hard. Her mother's body was shaking and she was emitting a deep coughing sound.

She was laughing.

"We did look pretty hysterical! Oh, and look Mom," she said pointing over the bed, "the curtains are open! I'll bet the neighbors saw it all."

Judith leaned over the bed and grabbed her mother around the shoulders, hugging her hard as she laughed and wiped away the tears trickling down her cheeks. Then, as disjointed a thought as it was, Judith put her face up close to her mother's and said breathlessly, "You know, Mom, I was thinking, we need to get you out to the apple festival in Julian this year. You've never been there."

27

IT WAS THREE-THIRTY. Dead time in the afternoon. The morning calendars had long since been called and the trials scheduled for the day were out and into the departments they'd been assigned to. The longer trials would wait until the judges were ready to proceed with them. The attorneys assigned had already talked with the judges in open court, or had spent time in chambers with the assigned judge setting the dates for jury selection and opening arguments. Some of the trials, the shorter ones taking one to three days from opening statement to jury instruction, had begun already.

The afternoon calendars had been called at one-thirty in the presiding department and assigned out to trial departments as well. Along with the afternoon trials, the special hearings for the day were sent out: the probation revocation hearings, mental health calendar, and the motions calendar. Special departments existed to handle these matters and one judge was assigned to each courtroom department.

Judith's office was quiet. As part of her daily routine, she had reviewed the files and reports from her deputies in each of the calendar departments. There were no conflicts; no attorneys needed to be in two places at the same time the next morning. Nothing was worse for a trial deputy than having to appear before two judges at the same time.

Farrell appeared at her door. "How'd it go today?" he asked.

"Fine, no problems anywhere. Calendars are set for tomorrow."

Farrell walked in and stood before Judith's desk, glancing down at the case files stacked neatly to her right. At her left, at the top of her desk, was a distinctive, legal-sized white envelope, unopened, addressed to "Judith Thornton, Chief Assistant District Attorney." He noticed it was marked PERSONAL AND CONFIDENTIAL. It was from the state bar's judicial evaluations committee.

If a vacancy on the municipal or superior court arose, the governor decided which of the persons who had sent in applications should be evaluated by the state bar. The judicial evaluation committee then sent out hundreds of evaluation forms on individuals the governor's office was considering for appointment to judgeships.

All one needed to do to stop an appointment was to assure the governor's officer never sent the name to the bar for evaluation. The forms were simple and direct. They asked what the skill level of the candidate was, known health problems, and potential biases.

An envelope like the one on Judith's desk could hold the evaluation form for one candidate or several. The bottom line was that they'd all done something she hadn't—they'd cleared the first hurdle—the governor's office.

"Whose names are down?" Farrell asked, knowing her response.

"I don't know," she said nonchalantly. "I didn't look. It wasn't me though." They both knew there was only one judicial opening left. "You know as well as I do that the word's out. I'm after Steele. I've gotten three telephone calls from attorneys I know in civil firms asking me if it's true about Steele.''

Farrell wanted to drop the subject. He tried to stay out of the personal agonies of his attorneys. But the mental health of his chief assistant was at stake here, if not the prosecution of the most significant and volatile case in years.

''It's just the first group. There'll be others.''

''I won't be in any of those either.''

''What makes you so sure?''

''My current caseload.''

Her caseload was limited to the Threadgill murder.

''They got to the governor's appointments secretary,'' she said matter-of-factly. She wasn't angry. She was resigned, subdued.

''Who got to the appointments secretary?'' Farrell asked, again knowing exactly who she meant.

''The money. Steele's friends. How do I know? The guys I don't drink with or play golf with on Friday afternoons.''

Farrell turned from the desk and walked the short distance to the office door. He closed it and returned to the chair facing Judith's desk.

''You going to scold me or something?'' she asked mockingly.

''No, I'm not going to scold you,'' he said, mimicking her.

''Thanks,'' she said. There was a long, thoughtful silence.

''You know, Larry, I love this system. I've never wanted to do anything else with my life. I've done all the grunt jobs, the rotten calendars, the miserable hours. I've looked the other way at the judges who call me 'hon' or wink when they think their clerks aren't looking. I can put up with all that. But I hate, *hate*, the hypocrisy. It doesn't matter how good you are or how much you can contribute. It's who you know. Who you schmooze with. And God help you if you offend someone."

"You think that's why your name's not in that envelope?" Farrell said, brushing his hand over the envelope Judith had placed so prominently at the top of her desk.

"Isn't it?" she asked.

"How the hell do I know. Do you really care that much? Does your exclusion from that group there in that envelope really hurt *that* badly?" He expected her to say she didn't care; that it didn't matter. He expected more from her than he got.

"Actually, yeah, it does." Her voice dropped perceptively. "Do you think it's petty of me?"

"No. It's beneath you." He was looking right at her, and she at him. His voice was direct, honest. "Mind if I open it up?" he asked, reaching for the envelope.

Farrell beat the end of the envelope on the desktop, then ripped the top end open. He pulled out a single sheet of paper and read it. Judith could tell it was not the evaluation forms she thought it was. Same envelope. Same sender. Different message.

Farrell's face was emotionless.

"It's an announcement," Farrell said, his eyes still on the letter. "The commission's got a vacancy. This is the notice of a resignation." He threw the letter ever so gently toward her. It landed gracefully, face up in front of her.

"Goddamnit Judith," he said, whispering, "I don't personally care how you feel about the *powers* out there. What're you going to do about it?" He allowed a brief pause. "Nothing. You're not going to do anything because there's not a whole lot you *can* do. They'll always control your destiny and mine too. At least they'll try.

But goddamnit that's what makes this job so important. Your willingness to say 'I don't give a damn' for the parties and the social events and the golf tournaments and the schmoozing with the big guys. It's what sets you apart. Don't you understand? It lets you file murder charges against them or tax fraud when you have to. You start feeling sorry for yourself and the goodies these guys aren't going to pass out to you if you're not a good girl, and you're no use to me, or this office.''

She was silent and he sensed he'd struck all the chords she needed to hear.

"I've known you a long time, Judith. I've seen you in the rough times and you've seen me at my best and worst too. Don't compromise the best part of you. Whether you get any appointment to the bench is in the laps of the gods. It's not up to you or me. I've seen people toss away what they believe in for those appointments. I've seen them used ... paying big money for fund-raiser tickets for candidates so they can be at the top of the line for the judicial appointments. I've seen 'em change their names so they're the right ethnic group. They get the appointments, sure. Is that how you want to get yours? Hell, if you don't care why you get appointed, just wait for the next election and make a big contribution. I'll personally call the governor's office and I'm sure your name will get shaken loose up there. Then you can save yourself all this grief.''

Farrell rose and walked to the door. As he opened it and left her office, he turned back to Judith.

"Don't fit in, Judith. Don't ever fit in. I know how badly you want this. And I know why you want it. . . . If I could give it to you, I'd do it. But I've known you long enough and well enough to know how you want to get it. On the merits. Your merits. So don't feel badly.''

Farrell left Judith sitting there at her desk, looking at the letter of resignation and wishing she didn't want an appointment quite so badly.

28

THERE WERE RISKS involved in filing a criminal case too early. If a jury came back with a verdict of not guilty, they could never again prosecute Steele for murder, even if an eyewitness with a photograph of the crime were to walk through the door. It would be double jeopardy. But if they waited too long, the scant evidence they did have could just disappear and with it, any hope of a conviction, ever. It was a judgment call filled with what-ifs. But after endless hours of self-debate, Judith had decided they must proceed. They ran a greater risk of losing all of their evidence if they waited than getting a conviction now.

"It's all going to disappear, Larry. The mural, Slic. Maybe the statue. We can't afford to wait."

Farrell was unemotional. In such things he could divorce himself from the alleged perpetrator, in this case Steele. He turned to his investigator.

"Pike?"

"I say we move on it now."

"Do I file through a preliminary hearing or grand jury indictment?" Judith asked.

Most cases are initiated by the public filing of a criminal complaint followed by a preliminary hearing before a judge to see if there is enough evidence to hold the defendant for trial. A smaller percentage of cases were investigated and charged through the secret county grand jury process.

Her question was not academic. The grand jury was a proceeding that would occur behind closed doors. The target of the probe is not present. Nor would an attorney for Steele be there. Nor would Steele necessarily know he was the target. The prosecutor would call the witnesses in and present her case to the grand jury. At the end of the presentation the jury would decide if it would issue an indictment.

The advantages of pursuing a grand jury indictment were several to both Judith and even Steele. Judith would have almost complete control over the presentation of the evidence. Because the process would be closed to the public, the newspaper press and glare of TV lights would be eliminated. At the same time, Steele's privacy could be maintained or at least controlled for a time. It could shake a weak case loose with a minimum of grief. In sensitive cases involving high-profile targets like Steele, the grand jury was the route to go.

Aside from the media circus a public inquiry would cause, careers were at stake. Reputations would shatter. The damage could be irreversible. And everyone's future was at risk. Steele, Larson, Farrell, and Judith. They were all, for entirely separate reasons, bound up together in this.

The choice made between preliminary hearing or grand jury would determine how much of an uproar the district attorney wanted to cause. It was not the kind of choice Judith would make alone.

Farrell took a long drink from his coffee cup. "My preference is to use the grand jury, Judith." He'd taken hundreds of cases to the grand jury and knew its benefits well. "We also need to consider Steele in this. The evidence against him isn't strong. There's a chance we won't have enough evidence to hold him for trial whichever way we go on this. If we're wrong, we run the risk of subjecting him to needless pillorying. Not to mention our office's reputation. The confidentiality is going to protect us all, and I mean legitimately protect." Judith had winced when he said they might be wrong about Steele's guilt. "I know you're convinced he's guilty. I think he is, too. We wouldn't be proceeding if I didn't think so, Judith."

"I've been thinking about this, Larry. I think there may be practical problems if we go through the grand jury."

"What problems?"

"If we use the grand jury and witnesses testify, then disappear, we can't use their grand jury testimony at trial. If we lose a witness after the preliminary hearing, we can introduce the testimony at trial even if they're not there."

"You're thinking about Mrs. Carpenter?"

"Right. And Slic. We need to get them on the stand and let Larson cross-examine them. Then we can use their testimony if Mrs. Carpenter's mental condition deteriorates and Slic disappears."

"Any other considerations?"

"How I deal with Larson. He's the key to this. He may have the murder weapon. We limit ourselves if we go the grand jury route."

"Let me think about it. I disagree. But you're the one who's got to deal with the cameras and media in this. I hope you're prepared because you haven't dealt with the kind of pressure this is going to generate. You think a few powerful people are tough to contend with; just wait."

"I've set aside any immediate plans for a judgeship."

Farrell was smiling. "I know, you're just waiting for the right political climate. And just how are you going to shake the statue from Larson?"

"I've got a few ideas. . . . By the way, Larry, Mike Richards is our forensics expert. Do you know if he's a good artist?"

"Artist? Well, he's done some great charts and drawings for our county forensics seminars. Any particular reason you're asking?"

"No, not really."

The way she looked at him, though, said something else.

She had something up her sleeve.

Had Steele been just anyone, his arrest would have taken place as soon as the warrant was obtained. Police officers would have been dispatched to his residence or place of work. He would have been handcuffed and escorted to the police station seated in the back seat of a black and white patrol car. He would have been fingerprinted, photographed, and, if he was lucky, bailed out.

But Steele wasn't just anyone. He was a sitting judge. He would be asked to surrender himself with his attorney present if he wished. He would be booked and if it were determined he was a flight risk, bail would be posted. It was likely he would be released on his own recognizance.

The following morning, Larson was called by Judith Thornton and told to surrender Steele at the San Diego Police Station downtown for booking.

Larson was terse in his acceptance of the terms of surrender, extracting a promise from Judith that his client would be treated with respect, and he could make an immediate plea Steele be released on his own recognizance.

Nothing, however, could keep the press photographers

away once word spread amongst the district attorney and court staff that Steele was surrendering himself on one count of murdering William Threadgill. They lined the sidewalk and shouted unanswered questions as Steele was hustled into the police station by Larson, then two hours later was hustled back outside into Larson's waiting auto. He was free on his own recognizance.

29

IN AN ERA of growing political correctness, the annual Hi-Jinx dinner was an anachronism. Begun in 1960 by a group of attorneys in San Diego, it had reached its height of popularity in the early 1970s.

The idea for the dinner was innocuous and meant solely in sport.

Once a year, in the spring, the members of the organizing group sponsored a dinner attended by the elite of San Diego's legal establishment for the sole purpose of making fun of themselves and everyone else around them. Tasteless awards were presented to those who had committed some faux pas during the year, or to someone who had "offended" the establishment. The list of past offenders read like a who's-who of the important and successful: bar association presidents, senior partners in prestigious law firms, and even highly placed government officers. The highlight of the evening, however, was the introduction of the judge or attorney who received the Golden Ass of the Year Award for offensive conduct. The winner need not be present to receive his trophy, consisting of some obscene or cast-off item. It was all in humor, a release of tensions and opinions that could not be displayed in public.

No harm was meant to anyone and the horribly off-color jokes and obscene skits performed had carried no sanctions. The one cardinal rule was that no one was allowed to attend the dinner except attorneys and judges. No guests. No spouses. And absolutely no reporters.

In the last decade however, the winds of fate and demographic changes within the San Diego Bar conspired to limit the revelry at the time-honored event. Gone were the days when a small group of Anglo attorneys and judges controlled the power structure within the legal profession. Increasing numbers of Latino, African-American, and women attorneys created splinter groups, independent bar associations; each applying pressures and flexing increasing political muscle.

The death knell for the Hi-Jinx dinner had sounded three years earlier when the women's bar, already having established its identity, had been asked to prepare an act for the dinner. The invitation was intended as an assault on the aggressively feminist stance of the women's bar.

True to the tradition of the dinner and intent of the invitation, the women were asked to prepare a chorus line routine. The organizer of the women's skit, a tough, sexy, five-foot-nine redhead named Anne Rhea, agreed to it and signed on to choreograph the much-anticipated production. She promised the event organizers the skit would be all that past skits had been, and more. She even offered a list of the city's more physically endowed attorneys as the participants. On promises the routine would be consistent with the goals of the evening's entertainment, the dinner organizers skeptically waived their traditional prescreening of the skit.

The night of the performance, the ladies were introduced to the hoots and howls of the audience. On cue, a chorus line of women attired in fluffy white, head-to-

toe rabbit costumes, hopped onto the stage, danced around in a circle and left. The audience, bewildered and humiliated by a spoof on themselves, vowed never to invite the ladies to perform again, at least not without adequate supervision. For the ladies' part, they had won a dramatic victory.

The Hi-Jinx dinner was never the same again.

In the past three years the Hi-Jinx dinner had suffered from lack of attendance and the creativity of earlier years. The explosion in the number of women attorneys and with it the emergence of a powerful women's bar had brought the event into disrepute, an example of what was no longer politically correct. This year's dinner was billed as the last.

Farrell had cajoled Judith. "It's the last Hi-Jinx. I'm expected to be there. I can't take my wife and I don't want to go alone."

"You shouldn't be going at all, Larry," Judith said, a look of disgust twisting her lips to a snarl. "I don't have time for that stuff."

"One dinner is all. It's not going to be the past garbage. We've all been promised it's just a farewell of sorts to a tradition . . . a very old tradition. They're asking all the large firms and government agencies to send a representative."

Judith picked up the invitation, a simple white card with italicized print.

"And you believe them? It's at the Casson. Nice restaurant. Fifty dollars a ticket. Who's paying?"

"I'll pay. All the proceeds are going to Tanner Children's Receiving Home."

"I'll think about it."

"You can rub shoulders with the rich and powerful. Every one of them will be there you know. . . . "

"I said I'll think about it. What day's it being held?"

"Two weeks from tonight."

"That's about the time Steele ought to be facing his preliminary hearing. Are you sure you want to go out in public?"

"That's why I need someone to go with me. Whatever happens I'm going to need some support. And a nice dinner out wouldn't hurt you either." He was smiling. Farrell was the last person to need emotional support during the filing of a tough case.

"Okay, I'll be your date for the evening. Bring a note from your wife and no funny stuff, okay?"

30

WHAT'S YOUR LINEUP this morning?" Pike asked as Judith carefully loaded her files into her brown leather briefcase.

"I'm calling Antonio, then Mike Richards."

"That's it?"

"That's *it*."

"No Ida Carpenter?"

"No Ida. I'm building the prelim around the mural, Slic's observations, and the artifacts. Ida's competency problems are better dealt with at trial. If I put her on it might taint the entire hearing."

Pike raised his eyebrows and shook his head.

"Good luck," he said.

"I'll meet you downstairs."

It was a zoo.

Cameras from every local television station lined the crowded hallway well before the eight-thirty calendar call. The case of the People against Steele was going to be sent to Department 34. There was no local judge who felt comfortable sitting in judgment on a colleague. It was almost too much to ask of any judge, no matter how

245

distant they had been from Steele. For that reason Judith had not protested when Larson suggested they request the state administrative office of the courts assign a visiting judge from some other part of the state. A list of names had been proposed, and between Judith and Larson, they came up with a list of four acceptable prospects. In the end, Joel E. Turner, a retired judge from Santa Clara County, in Northern California, was sent to San Diego to preside at the preliminary hearing.

Turner was seventy-two. A brilliant, hard-working judge, he had been forced two years earlier into retirement by a California law which states a judge who remains in office past his or her seventieth birthday loses a portion of retirement benefits. It was meant to encourage retirement of those judges who should have retired at an even earlier age. Unfortunately, it forced the retirement of jurists like Turner, who still demonstrated the skill and energy of judges half their age.

Turner brought with him more than energy and skill. He brought a reputation of iron-fisted justice. He called the shots as he saw them. No politics. No fooling around with the law. No silly games and juvenile antics in his courtroom. Attorneys needed to know the law and their case. His deep booming voice had sent more than one unprepared attorney back to their office shaking. A black man who had been born in the Bronx and came through the system the hard way, he had been dubbed "Darth Vader" by the defense and prosecution during his fifteen-year tenure on the Santa Clara Superior Court.

Judith avoided all discussion with the press as she left the presiding department and headed for Turner's courtroom on the fourth floor. She edged along the wall and around a bright pocket of light from the television lamps. In the glow of the intense white glare stood Larson in, of all things, a gray three-piece suit. Judith had never seen Larson in court in anything but corduroy, usually brown. For Steele though, a different aura was called for. One of skill and polish. Judith wondered if this new veneer signaled a return to decorum in the courtroom as well. She could hear him talking into one of the microphones as she passed.

"There is no question of Judge Steele's innocence. This is a fabricated charge which will, at the appropriate time, be thrown out of court."

Standing next to him was an unsmiling Steele.

The courtroom was filled to standing room only with the press and the curious. Threadgill's widow was not present in court. After discussions with her it was concluded she need not attend. She was not going to be called as a witness and she had no desire to face the multitude of questions that would have been thrust at her.

This was, for all intents and purposes, the Judith Thornton show. As in any preliminary hearing, the defendant was not required to put on any evidence at all, and most defense attorneys did not. They watched the prosecution witnesses and then argued based upon the evidence presented.

Judith had her photos of Threadgill lined up and marked for evidence. She had her enlarged photos of the mural and the face that was so clearly Steele. What she didn't have was a murder weapon. And so this preliminary hearing was going to be somewhat different in its approach since it was as much Larson she was after as Steele.

Most judges called for order upon their entrance by requiring the audience stand to the bailiff's, "All rise, the honorable judge whoever presiding." This morning the courtroom clamor was silenced as the bailiff yelled, "Remain seated and come to order." Turner entered, took the bench, and began.

"The case this morning is the People of the State of

California against Marcus Steele. The charge is murder in violation of Penal code Section 187. Can I have appearances for the record please?'' He looked at Judith. She stood.

"Judith Thornton, chief assistant district attorney, your honor. I would like to designate at this time Mr. Pike Martin as my investigating officer.''

"Very good, Mrs. Thornton. Officer Martin is hereby designated investigating officer. Mr. Martin I presume is the gentleman now taking a seat next to you at counsel table?''

Pike had entered the courtroom as Judith was introducing herself. He slipped in next to her at the counsel table.

"Yes, your honor, this is Detective Martin.''

It was common practice for defense counsel to request all witnesses for the prosecution leave the courtroom at the beginning of the preliminary hearing. They were called in one at a time so as to keep them from hearing each other's testimony. The one exception was the investigating officer. Even though he might be a witness, he was permitted to remain throughout the hearing.

Judith sat down as Larson stood at the next table.

"Alan Larson, Your Honor, representing Judge Marcus Steele in this matter. Judge Steele is seated to my left. We request all witnesses remain in the hallway outside the courtroom until called.''

"Very good. All witnesses who are here please wait in the hallway until you are called and I instruct you not to discuss your testimony amongst yourselves while you are waiting.''

"Your Honor, we have only four witnesses this morning. Detective Martin who is next to me here, Dr. Mike Richards, Dr. Henry Tegler, and Antonio Perez. I will ask Dr. Richards and Dr. Tegler to wait in the hallway since Mr. Perez is our first witness.''

"Dr. Richards and Dr. Tegler, please take a seat outside in the hallway. And please refrain from speaking to anyone about this case while you are out there. Mr. Perez, please take the stand."

Slic stepped forward into the well of the courtroom through the short swinging wood gate. Unsure where he should stand, he headed toward the witness stand. The clerk stood and motioned for him to stop and step closer to her.

"Please raise your right hand."

Slic started to raise his left hand then quickly raised his right. There were muffled snickers from the audience.

"Do you swear to tell the whole truth and nothing but the truth, so help you God?"

"Yeah . . . yes, I do."

"Take a seat there on the witness stand please, Mr. Perez," the clerk said, motioning to the wood podium next to the judge's bench.

Judith watched Slic climb the four steps and shift uneasily into the oversized leather chair. He looked stiff and uncomfortable in the sport coat and tie he had borrowed from his cousin. He glanced across the courtroom. Judith knew how he felt. He had never had so big an audience. A sense of the importance of the morning, of himself and what he had to say at that moment, had no doubt overtaken him. That was exactly what the courtroom bench and witness chair were supposed to do. That was the reason why the judge's bench towered even more noticeably over the witness chair and courtroom.

Height was a jealously guarded tool of justice. One of the greatest arguments in the last several years had been the county's attempt to build two new courtrooms with judicial benches almost eyeball-to-eyeball with the taller members of the bar. For the senior members of the bench who might have first pick of these new courtrooms, the proposal meant all-out war. With appropriately placed pressure, the benches were raised.

Slic glanced up at the black man next to him. Despite his own preeminence in the courtroom, the judge dwarfed him.

Judith stepped from her desk.

"Your Honor, may I approach the witness?"

She would not ordinarily act with such propriety. Most of the judges did not require such procedure. Her research, however, had indicated Turner did. She wondered if Larson would behave himself.

"You may."

"Thank you, Your Honor. Mr. Perez, can you state your name and spell your last name for the record?"

"Antonio Perez. A-n-t-o-n-i-o P-e-r-e-z."

Question by question, Judith took Slic through his friendship with Colon and his observations of Colon's painting. She was able to ask whether Colon had ever expressed concerns that what he was painting was not correct. She could not ask what Colon had said to him, however, since that was hearsay, and with only certain exceptions not present in her case, hearsay was not admissible.

At the end of Slic's testimony, Judith had established that Colon had painted what he had seen on the night of the murder. Surprisingly, Larson had agreed to stipulate that the man lying dead in the mural painting was Threadgill, that William Threadgill was in fact the person who had died, and that the cause of his death was bludgeoning.

Then it was Larson's turn to cross-examine Slic. His first question indicated he was going right for the jugular.

"Mr. Perez, are you not also known as Slic?" He slurred the boy's nickname, purposely emphasizing his disapproval of the boy's pastime.

Slic looked furtively toward Judith. She had prepared him for this. While she had no intention of discussing his freeway antics in court, she knew that Larson had the police reports and he had all of Slic's history.

"I . . . I refuse to answer on the ground that my answer might incriminate me."

"Ms. Thornton, are you aware of this . . . complication?" Turner asked.

"Yes, Your Honor, and I suggest that before we go any farther with Mr. Perez, he be permitted to speak with an attorney. The district attorney's office is prepared to invoke the immunity procedures of the Penal code and compel Mr. Perez to answer. Without the immunity of Mr. Perez, he will undoubtedly not answer the questions Mr. Larson wants to ask. I will be candid with the court. The questions Mr. Larson seeks to ask do go to the witness's truthfulness. If he does not answer them, Mr. Larson can claim he is not able to properly cross-examine the witness and he will, I am sure, ask you to strike all of the testimony of Mr. Perez."

"Is that where we are heading, Mr. Larson?"

"I certainly am, Your Honor."

"In that case, Mr. Perez, you may step down. Do we have an attorney available to talk with Mr. Perez?"

Judith stepped back toward her desk. "Yes, Your Honor. I took the liberty of notifying the public defender's office and Mr. Hewlett is here to speak with Mr. Perez. This might take more than this morning because there is another jurisdiction involved in any grant of immunity. The offenses Mr. Perez is charged with are prosecutable by the city attorney. To be safe, we will need their concurrence. I'm sure Mr. Perez's counsel will insist on it."

"Will we want Mr. Perez back this afternoon?" Turner asked.

"If the court and Mr. Larson do not mind, I do not

think we will be ready again with Mr. Perez until tomorrow morning.''

Turner looked down at Slic. "Mr. Perez, counsel is
here to advise you. You may step down. You are ordered
to return to this court tomorrow morning at eight-thirty.
Don't be late. If you're not here when I begin, I'll issue
a warrant for your arrest. Do you understand?'' Slic nodded. "You may step down. And you may call your next
witness, Mrs. Thornton.''

"The People call Henry Tegler.''

The bailiff walked quickly to the back door of the
courtroom and poked his head outside into the hallway.
When he emerged, Dr. Tegler was following him.

Judith wasted little time on Dr. Tegler's qualifications.
She established he was an authority on the early California Indians and handed Larson a set of four eight-by-
ten black and white glossy photos to examine before she
handed them to the witness.

Larson was rubbing the palm of his right hand on the
top of his desk as he handed them back to Judith.

"Dr. Tegler. Can I have you examine the object in
this photo please and tell me what it appears to depict?''

"Certainly." He looked at the photograph and handed
it back to her.

"This item which is depicted in that photo appears to
resemble an early California Indian artifact of the type
used by the Chumash in Santa Barbara County.''

"Can you tell the court what you base that conclusion
on?''

"Experience. I have collected and identified many
such objects. And as I stated, it *resembles* Chumash art.
I'd have to examine it closely to make a positive iden-
tification.''

"Can you estimate the value of such an object if
found in San Diego?''

"Well, it is especially rare in and of itself. If found

here it is particularly rare. The Chumash are not believed to have traveled this far south. I cannot place a monetary value on it.''

Larson was suddenly standing.

"Your Honor, I object. I fail to see the relevance of this photograph.''

The judge nodded in the direction of Judith.

"Mrs. Thornton?''

"Your Honor, I will tie this into a possible motive for Mr. Threadgill's death.''

"Okay, Mrs. Thornton. I'll overrule the objection. We'll see how you tie it up.''

"Thank you, Your Honor. No further questions of this witness.''

"Mr. Larson?''

Larson sat down. "No questions, Your Honor.''

The court was moving quickly, ignoring the normal morning recess.

"Your next witness, Mrs. Thornton.''

"Pike Martin, Your Honor.''

Pike's testimony was brief. Judith showed him the photo previously shown Dr. Tegler and he explained how he took the photo himself beneath Silverado Estates. He had previously prepared an elaborate plastic overlay of the exact location of the cave where the photo was taken. When placed over a plot map of Silverado Estates, the location of the object lined up almost exactly with the boundary between the Threadgill and Steele properties.

Again, Larson declined to press the witness. He was clearly relying upon the obvious gaps in the prosecution's case. So what if she could show a valuable article was underneath the Threadgill property? Or Steele's for that matter. Without more, it was a weak motive at best.

Judith knew exactly what Larson was thinking. He was thinking he was safe. But she was about to deliver the final blow of the morning, one which she hoped would jar Larson sufficiently to force his hand and perhaps deliver the murder weapon to her.

Judge Turner shuffled his notes.

"Mrs. Larson, do you have a final witness for this morning?"

"The People call Mike Richards."

Judith looked at Larson and held her breath. She leaned toward Pike.

"Watch Larson and Steele. I may not be able to see them when I'm asking the questions."

Richards, already a veteran witness of hundreds of trials and preliminary hearings, many before Steele himself, had already positioned himself confidently at the clerk's desk and had his hand raised, ready to take the oath. It was administered quickly and he took his seat on the witness stand.

In order for an expert to testify and offer an expert opinion, it was necessary for the side seeking his testimony to establish he was, indeed, an expert. In a significant case where the verdict might hinge on the expert's opinion, hours, even days or weeks might be taken up with the parties battling over the witness's qualifications. The show, of course, was for the jury, to persuade it to accept or reject the expert testimony. The problems were exacerbated with cases that were a battle between experts. At the preliminary hearing stage, however, there was no jury to persuade. Even if an attorney had some doubt about an expert, as a matter of courtesy and saving time, the parties generally stipulated to a witness's expertise. Most judges presiding at preliminary hearings expected the courtesy and nothing irritated them quite as much as an attorney who decided to play hardball at the prelim by requiring everyone sit through the tedious qualification of a known expert.

"Your Honor, for purposes of the preliminary hearing

only, Judge Steele will stipulate to Mr. Richards's expertise.''

Judith leaned over to Pike. "See how polite he's become?"

"I'm still checking my paper cups," Pike snarled. He looked toward Larson and when he was sure the attorney was watching him, he picked up the stack of paper cups next to the water carafe on their desk and looked closely at them.

Pike was referring to the incident during the Bobby Engle trial, when he poured a cup of water during Judith's argument to the jury and found the water trickling out of the bottom of the cup, down his arm and onto the desk, much to the delight of the jury and spectators. He firmly believed Larson, known for such antics, had stuck a pin through the entire pile of paper cups on the prosecution table. Pike had never forgiven him the perceived indiscretion. He wanted him to know he was watching.

"Thank you, Mr. Larson." Judith stood, becoming animated at the prospect that a dramatic incident was about to take place and only she and Larson would know what it was. She glanced toward Larson. He had leaned back, obviously unconcerned with Richards's testimony. All things considered, that was understandable.

"Good morning, Dr. Richards. Will you tell the court what your profession is?"

"I am a deputy medical examiner for the medical examiner's office of San Diego County."

"Will you give us a nutshell idea of what that office does?"

"Well, we are doctors who investigate deaths that come into our office. They include all people who die of non-natural causes, as well as people who die without a doctor in attendance. Our investigation of these deaths usually includes doing an autopsy examination on the body.''

''Will you tell us generally what education and training you have that qualifies you to hold a position such as that?''

''Sure. I'm a medical doctor. I have an MD degree. I did a year internship training. I trained in the field of pathology, general pathology, which includes what is known as anatomic pathology and clinical pathology. After completing that residency I did specialized training in forensics pathology, which is what I'm practicing as a medical examiner. And I'm board certified in all those three areas of pathology. I've been working in forensic pathology exclusively now for about six years.''

''Can you give us a general idea of the number of autopsies you have performed?''

''Oh, I have done about 2400 autopsies.''

''Doctor, did you conduct an autopsy on an individual identified to you as William Threadgill?''

''Yes, I did.''

''Where did that take place?''

''That was at the medical examiner's office.''

''And when you conducted that autopsy, did that include an examination of the entire body?''

''Yes, it did.''

''Can you describe any evidence of injuries that you found to the head of William Threadgill?''

''Sure. The most striking thing was an extremely large laceration or tear of the skin which went across the entire left side of the head. It was about eight inches long. It was jagged. There were also a couple of tears of the skin near this large one, but below it. And there was one small one that was just below the nose on the face.''

''Doctor, from your examination of the largest laceration, did it appear that it could have been caused by one single impact?''

"Well, it seemed to be more than one. It is so complex that the impression I had was that it was caused by probably several lacerations that just tore together into a larger wound."

"And the gray area shown, is that an actual separation of the skin?"

"It represents that, yes."

"Was there some flapping out or undermining of some of the tissue surrounding this laceration?"

"Yes. The tissue underneath between the scalp and the skull was also torn in areas next to where this large tear was so that it would make the scalp loose. That's what we call undermining."

"Doctor, based on your examination of the laceration and the skin, and also the damage to the bony structures underneath the skin, can you give the court some general idea of the type of instrument or type of object that would be used or that would cause this kind of injury?"

"Well, these are representative of what we call blunt force injury, meaning that it is an impact with a blunt object.

"The injuries themselves do not have any particular pattern that would tell us specifically what kind of instrument it would be, but it is some kind of a blunt instrument with possible sharp edges at the extreme ends."

Judith glanced toward Larson. He was reading a report. She moved from her desk toward that of Larson. Her movement caused him to shift as well, diverting him from the report to the witness. She wanted Larson's undivided attention.

"Doctor, did you find anything in your examination of the skull that was foreign to the human body or the tissue themselves?"

"Yes."

"Can you tell us what that was?"

"Sure. You can actually see it in several of the photos we took. There were three areas on the skull adjacent to the portions of these fractures where there was a very fine white particulate material that actually had rubbed off onto the skull."

"If I can help here, we have five photos of Mr. Threadgill's wounds. They have been previously marked as exhibits and if Mr. Larson doesn't mind, we would move to introduce them at this time?"

"We have no objection, Your Honor," Larson said, his attention now clearly fixed on Judith.

"They are admitted, then," Turner said.

"Your Honor, may I approach the witness?"

"Feel free, counsel."

Judith handed the photos to Richards.

"Dr. Richards, take a look if you will at these photographs. Did you find anything you consider unusual in and around Mr. Threadgill's wounds?"

"Yes. That's where I found a substance commonly known as talc."

"Is the substance also known as steatite?"

"Yes, it is."

"Could the talc have come from the ground when Mr. Threadgill fell from his wounds?"

"No."

Richards was a good witness. And his experience on the stand was obvious. A good witness never gives more information than the question asks for.

"Why not?"

"One, there is no talc in the soil where he died. Second, it was embedded too far into the skull to have been caused by his rolling on it."

"Did this lead you to any conclusion about the nature of the instrument used to kill Mr. Threadgill?"

"I concluded the implement or implements used to kill him were made of, or contained, talc."

"Now, Dr. Richards, I have a few questions about the wounds. Can you offer any further conclusion about the kind of implement that caused the wounds?"

"Well, I want to say that at first we thought there might be more than one weapon."

"Why did you think that?"

"Well, because along with the blunt instrument trauma there were slashing marks involved in the same areas as the blunt trauma."

"Is that common?"

"Not really. Usually you see one or the other. Especially if there was only one attacker involved. It's pretty hard for someone to kill a person with two implements."

"Have you been able to formulate any idea as to what this murder implement looked like?"

"Yes, because it had to have the characteristics of both a blunt and sharp object as held in one place by the attacker."

Judith took the photos from her witness and handed them up to the judge to examine. She was not one for dramatics. It could backfire before a jury. But here, she was safe. And the risk was going to be worth it. She had talked with Richards earlier. He knew what she was looking for. What *she* was looking for was plausible and if asked in the right way, she would get what she wanted.

"Dr. Richards, I have set up an easel here in front of Mr. Larson. I'd like to ask the court if I can have you step down and approach it." She looked at Turner.

"Go ahead, you can step down."

"Now, Dr. Richards, can you offer us any diagram or drawing as to what this object might look like? If there are several possibilities, I'd like you to draw those for us."

Richards picked up the black marker pen on the base of the easel and began drawing and verbally describing his drawing at the same time. He was savvy enough to know the record would otherwise never reflect what he was drawing.

"It could well have a base, like this. It's square at the bottom, giving the ability to be used in a clawlike manner. This could account for the slash marks and deep gouges. Now, the blunt trauma from the same instrument could have come from further up the base like this."

Judith watched Larson lean forward, suddenly, intensely, interested.

"You've drawn what one could say looks like a statue."

Larson did not object to her conclusion.

"That's correct."

Judith again looked at Larson. The color had drained from his face. He recognized the shape Richards had drawn. It was the shape of the statue sitting on his office bookcase. It was the statue his own client had given him.

She had hit her mark. Judith turned away quickly. She did not want to give Larson the impression she remembered where that shape had been last seen by her. *Did he remember her visit to the office? She had held it. She had pointed out its uniqueness and the stain on it. My God, she had even asked where he got it and he proudly pointed out it was a gift from Steele. There you go, Alan. Take that. Remember this technique? You taught it to me in the Engle case. You destroyed a young woman's life using this artistic technique.*

"Your Honor, I'm through with this witness. Perhaps Mr. Larson would like to cross-examine?"

Larson was on his feet. "No, Your Honor. Given our position we have no need to cross-examine Dr. Richards."

"Dr. Richards, you are excused and free to leave. Counsel, it's noon. We stand in recess until one-thirty."

Larson left the courtroom with Steele. He did not

make his usual stop to chat with the multitude of reporters who were gathered in the hallway outside.

As soon as they were clear of the reporters, Pike turned to Judith.

"What in God's name happened to Larson? I was watching him. He turned several shades of white. And I've never seen him dodge the press."

"The statue, Pike. The statue in his office."

Pike stopped in his tracks. His eyes widened. "Hey," he said in mock anger, "I'm your investigator. You're supposed to let me know these things."

"And spoil my fun? No, this one was mine, Pike. Let's grab lunch."

They settled for a sandwich shop with nice high-backed booths.

"The question now"—Judith paused between sips of hot coffee—"is what Larson's going to do. If he confronts Steele directly and Steele admits he killed Threadgill with the statue, he's got to turn it over to us in a reasonable time. He knows that. My God, can you imagine Larson walking in to us with a murder weapon. If he doesn't confront Steele, he's safe. He has no information on which to feel compelled to act. But, he's got to know I've seen it. And I'm sure he's wondering when and if I'm going to remember."

Pike was beside himself. "Shit I haven't seen nothing like this in years, maybe a decade even. But what if he dumps it?"

"I don't think he will. Not yet. I don't think he's going to move that statue one inch in any direction just now. If we remember and ask him for it, and he doesn't have it, he's going to find himself an accessory to murder. He's in the proverbial tough spot."

"How long are you going to let this go on?"

"I don't have any intention of letting this go for more than forty-eight hours. Then we move. If he doesn't bring it to us voluntarily, we start asking questions. Then all hell's going to break loose.''

"It's a risk, Judith.''

"I know. But we still don't have probable cause to go get it from him. He'll find some way to get rid of it. He doesn't want it.''

"The question now is, what's he going to do this afternoon?''

Judith's question was answered before she could get back into the courtroom. Stopping at her office for messages, her secretary flagged her and Pike and delivered the news.

"The clerk from Department 34 called fifteen minutes ago. Mr. Larson got very ill at lunch. He called in. He won't be in court this afternoon. The Steele prelim has been continued to next Monday. Steele has notified the court it's okay with him to have the break in the hearing.''

"Monday! It's Wednesday. That's a week!'' Pike exclaimed.

"Larson's so ill he won't be in tomorrow and Turner has to go back to Santa Clara on Friday for some special hearing he's got set up there. He can't go with the prelim any earlier. He thought this would be two days at most.''

"So Larson's sick,'' Pike muttered.

"I'll bet he is,'' Judith whispered back. "I'll just bet he is.''

31

IN THE SILENT solitude of his office, Alan Larson read and reread page 201 in the blue paperback edition of the rules of professional conduct. Rule 3-100 was clear.

> It is the duty of a member of the California Bar to maintain inviolate the confidence, and, at every peril to himself or herself, to preserve the secrets of a client.

The definition of "secrets" seemed so very simple. So straightforward.

> "Secrets" means any information obtained by the member [attorney] during the professional relationship, or relating to the representation, which the client has requested to be inviolate or the disclosure of which might be embarrassing or detrimental to the client.

It was the last line that was of significance. Did Larson possess information that would be embarrassing or detrimental to Steele? He certainly did if the statue on the shelf behind him was the implement used to bludgeon Threadgill to death.

This much Larson could keep secret. Indeed, the professional conduct rules seemed to require this much he must keep secret.

The law, however, was seldom so simple in application. Larson continued reading and cross-referencing to the case of *Washington v. Olwell*, a 1964 case from the Supreme Court of Washington. The case cautioned there was a balance to be maintained between the attorney-client privilege and the public interest in criminal investigations. The language was strong. The attorney should not be a depository for criminal evidence (such as a knife, other weapons, stolen property, etc.) which in itself has little, if any material value for the purpose of aiding counsel in the preparation of the defense of his client's case. Such evidence given the attorney during legal consultation for information purposes and used by the attorney in preparing the defense of his client's case could clearly be withheld for a reasonable period of time.

Larson read on. "It follows that the attorney, after a reasonable period, should, as an officer of the court, on his own motion, turn the same over to the prosecution."

What then was his obligation? If he was piecing the law together correctly, he was obligated to keep his possession of weapons obtained from a client secret for a reasonable time then turn them over to the prosecutor.

Alan Larson had lived this dilemma before. The defendant who arrived, sobbing, in his office, murder weapon in hand, pleading for help. He knew just what to do. First, you got your client calmed down. You prepared them for the inevitable surrender to authorities. You walk them through the arrest. The booking. Hopefully, the release on bail. The weapon was turned over to the police and Larson's hands were washed of the murder weapon.

The scenario varied at times. There was the woman who told him where she buried the knife. He waited a day, then told the police.

But never in all of his years of practice had a client dropped a murder weapon on him without telling him. He had never been made a dupe that way. Of course, he could be wrong; perhaps the statue was not the murder weapon and he had been the victim of an unscrupulous assistant district attorney.

He had not broached this with Steele. He had bid the judge a hasty goodbye after the morning session, telling him he wasn't feeling well. It was true. A sledgehammer had been dropped on him by Judith Thornton.

Now, in his office, Larson paced nervously, stopping periodically to examine the statue. It was possible the soapstone finish was marred and stained. Then again, it might be blood. Threadgill's blood.

His options were several. He could ask Steele directly about the statue, and if Steele admitted the statue was a murder weapon, he would turn it over to the DA and hope for a plea bargain because that was as clear an admission of his client's guilt as he could come. But the option required he violate one of his own cardinal rules of representation. He would have to ask Steele if he'd murdered Threadgill.

Larson never asked his clients if they were guilty. He considered guilt or innocence an unnecessary albatross around the neck of a good defense attorney. You address the truth of guilt if you need to in order to defend your client. Why? Because every person was entitled to the best representation he could give them whether they were guilty or not. He did not understand attorneys who insisted on knowing "the full story" before they would represent someone.

The truth burdened him. More than that, it burdened the justice system. And he was not alone; his was no aberrant attitude.

On his wall hung a framed quotation from the dissenting opinion in *United States v. Wade*, a 1967 case from the United States Supreme Court Justice Byron White:

> Law enforcement officers have the obligation to convict the guilty and to make sure they do not convict the innocent. They must be dedicated to making the criminal trial a procedure for the ascertainment of the true facts surrounding the commission of the crime. . . . But defense counsel has no comparable obligation to ascertain or present the truth. Our system assigns him a different mission. . . . Defense counsel need present nothing, even if he knows what the truth is. He need furnish no witnesses to the police, reveal no confidences of his client, nor furnish any other information to help the prosecution's case. If he can confuse a witness, even a truthful one, or make him appear at a disadvantage, unsure or indecisive, that will be his normal course. Our interest in not convicting the innocent permits counsel to put the State to its proof, to put the State's case in the worst possible light, regardless of what he thinks or knows to be the truth. . . . In this respect, as part of our modified adversary system and as part of the duty imposed on the most honorable defense counsel, we countenance or require conduct which in many instances has little, if any, relation to the search for truth.

Larson believed in the quotation with all his heart and soul. Despite the misgivings he felt for what Steele may have done to him, he would not place his client in a compromised position. If he had unloaded the murder weapon on him, Steele had to have been desperate.

Larson paced on until his shirt was sticky with perspiration. It was 4 P.M.

His rationalization of Steele's conduct gave way to another question. What should he do with the statue? Judith Thornton had seen it. Had she recognized it? Was all of that business this morning a setup to get Steele?

Or to get him?

He knew the prosecution had no way to obtain a search warrant. They were waiting for him to make a move maybe. No, Judith Thornton was too professional to go after him personally like that. Now, that Pike Martin . . . maybe. He might try to maneuver an accessory charge on him.

Larson picked up the statue and held it tight. He had been pushed to the limit. He didn't know if the statue was a murder weapon and he didn't want to know. If he got rid of it now, he would have violated no law, no ethical tenet. He was, in this, still representing a client, a very well known one whose life and career rested in his hands as surely as this statue did.

Larson looked down at his desk. On the top of the pile of the days' mail sat the invitation to the annual Hi-Jinx dinner and show. He had read it the week before and had reserved a table for himself and eight other attorneys. A white mimeographed letter tucked inside the invitation was suddenly of intense interest to him. He opened the invitation envelope again, fumbling with the boldly printed note:

As part of this year's ceremony, our final Golden Ass of the Year Award will be presented. We are looking for white elephants you may have lying around your office or home. Deliver them to Jeff

Martin at least one day before the dinner. One and only one of the contributions will be presented to this year's Golden Ass! A generous gift of a weekend vacation at Cabo San Lucas (for two!) will be presented to the person whose contribution is selected as our Golden Ass Award.

Larson's eyes fixed on the statue. He had a contribution to make.

Before he learned the truth.

32

THE FOLLOWING MONDAY, Judge Turner was back on the bench. Slic was in court, ready for cross-examination by Larson. By this time, Judith had secured a three-way grant of immunity for him from the city attorney, her own county office, and the state transit department. The logistics had not been easy, complicated by the fact that Slic had managed to offend at almost every level of government. In return for Slic's testimony in the Steele case, all three jurisdictions had agreed they would not prosecute him for any of his tagging vandalism occurring up to the day of the testimony.

"I believe, counsel, that when we recessed at the end of last week, we had concluded the testimony of Doctor Richards. We will resume the cross-examination of Antonio Perez. Mr. Perez, please resume the stand."

Antonio, still looking stiff and awkward in his suit and tie, climbed back onto the witness stand and sat bolt upright, staring intently at Larson.

Surprisingly, even after the shock he had received from Judith, Larson seemed reinvigorated. He glanced at Judith and Pike from time to time, smiling. During the first recess, Judith and Pike conferred, wondering aloud how, and if, Larson had met the volley thrust at him by the forensics expert turned artist the prior week.

Larson wasted no time ripping into Slic. His questions hammered away at Slic's credibility. *Hadn't he broken the law? Why should anyone believe him now?* In the end though, it was a draw. There was no jury to play to and Larson knew whatever Slic's past, his brief testimony would not greatly influence Turner.

Following Slic's testimony, Judith rested her case. Larson introduced no evidence on behalf of Steele, choosing instead to put the People to their test and argue that the amount of evidence introduced by the prosecution was not sufficient to bind Steele over for trial.

"Your Honor, in my relatively short career in criminal law, I have had the opportunity to participate in a substantial number of cases. However, I have never been witness to such a travesty as this. If I may detail the evidence presented. One, a mural. A mural with Judge Steele's face on the body of a person who has bludgeoned someone. That 'someone' depicted on the mural is William Threadgill. The artist is dead. His meaning in painting my client will always remain a mystery. Was he sane? Crazy? Judge Steele will never be able to answer those questions. Neither will this court. Certainly, the prosecution hasn't. Two. We have the testimony of a known criminal that he knew the artist. The artist set about to paint the murderer. Beyond that we cannot go. It is hearsay of the rankest level. Three, we have a photograph of an item that appears to be a Chumash artifact. It's found under Silverado Estates. A motive? The prosecution has failed to tie this in any manner to my client. 'Weak' is too strong a word for this attempt to establish a reason for William Threadgill's death. And finally, we have Dr. Richards. He has drawn an object. It looks vaguely like a statue. He has found talc in Mr. Threadgill's wounds. Even if the prosecution has somehow drawn a thread from the Chumash items under Silverado Estates to the object or objects that may have been used to kill Threadgill, where is the finger that points to my client, Judge Steele? A criminal tagger? An unexplained mural? Not enough, Your Honor. It's just not enough. We ask you to do what the evidence cries out for. Dismissal of all charges.''

''Mrs. Thornton, you wish to argue in rebuttal?''

''Yes, Your Honor. Our case rises and falls on the word of Gui Colon. It is Colon who painted what he saw. And he saw that man''—she pointed to Steele—''kill William Threadgill. Your Honor, to bind this case over to superior court, all the People need show is a reasonable suspicion the defendant murdered William Threadgill. We believe that showing has been made.''

Turner collected his yellow-lined note tablets and leaned over his bench.

''Court will be in recess until eight-thirty tomorrow morning, Counsel, while I consider the evidence.''

As with most good judges, Turner had not ruled from the bench immediately upon the close of the evidence. Even when Turner knew how he was going to rule in a case, he placed time and distance between the last witness, or the last argument by the attorneys, and his ruling. The distance gave him some time to reflect. In all cases it emphasized he was, indeed, thinking about what the parties had presented to him.

Turner was not the only one reflecting on the evidence.

The afternoon Judith rested her case, she, Pike, and Farrell met to discuss the possible scenarios and how they would handle each of them. They were glum-faced as they sat around the circular wood table in Farrell's office.

Pike's prediction was blunt. ''If you ask me, based on the evidence presented he won't be bound over.'' Farrell was more Socratic. "Judith, how would you decide if you were Turner?"

"I wouldn't bind him over, Larry." Her response was quick, unfettered with diplomacy.

"And so now where does that leave us?" Farrell asked.

Judith rose and walked toward a wall lined with California codes. She reached for her copy of the Penal code and flipped through the index. Of the more than four thousand statutes relating to the state's criminal law, there were approximately twelve dealing with dismissal of criminal actions.

"I just want to check to make sure here. . . . This is it. Penal code Section 1387 is the one I was looking for." She read in silence, then returned to the table and sat down. "If the court decides there's not enough evidence to hold him for trial, he's going to dismiss the charges. There's not a whole lot we can do. We can take the case up to the superior court and have them decide if the lower court erred. The problem is, the superior court isn't allowed to reverse Turner unless it can say as a matter of law that he was wrong. That's pretty hard to do when he's evaluating evidence like ours that really could go either way. We'll never get the superior court to overturn it."

"What if *we* dismiss the charges? Are we in any better shape?" Pike asked.

Judith continued reading, thumbed through the pages of the code, and summarized her finding.

"We could bring our own motion to dismiss and my guess is that Turner would buy into it and grant the motion. But we'd look like fools. I'd prefer not to deal with that. It's not an option as far as I'm concerned. The bottom line is that whether we ask for a dismissal, or Turner grants it on his own, we can refill the charges only in a couple of pretty strict instances. But, one of them is this: we can refill if we find substantial new evidence that was not known before the refilling and which we wouldn't have known through the exercise of due diligence."

"How about the statue?" Pike asked.

"Right. The statue. We don't know if it's the murder weapon. And besides," Judith added, "we didn't have enough for a search warrant on Larson. And we still don't. I say that doesn't add up to a legal obligation to secure it."

"Someone could make an argument we didn't seize it and should have tried again," Farrell said.

"They can make the argument, sure, and we have our response," Judith shot back. "We did all we could. It's in the record." She paused, slapped the book shut, and gave Farrell her final recommendation, the only recommendation possible. "If it's dismissed, we say our investigation into Threadgill's death is continuing and we see if we can get hold of that statue."

Turner was not a man who minced words or agonized over decisions. He called the shots the way he saw them and let the higher courts tell him when he was wrong. When they did, he read their opinion, knew not to do it again, and then he put it out of his mind.

Turner, though, was struggling over the Steele case. Not because the defendant was a sitting judge. Turner did not know the man, had no connections with the bench or bar in San Diego, and was leaving town as soon as the matter was completed.

It was the preliminary hearing bindover standard that bothered the hell out of Turner on this one. In order to bind Steele over to superior court he would have to conclude there was probable cause to believe Steele committed the offense.

The parties had agreed that the painting on the mural

was Steele. But without the artist present to explain what he saw or why he painted Steele as a murderer, the case against him was weak at best. This was a case screaming out for dismissal.

Indeed, stepping back from the specific evidence, the case as a whole struck Turner as almost comedic. A face on a wall? Some half-crazed artist obsessed with painting one last mural? The prosecution's chief witness was a kid whose claim to fame was hanging out over freeways to see how much of a risk he could take short of killing himself. This was not the stuff that strong cases were made of, especially not murder cases. Turner's desire was to save the judicial system the grief and expense of trial and force the People to come up with more.

On the other hand, when the evidence was looked at one piece at a time, there was more. What motivation did the kid have to lie? None really. Despite the ranting and railings of Larson, the kid, Slic, had come forward in part because of his respect for the artist.

And then there was Steele himself. With the preliminary hearing, more than any other hearing a judge might sit on, the resolution was pitted in your gut, and something in Turner's gut was telling him to trust his instincts. What had his instincts told him here? It was not as much what, as when, this feeling had been aroused. There had been just a moment when the expert had drawn the possible murder weapon when. . . . He couldn't say what, but Turner had focused on the man and had seen something in that man's piercing eyes . . . a confusion . . . a fear. It was a feeling that had made him curious. Curious enough to want to be sure he had seen and heard all the evidence available. And that meant personally viewing the mural.

From the start of the case, Colon and the mural had intrigued Turner. He had the photographs of the mural that had been entered into evidence but because of the size of the mural, its depiction could only be accomplished by a series of four shots from a distance that did not allow for his seeing detail. His experience and intuition told him that, despite his feelings, before dismissing, he wanted to see the mural personally and up close, and he needed to do that at the same time of day and in the same light as Colon had painted it. And that meant convening court at 7 A.M., just after the sun came up.

At 7 A.M. sharp, Judith drove to the Thulis' house and parked across the street. Steele, Larson, and Turner had been notified of Turner's visit to the mural, and had already arrived and were standing together, exchanging pleasantries unrelated to the case. Within minutes, the court clerk joined the group.

The parties had agreed the reporter need not come along because they planned to do nothing more than go down to the mural, view it, and leave. Any problems that developed could be placed on the record later that morning when court convened downtown.

The group walked single-file down the hill and took various positions at the base of the mural. Larson and Steele examined it and then gazed out onto the canyons, lapsing into discussion on the property values of the area. The others silently examined the mural, noticing only casually that Turner had positioned himself directly in front of the painting of Steele. His attention was riveted on the painting of Steele's face. On his eyes. In them Turner saw anger, and fear. Blind fear. The same fear he had seen on Steele's face, in his eyes, when Dr. Richards drew the possible murder weapon. Steele had frozen at the defense table and panic had overtaken him.

Truth, it is said, is two people seeing the same thing at the same time. Standing before the mural this morning, Turner saw what Colon had seen in Steele's eyes as he bludgeoned Threadgill to death. And Turner himself had seen that look on Steele's face. In court. When the prosecution expert had drawn the murder weapon.

It was a judicial revelation incapable of words, the type of intuitive revelation a judge never puts on the record. How would Turner ever describe what was happening to him, to his judgment, as he stood before the mural. What words could he use? No one had seen what he had seen from his bench, and what he was now seeing in the mural. Colon had seen the murderer and the murderer was Marcus Steele.

After several minutes, without comment on his observations, Turner indicated he had seen enough. He ordered the parties appear in his court at 9:30 A.M.

Neither Judith nor Pike had any kind of read on Turner as he entered the courtroom. The end would be mercifully fast, accompanied by the hollow feeling that only one who has suffered the public humiliation of losing the big case can explain.

"Counsel, I've examined all the evidence and it is the court's opinion that the evidence is sufficient to hold the defendant to answer. The defendant is ordered to appear in superior court fifteen days from today to enter his plea. He may remain free on his own recognizance."

The courtroom was silent. Then Larson was on his feet, trying in vain to get Turner to explain his ruling, to set out in the record what evidence, what hard evidence, there was of Steele's guilt.

"I've ruled, Counsel. The record will stand on its own."

In declining to elaborate on his ruling, Turner allowed an appellate court to find its own reasons in the record to uphold his conclusion, unfettered by Turner's logic or reasoning.

Nowhere, however, would the record reflect what

Turner had seen and felt, and thus what had been the heart of his decision. His rationale would find its way into the broad presumption of appellate review: reviewing courts, able to examine only cold records, do not second-guess the intuition of a trial judge's observation of the witnesses and parties from the lofty position of their judicial benches.

Judith closed her file as Larson and Steele sat in stunned silence. The reporters pressed close to the gate separating the spectators from the court personnel. Judith exited the courtroom with Pike, politely declining to speak with them. When Judith declined to speak, the crush of reporters shifted to the defendant. Larson and Steele lingered to express their indignation.

"It's not over, is it, Judge Steele?" she heard a reporter yell toward a red-faced Steele.

Judith knew it wasn't over. Not by a long shot. But if she was going to make a verdict stick, she needed more than she'd given to Turner. Even to her, Turner's ruling was inexplicable. The case was still alive, but it was going to have to be tried.

"Can you believe Turner?" Pike asked as they left the courtroom. "He must have seen something we didn't."

33

ELIZABETH WAS SPENDING the weekend with her father. There was no reason for Judith to be nervous or feel rushed getting ready for the Hi-Jinx dinner, but she did. As the evening progressed, she began to realize the problem was that she did not want to attend.

She dressed, purposely bypassing the sexier reds and blues in favor of a conservative black dress with a white lace collar, something that would let her better blend into the crowd. The last thing she wanted to do this evening was to draw attention to herself.

It had been a difficult week since Steele was bound over for trial. First, there had been the question of the mural. Now that it had become the focus of a notorious murder trial, no one was anxious to have it removed. The Thulis had returned from their European vacation and upon learning the events preceding their return, they agreed to allow it to remain on their property, at least until the criminal charges against Steele were resolved.

The newspaper articles had been another matter. Two articles had appeared immediately after the bindover. They had been fairly straightforward. The headlines, however, were editorial comment. She had clipped them

and they were laying on her bedroom dresser. RE-
NOWNED JUDGE TO STAND TRIAL. WELL-KNOWN JURIST
CHARGED IN MYSTERY MURDER.

At five-thirty Judith drove to the Casson Restaurant,
where the dinner was being held. Farrell had suggested
they meet at the door at five o'clock so that they would
have time for a drink and conversation before dinner.
Judith, however, was seeking to minimize her exposure.
She intended to have dinner and leave.

Farrell was standing at the door surrounded by a
group composed of deputies from the office and attorneys she recognized as civil attorneys.

"I didn't think you'd make it," Farrell said. "Our
table is number thirteen. It's close to the door at the far
wall. I'm sorry. . . . I should introduce you. . . . Obviously you know these gentlemen." He motioned toward
the deputies. "And, this is Peter Kelleher from Town-
send and Kelleher, and Michael Henderson with Hills-
borough."

She knew them both by sight. Kelleher and Henderson
were senior members of two of San Diego's most prestigious law firms.

Kelleher extended his hand. "Good to meet you, Mrs.
Thornton. May I call you Judith?"

"Of course."

"I've seen you in the newspaper recently. You certainly have your hands full."

"I think dinner's on," Farrell bubbled. "The salads
were being set."

Judith and Farrell and the deputy district attorneys occupied one of the ten-place tables. The dinner was a
relaxing one with talk centering around the usual hier-
archy and escalation of thought: caseloads, the state of
the office, and finally, the state of the criminal law in
general.

As dessert was being set, the room lights lowered and

the lights came up on a stage set up at the front of the room. Thomas Sullivan, president of the club, took center stage. Perhaps it was the shift in light in the room, but when the lights on the stage alternated, Larson suddenly came into focus, sitting at a table on the far side of the room. Surrounding him were people she recognized as being from the public defender's office. She surveyed the room and finally spied Steele, sitting near the front of the room at a table reserved for officials and the judiciary.

Sullivan smiled and raised his hands to silence the applause.

"Thank you, counsel, honorable judges, and colleagues. . . . This is a very special night for us tonight; a sad night because it marks the passing of an era, an era we will likely never see again."

Boos echoed through the audience as Sullivan again held up his hands to silence the group.

"Now, now . . . while we have seen tremendous growth and change, some things remain the same . . . our friendships, our memories and . . ."

Here he paused.

"And our annual recognition of the one person who in the opinion of the club has earned our censure as the one who has insulted the tenets of camaraderie and, in a word, has done the stupidest thing of the year!"

A cheer echoed through the room.

"I won't delay this. . . . I know you all want to get back to your guests and your conversation. Our winner this year is a woman whose face has recently graced the pages of our local papers because she is involved in an investigation of significant magnitude. . . . "

The room began to buzz, an electric current directed toward Judith's side of the room.

Farrell leaned over, his face at her ear.

"There's still time to get out of here. . . . "

"No. If it's mine I'll accept. I just hope it's lots of money."

"Not a chance," he whispered back.

In the background, Sullivan's voice continued. Judith's eyes were fastened on him, trying to ignore those at neighboring tables who had begun to stare and point in her direction.

"This year's winner is Chief Deputy District Attorney Judith Thornton. I'm told she's here tonight! Judith. Where are you?"

Judith stood, humiliated but smiling, and began walking toward the dais. Ahead of her stood Sullivan, a large package in his outstretched hands. It was wrapped in silver paper with a very large pink ribbon.

Judith accepted the box and heard the first chants rise from the back of the room.

"O-pen it. O-pen it!"

Sullivan smiled and addressed the crowd.

"It appears there is some sentiment, Judith, for you to open this gift. As you know, our annual gift is a rummage contribution . . . but this year's gift is unique. Go ahead!"

Judith placed the package on the podium and quickly slid her fingers under the edges of the wrapping, then the ribbon. The box was heavy. As the lid slipped off, her eyes widened.

In the box, amidst an ample supply of plastic bubble pack, was *the statue*.

Judith replaced the lid.

"Judith! Aren't you going to show us what it is?" Sullivan cajoled. "Our donor is somewhere out there in tonight's audience, and doesn't know his, or her, donation was selected! But they will when our gift certificate arrives in the mail!"

It took Judith a few minutes to recover her senses. Her heart racing, she leaned toward the microphone and in a raspy voice that surprised even her, whispered, "Thank you." The room erupted in applause.

Back at her table, Judith handed the box to Farrell.

"Don't take it out, Larry. Look inside but don't take it out . . . I don't know if he knows his was picked."

Farrell lifted the lid.

"My God . . ." was all he could manage initially.

He covered the box again and looked at his watch.

"Let's go," he said.

Judith gathered her purse, shoving the evening's program into it. She looked one last time across the room. Larson was engaged in an animated conversation, oblivious to the doom about to befall him.

34

LARSON FOLLOWED THE winding cobblestone walkway from the street to the gray Tudor house. The chandelier in the dining room was on, hundreds of pieces of Austrian crystal, prisms sparkling flashes of blue and red. The automatic sprinkler system had shut off minutes before, leaving the plants lining the path dripping wet and the air moist and cool. Larson had called Steele before coming to the house tonight. He needed to begin the strategy that would carry them victoriously through the coming trial, and he was anxious to begin his plans.

Steele was waiting in the library, a large, wood-paneled room with bay windows overlooking the expansive yard and the canyon beyond. The light was more subdued than one might expect for a meeting with one's attorney. The sole illumination came from a small Tiffany desk lamp and the four wall sconces.

Steele was sitting behind his antique desk, a Louis XIV he and his wife had found two decades before on a trip to Europe. Its gold trim seemed appropriate for a man of distinction. A casual glance around the room without strong light gave an instant portrait of Steele's life. His career and family surrounded him. Pictures of him and his wife on trips, and the children and grand-children at play. The silver and crystal of awards and presents lined the bookshelves, defined the accomplishments.

"Can I get you some coffee, Alan?"

"No thanks, Judge, I'm trying to lay off the stuff. Maybe some tea later on."

"Have a seat then, we'll just chat for now."

"I want to launch right into this, Judge. I'd like to talk about your defense, get some ideas how you might like to approach the issues and the evidence."

Steele sighed. "I want to enter a plea of guilty, Alan."

Larson sat stunned, for a moment unable to speak. When he found the words, they were stiff and far more lawyerlike than he might have chosen had he had time to reflect.

"I'd advise against that, Judge."

"I want to talk about what happened out there by the mural."

"You don't have to."

Steele shook his head. "No . . . no . . . I want to. I need to."

"You don't have . . ."

"Yes, I do. I do need to talk to someone. To explain. I . . . killed Threadgill. You know that, don't you?"

"Actually, I hadn't spent much time on that conclusion."

Steele smiled. "Ah . . . I often wondered Alan, if you ever asked your clients about their guilt or innocence."

"I don't."

"Tell me, I'm curious. Does it help you not to know if we're guilty?"

"It helps. Knowing slows me down. It's not relevant. Everyone's entitled to the best representation I can give them."

Steele nodded, understanding. "You're a good attorney, Alan."

"Not great?" Larson was kidding but the invitation was there and Steele accepted it.

"I'll be honest, shall I? No, you're not a great attorney, Alan. You win all the awards and damn, you win your cases. But you're not a great attorney. Please, don't be offended. I've seen a number of really great attorneys in my time. Some have been flamboyant. Others have been great orators. A few have been downright nice. But the thing every one of them had was a completeness and depth in their preparation. They won their cases, not necessarily because they were brilliant, but because they dug and investigated and found evidence then knew how to use it. They found the truth. They were looking for the truth. You manipulate the system too much, Alan. It's too much of a game; less love of the ethic and more a thumbing of your nose at authority. You haven't seen the real beauty of the system, or your role in it. You know that's given me problems in the past." Steele's face suddenly saddened; a man whose sense of propriety had brushed up against his own indiscretion.

Larson was unmoved. "You know, Judge, we can beat this. The people don't have the evidence. They have a mural with no artist to say what he painted. And that's the strongest evidence! You've got to let me try."

"And gain what?"

"A verdict . . . your career. Your life, man."

"And live with it all by myself?"

"If you can't do this for yourself, do it for your family."

"I've talked with my family already. They are prepared to stand by whatever decision I make."

"Jesus, how about the hundreds of people . . . the attorneys . . . who look up to you? You're a hero to those people."

Steele laughed aloud.

"Hero? I'm not a hero, man. A hero is a person who has a conception of what is right and then does what's right—what he believes in—in the face of over-whelming resistance. I've known some lawyers who've been heroes; men like Clarence Darrow, who were ab-solutely committed to the idea that every human being is entitled to a vigorous and complete defense no matter who they are or what they've done. And they've pre-sented their cases in the face of overwhelming hatred. Without gimmicks. With only an inexhaustible search for truth. Me? I'm not in that grouping. In the end, all I've succeeded in demonstrating is something I, more than anyone else, already know, and that's that humans are capable of doing horribly evil things to each other, for very weak reasons."

"I wouldn't do what you're wanting to do."

"I know you wouldn't. Can I tell you what hap-pened?"

"No ... but I think you're going to."

"I need to tell you ... and besides ... you are still my attorney."

"If you're going to tell me what happened at the wall, you'd better start at the beginning."

"Let me think where the beginning was. Everything just blurred after a while. Come outside with me. Maybe it's better if I show you."

Steele stood and led Larson out of the library into a large family room. He pressed a button on the wall and instantly, lighting flooded the backyard. The pair stepped outside through a large sliding glass door onto a gray slate patio.

Steele pointed out over the backyard. "There," he said. "That's what started it all."

"Your yard?" Larson asked.

"My roses. There are at least sixty different types of

roses out there. Some of them are prize winners. Grand prize winners. They've been out there for years some of them.''

"What have they to do with Threadgill?" Larson asked.

Steele rubbed his eyes. He did not answer Larson's question.

"I told the fool I'd buy the land from him. Six feet. That's all it would have taken. A six-foot strip of dirt. Just to have left the plants intact. That's all I was asking.''

"You mean Threadgill?''

"You see that tennis court there?''

Larson squinted. To the west was a tall chain-link fence.

"It's Threadgill's tennis court. He brought the goddamned thing clear up to the setback. It was legal. But it destroyed twenty of my best rose bushes. Including the three I had taken from my mother's yard when she died six years ago. There's no way they can be replaced.''

"You fought with Threadgill about the roses?''

"I offered the man money. I offered to pay him for the land. He never even responded. I came out here that night and they were gone. Just like that. The machines just . . .'' He stopped, too emotional to continue.

"Was this the night Threadgill was killed?''

"I lost myself. I went looking for him and I saw him walking. He did that. He walked all over the neighborhood. I followed him down to the wall. I just wanted to know why. Why did he do it. He laughed at me. Can you imagine a man like that laughing at me? He was like that. If something got in his way he stepped on it. I could feel myself losing control . . . I just exploded.''

"The statue . . . did you take it with you?

"No. It was out there on the ground. I hadn't the

slightest idea what it was. I thought it was a rock. Some of the kids around here go into the tunnels. They must have brought it out.''

''But, why'd you give it to me? Why didn't you drop it in the bay or throw it in a garbage pail and be done with it once and for all?''

''I thought about it. But I couldn't make myself do it. I guess I needed to give it to someone.''

The two men stood looking over the field of roses until Steele sighed and turned back to the house. Larson followed in silence.

At the back door Steele turned to address him. ''Tomorrow I'd like you to communicate my desire to plead guilty.''

Larson was still agitated. ''Surrender isn't something I do very gracefully, Judge. If you won't go to trial on this, will you please let me see what kind of plea negotiation the People are willing to discuss? They have no credible evidence. None. And they know it. Just give me a chance. That's all I'm asking. Before you give up and spend the rest of your life in prison let me use some of those skills you find so . . . what was the word you used?''

Steele smiled. ''Manipulative. I think that was the word.''

''Some of those manipulative skills to get this reduced. I can do it.''

''If you can do it diplomatically, Alan. With some degree of . . . honor.''

''I'll give it my best shot, Judge.''

35

FARRELL AND JUDITH sat, coffee cups in hand, across the table from each other. It was 6 P.M. Farrell's office was quiet.

"We need to be careful, Judith. We can't give away the store and we can't allow there to be an appearance we're giving away the store because it's a judge involved."

"It doesn't matter, Larry. Any sentence other than murder is going to look like we've capitulated."

"But that's our job. Read the evidence . . . arrive at a fair disposition. I've looked at Steele's statement. It's possible if we go to trial we'd end up with a second-degree murder. There's no premeditation but he intended to kill Threadgill."

Judith frowned and shook her head. "I don't know, Larry. He's got a good argument there was a sudden quarrel or heat of passion, and that's manslaughter."

"But the provocation has to be the kind that would naturally excite and arouse passions."

"Pike said it a long time ago when this first started. Boundary disputes arouse passions. They're the worst. Neighbors fighting over views obstructed by trees. How many homicides have we had where the actors were fighting over land? Too many to count.''

"And us thinking it was wealth and fame, a treasure underneath the ground. It was a bunch of rose bushes. Scrawny woody shrubs with thorns. They aren't even pretty except a fraction of the year. It wasn't greed, just good old anger, sheer anger."

"You know, Larry, we don't have many options. Steele wants to plead guilty. He doesn't know yet that we have the statue. It's the strongest evidence we have and it's still going to be tough to tie it to Steele. We can't get prints from it. Even if we can establish it's the murder weapon . . ."

"You can tie it to Larson. That'll tie it to Steele. But you know what that'll mean, Judith."

Judith nodded. "Yeah. We nail Larson along with Steele."

The two silently mulled over the thought. It was the kind of thing a prosecutor might contemplate in the heat of battle. But here it was. The actual power to force an ethics investigation against an adversary who'd skirted the lines of propriety. Again.

"It's your call on Larson, Judith. I'll live with whatever you decide. As to Steele, we don't have strong enough evidence to force this to trial. I say let's accept voluntary manslaughter if he'll plead. In the end, it's a fair disposition."

"Do you want me to talk sentence with Larson?"

"We leave it to the court."

Judith rose to leave. "I'll contact Larson first thing in the morning. You know, Larry, if we take a plea we'd be getting a guilty verdict with virtually no strong evidence. That's the bright side." As she was almost to the door, Farrell called after her.

"Judith, how about the kid, Slic?"

"His family's moved back to Mexico. I don't know

if he went with them. We have his moniker now. If we
see Slic up in the heavens we know who we're after. He
wouldn't stick around here. I like to think Colon had
some effect for the good on the boy."

"See you tomorrow, Judith. Let me know if Larson
takes the offer. And, Judith?"

"Yeah."

"Let me know what you decide to do about Larson."

At the doorway, Judith turned back to Farrell. "I've
already decided."

Epilogue

━━◆━━

JUDITH WAS HEADING home from the office. On the car seat next to her was a rental tape—*Die Hard*. Her mother would love it.

It had been three months since Steele entered a plea of guilty to voluntary manslaughter and the case had come and gone like hundreds of others. Following a flurry of publicity and stories of fallen heroes, he was in prison. She was perceived the heroine whose courage in the face of overwhelming political pressure now brought renewed expectation of a judicial appointment.

As for Larson, she would be facing him in court tomorrow morning and checking her paper cups for pin holes. In the end, Judith had deferred to the thin line separating their respective roles in the criminal justice process.

Justice, or something akin to it, had been achieved. And almost everyone had emerged intact.

As she passed the Fairmount Avenue exit, Judith looked up toward Silverado Estates. The mural was gone. Erased by a new layer of pink-tinted concrete. Dissed, she thought. But it had had its moment of truth, its one moment in time when somehow, some way, one other person had seen what Colon had seen and art had been a handmaiden to justice.

As Judith's car turned and sped along El Cajon Boulevard, she looked up at the water tower looming over the public tennis courts, and her eye was drawn to the top of it. It was the highest point along the wide, busy street. Stupid fool, she thought. Unmistakable printing proclaimed in vivid red letters what had not been there the day before:

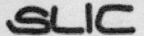